An Heiress to Remember

"What is that look, Dalton? If I didn't know any better I'd think you wanted to kiss me."

"Don't tempt me," he said sharply.

"Or what?" Beatrice challenged.

"Or I just might."

"Oooh," she breathed. "Oh I am so . . ."

"So what, Beatrice?"

Dalton took a step close, too close. There were mere inches separating their thundering hearts. He either wanted to kiss her or throttle her, and it took all of his self-control to keep himself in check.

This was not usually how he conducted business.

He would never stand so close.

He would never feel so much.

He would never think of kissing.

That's what this felt like. A prelude to a kiss. An up-against-the-wall, cannot-even-breathe, about-to-explode, scorching kiss. One long overdue.

By Maya Rodale

The Gilded Age Girls Club
AN HEIRESS TO REMEMBER
SOME LIKE IT SCANDALOUS
DUCHESS BY DESIGN

Keeping Up with the Cavendishes
IT'S HARD OUT HERE FOR A DUKE
LADY CLAIRE IS ALL THAT
CHASING LADY AMELIA
LADY BRIDGET'S DIARY

The Bad Boys and Wallflowers Series
THE BAD BOY BILLIONAIRE: WHAT A GIRL WANTS
WHAT A WALLFLOWER WANTS
THE BAD BOY BILLIONAIRE'S GIRL GONE WILD
WALLFLOWER GONE WILD
THE BAD BOY BILLIONAIRE'S WICKED ARRANGEMENT
THE WICKED WALLFLOWER

The Writing Girl Romances Series
SEDUCING MR. KNIGHTLY
THE TATTOOED DUKE
A TALE OF TWO LOVERS
A GROOM OF ONE'S OWN
THREE SCHEMES AND A SCANDAL

Maya Rodale

An Heiress to Remember

❊ THE GILDED AGE GIRLS CLUB ❊

AVONBOOKS

An Imprint of HarperCollinsPublishers

AN HEIRESS TO REMEMBER. Copyright © 2020 by Maya Rodale. All rights reserved. Printed in the United States of America. No part of this book may be used or reproduced in any manner whatsoever without written permission except in the case of brief quotations embodied in critical articles and reviews. For information, address HarperCollins Publishers, 195 Broadway, New York, NY 10007.

First Avon Books mass market printing: April 2020
First Avon Books hardcover printing: March 2020

Print Edition ISBN: 978-0-06-283884-1
Digital Edition ISBN: 978-0-06-283885-8

Cover design by Guido Caroti
Cover art © Paul D'Innocenzo 2019

Avon, Avon & logo, and Avon Books & logo are registered trademarks of HarperCollins Publishers in the United States of America and other countries.

HarperCollins is a registered trademark of HarperCollins Publishers in the United States of America and other countries.

FIRST EDITION

20 21 22 23 24   QGM   10 9 8 7 6 5 4 3 2 1

For all the ladies who do whatever they please
Especially Seneca & Penelope

Prologue

New York City, 1879
One West Thirty-Fourth Street

*T*he duke was at the door. His Grace, the Duke of Montrose, had come calling at the Goodwin residence, all the way from Ye Olde England, on the hunt for an heiress to marry as dukes were wont to do these days.

But young Beatrice Goodwin only had eyes for the young, handsome boy who had climbed into her bedroom window.

By any definition, Wes Dalton was a nobody. He also happened to be the somebody she adored most in the world for many reasons, though one in particular claimed her attention now.

Wes Dalton knew how to kiss a girl. He'd been in her room less than a minute before their arms were around each other, mouths colliding, young love seizing the moment.

"You have to go," she murmured.

"I know," he said. Mumbled, really. Talking and kissing were not tremendously compatible. Kissing won out.

Arms and hearts entwined. Soft breaths. The sweetest taste.

"I have to go," he murmured.

"I know," she mumbled.

Beatrice and Wes were no fools; they knew the rules and the way of the world. There was a duke at the front door and Wes was a nobody sneaking into her bedroom and Beatrice . . . well she was just a girl. One who was in danger of forgetting her purpose. Why did her father work night and day, eight days a week, to earn a fortune if not so her mother could realize her greatest social ambitions by making a duchess of their daughter?

The duke was at the door . . .

Barney and Estella Goodwin hadn't done all that for Beatrice to marry Wes Dalton, a mere associate department manager at Goodwin's, the department store her family owned. Even if Wes was an excellent kisser who, when he was not kissing her, wanted to hear whatever she had to say.

Beatrice usually had lots to say, much to people's chagrin.

"We could run away," he suggested.

"We could," she agreed, laughing. Because he couldn't be serious. Then she lifted her gaze to his deep blue eyes and fell silent. He was serious.

Him. Her. Run away.

Her heart leapt at the prospect. Long nights with him, waking up beside him. The two of them taking on the world with nothing but their wits and love and fierce kisses.

But the duke was at the door . . .

It was a big risk. The biggest risk. Especially when the duke was downstairs, presumably now in the formal drawing room. It was not his first visit. But everyone understood that this was *the* visit. The one where he asked the same question Wes was asking her now. But with a guarantee of castles and parties and fancy dresses.

She cared about these things as much as the next girl, which is to say somewhat.

"I can promise you exactly nothing," he said and they both already knew it. "Just undying love. Run away with me, Bea. Right now."

If there was one thing she knew about Wes it was that the man had an enormous appetite for risk. Exhibit A: climbing into the bedroom window of his employer's daughter, who was an heiress about to receive a marriage proposal from a duke. Men ended up in the East River for less.

"When? And where to? And how—?" she sputtered.

Beatrice was not risk averse, but she did appreciate a plan. Her father's business sense may have been lost on her brother, Edward, but not her. She needed some particulars more than just a promise. An idea. A kiss. Some facts and figures would be nice. A plan would not be remiss.

"We'll catch a train this afternoon," Wes murmured as he kissed her neck and for a second she thought, *Maybe*.

"Wes, you're mad. Absolutely mad to suggest such a mad thing," she said. Finishing school never did manage to tame her blunt, impulsive speech.

"Madly in love."

"Is that what you call it?"

He pulled her close so she could feel how madly in love he was with her. He flashed a grin that had her heart bursting like fireworks. If this was the start of forever . . . she could do worse.

There was a knock at the door.

They jumped apart.

She opened the door a crack while Wes stayed out of sight, hiding behind the curtains.

It was a housemaid.

"I have been sent to inform you that His Grace is waiting. And your mother."

One was more fearsome than the other.

"I'll be there in a moment."

She closed the door. The curtains over her window fluttered in the breeze.

They both knew why the duke was downstairs, in the formal drawing room. There was only one reason British Peers of The Realm traveled so far afield. There was only one reason dukes condescended to call repeatedly upon new-money debutantes.

Fortune hunting was the sport of the day.

She was the prize.

"If not right now, then run away with me tonight," Wes said urgently. Because the clock was ticking on forever. Their chances to be together were dwindling. He grasped her hand. "You, Beatrice, are my one and only."

Her lips still tingled from his kiss. She wanted to know how this could work. Because she was tempted. The duke was . . . fine. He was a few years older, staid and remote and just . . . fine.

And Wes was divine. He only had to smile at her across the sales floor and she was floating on air. He had only to kiss her and she was thinking of throwing her whole future away for him.

She was young yet. Just twenty years old. That was a lot of future to throw away.

"And then what? Suppose I run away with you to Grand Central Depot right now. And then what?"

"You. Me. The rest of our lives. Starting tonight."

Tonight! Beatrice felt the walls closing in on her.

She knew what her mother and society expected of her: to marry, and marry well. Dress well, throw parties, associate with the right people. She knew the expectations so well that she scarcely even considered that there might be more. She adored Wes, but how was she supposed to give up family, friends, and a city she loved on some mad lark, with no plans?

Beatrice gazed at him. The dark hair falling rakishly into his ocean blue eyes. The line of his jaw, the curve of his top lip, the hands around her waist. She gazed at this boy she loved to kiss, who made her heart sing, who never told her to be quiet, who always asked her opinion. She *wanted* to run away with him. But she also couldn't help but wonder:

Where would they even go?

How would they eat?

Her father would fire him in a heartbeat. She knew how the world worked; powerful men protected their own and doors all over town would be closed to Wes. He wouldn't find decent work in this town. She would have to give up family, friends, and the city she loved to wander the world with a man who might not be able to support her at all.

It felt tremendously, grievously unfair that she should have only these two wildly extreme all-or-nothing options to choose from. What she wouldn't do to just . . . see how things went.

To pursue both paths without impossibly high stakes, or devastating repercussions. If only she had a little more time or freedom to explore. If only it wasn't a matter of either/or.

But the duke was at the door.

"I'll think about it." She pressed one more kiss on his lips. "But I have to go."

Chapter One

New York City, 1895
Sixteen years later

The first thing Beatrice did after the demise of her marriage was to return to New York. After nearly sixteen years spent languishing in a crumbling old castle in a remote corner of the English countryside, the city seemed like the place to go. When one had burned their bridges, ruined their reputation, and still smoldered with possibilities, what else could one do but escape to Manhattan?

The place was full of opportunities for second chances—as long as one was mad and daring enough to seize them. Beatrice was mad enough and daring enough. She didn't have other options.

Where else in the world was a divorced duchess to go?

Despite the best efforts of the duke, he hadn't been able to extinguish her spark. God knew he'd tried. She still shuddered thinking of his knock at the door. But all that was on the other side of the Atlantic. Good riddance.

Finally, unencumbered, Beatrice stepped onto the dock and into the churning crush of humanity. She breathed in deeply.

Some lumbering man beside her grumbled loudly, "It smells like—"

She thought *home* just as he said "garbage."

To be clear, it did smell like garbage. Hot, stinking garbage that had been left in the sun. It was a noxious mix of manure, refuse, and the seething mass of humanity inhabiting the island. Oh, the city did stink. But it was also home. Where she'd been born and raised, a place where she had loved and lost and left.

It felt good to be back. It felt right. Already she felt a shimmer of possibility that she hadn't felt in a long time. It was the magic of the city, welcoming her home.

Beatrice easily fell back into the brisk pace of a city person; the dowager duchess never managed to get her to move at the sedate pace of a duchess with nothing to do. Though Lord knew her ladyship had done everything in her power to slow Beatrice down, to silence her, to stifle her. The duke, too.

But she did not want to think of them anymore.

She didn't want to think of anything in her past. Beatrice only had eyes for the future.

She made her way along the dock, jostled by the crowds. Someone stepped on her boot and shoved her slightly to the side. People here were in such a hurry, all burning up with ambition and determined to get it done yesterday. All that energy urged one to go faster, try harder. It took extraordinary effort just to keep up. Some found it exhausting, Beatrice found it exhilarating.

The duke should have known better than to try to cow an American girl. A Manhattan girl.

She would have the last laugh because she was *here* and she had money and she was free.

Beatrice flashed a grin.

The dowager would say women of a certain age shouldn't grin. A certain age being six and thirty. Anyone would say she was old news and unmarriageable but oh, if she didn't feel like her life was only beginning.

The dowager duchess had no command over Beatrice now.

And what do you know if Beatrice didn't give a whoop of joy. Right there in the middle of the crowded docks.

No one batted an eye.

Because this was New York City and if you wanted to whoop for joy on the street, apropos of nothing, it was the least interesting thing that happened on that particular spot of sidewalk.

When Beatrice saw Henry, the family's long-time driver, she shot her hand in the air for a wild, undignified wave unbefitting a duchess. "Henry! Hello!"

He smiled when he saw her.

"Welcome back, Duchess."

"Oh, Henry shush. I left *her* back in England. I feel like Miss Goodwin again."

They sorted out the bags, and there weren't too many. She'd left most of her duchess dresses behind, as they were the sort of gowns one wore when languishing in a drafty old castle, trying to blend in with the woodwork.

It went without saying she had Other Ideas for her time in New York City.

"Henry, will you take us to the shop first?"

"Before you kiss your mother?"

"You know me, Henry."

"I do, Miss Goodwin. I do."

Henry expertly navigated the carriage through the mad crush on the docks and onto the avenue taking them uptown to her favorite place in the world. They moved slowly—traffic!—but there was so much to see.

Buildings she remembered had been torn down and rebuilt taller than ever before, in the newest cast-iron architectural styles—next to churches and dwellings that had been standing since before she'd been born. It was just like she remembered and wildly different at the same time. The old crushed up against the new. This was a city for constant reinvention.

For second chances.

And there it was ahead, a particular building rising up on the corner of Broadway and Tenth Street. Goodwin's, the greatest department store in all of New York. It was certainly her most favorite spot in the world.

Her grandfather on her mother's side had started a successful shop farther downtown, her father had taken over the business—and renamed it after himself—after marrying her mother. He'd built this magnificent department store on the Ladies' Mile. It was five floors of everything a man, woman, or child could ever want or need.

Her happiest childhood hours had been spent wandering through the shop, marveling at all the pretty fabrics, gloves, jewels, umbrellas, whatever. She tagged along after her father, as he discussed pricing strategies and merchandise displays and managed all the employees.

Goodwin's was where she experienced that magical rush of a girl's first love. Shopping. And her other first love.

Whatever happened to him?

The carriage rolled to a stop and Beatrice didn't waste a minute, leaping from the carriage and bursting in through the tall front doors.

It was just like she remembered.

The pink marble columns. The five-story open atrium. The old brass chandeliers.

But it all felt smaller and it didn't quite gleam as it did in her memories. All the energy out there on the streets came to a screeching halt in these once-hallowed halls.

A few customers wandered around the counters and displays, rifling through the selection of goods. This was not the vibrant, bustling scene of her youth. This was not the magical place that inspired hope and dreams of brighter days and better things.

Something had changed. Something had gone wrong.

The magic was gone.

What happened?

Edward, probably. With her father gone and the store failing to capture her brother's imagination, it had been left to plod along as it had always done, even as the city grew and transformed all around it.

With a heavy heart, Beatrice turned, pushed open the heavy doors, and stepped onto the street.

She was momentarily blinded by the sight of a tall, gleaming white building on the other side of Broadway. It was six stories high with a massive glass dome rising higher still. Massive sheet glass windows revealed colorful displays of hats and gowns. A crush of people were entering and exiting through a revolving door. The whole building was a hive of activity.

"Henry, what is that? I don't see a sign."

"That is Dalton's. It's so popular it doesn't need a sign," Henry explained.

I used to know a Dalton once. Funny, she hadn't thought of him in years and she'd already thought of him twice this morning. Ghosts of New York, she supposed. But never mind that, Beatrice had crawled through hellfire and agonies to be here, in the heart of New York City, and she wasn't looking back.

Chapter Two

The Goodwin Residence
One West Thirty-Fourth Street

*A*fter thoroughly enjoying the modern conveniences of her family's mansion—which she had been deprived of in the duke's drafty old castle—Beatrice dressed and went down to dinner.

"It's good to be home," Beatrice said and it was somehow the wrong thing to say because it reminded her mother of her daughter's failure.

A divorcée was bad. But to divorce a duke? It boggled the mind and was somehow a personal attack upon her mother, her values, and the sacrifices and plans she had made.

Her mother, Estella, smiled tightly.

"What is the news?"

"You know most of it from our letters," Estella said. Her mother's long missives detailing the births, deaths, marriages, and scandals of Manhattan society had always been a delight to receive and savor. But then Beatrice had to write back—with so much time and very little to report—and it'd been rather depressing.

Silence. Her mother sipped her wine. Edward, leaning against the mantel, sipped some spirits. What a homecoming.

"I went to the shop today," Beatrice said.

"Already?"

"I popped in on my way home from the ship. I had missed it desperately and couldn't wait to see it. You know it is my favorite place in the world. But things have changed. Or rather . . . they had not changed at all."

Beatrice looked from her mother to her brother, hoping for an explanation as to why the crown jewel of the Ladies' Mile was now a dispiriting building hosting last season's left-over merchandise, like a party that had gone on too long.

"We're going to sell it," Edward said, leaning against the mantel. In the fireplace were the smoldering remains of a fire that had been allowed to die out. But a few stubborn embers remained.

"Sell it!?" Beatrice exclaimed. "That's like saying you want to sell a heart or a lung. Edward, what are you saying?"

Edward shrugged. "It's a lot of bother for little return. Besides, we don't need it. Not with the rents from our various real estate investments. With the proceeds of the sale I can invest in Hodsoll's silver mine."

Her mother sat on a chair with her spine straight—there was simply no excuse for bad posture—sipping some wine.

"The shop isn't quite what it used to be, dear," her mother said. "Frankly, it's an embarrassment now. None of my friends shop there anymore. Terribly awkward. Best to just sell it and be done with it. Since we don't *need* it. We are assured a fortune if we invest in the Hodsoll's mine."

"You could—and I'm just thinking out loud here, and I am just a woman so what do I know," Beatrice began with her usual preface to any thought, meant to ward off her former husband's plentiful criticisms. "But . . . maybe you could try a bit harder to make the store successful?"

"Beatrice, your brother has been working very hard and circumstances are just beyond our control. Things never quite recovered after the recession in 1873."

"That was twenty-five years ago."

"And in 1893."

"Well, then. Something bad happened a few years ago. But what about second chances?"

Beatrice was a fervent believer in rising up from the wreckage of one's past mistakes. Of not giving up on oneself. She had *divorced a duke*, was exiled from English society, and crossed an ocean for her second chance. The least her brother could do was to *try* not to ruin a once-successful business.

"It's that damned Dalton's store is what it is," Edward said. "He had to go and build a bigger, newer store right across the street from ours. Things would be *fine* if it weren't for that."

DALTON.

She had known a Dalton once upon a time. She had even loved him, though she had lacked the courage of her convictions. To be fair, it was hard for a young girl to follow her heart when faced with the enormous pressure exerted by her mother, society, and the way of the world. But all that felt like another lifetime entirely. He'd probably gone out West to seek his fortune. He'd probably vanished from earth entirely. He certainly had no place in her head or heart anymore.

Not after what he'd done.

That was a fire that was nothing but ashes now.

Beatrice was just a woman, so what did she know about anything *but* she had to think that just because a competitor moved in next door didn't mean their store had to wave last season's white flag. Especially if the competitor was *Dalton*.

"What I'd like to know is what we ever did to him to make him come into our turf and steal our customers," Edward grumbled. He stared down at that last glowing ember and kicked some ash toward it with the toe of his shoe. Mother sipped her wine. He continued. "We'd been there for decades. We were there first."

"Have you tried updating the merchandise?" Beatrice asked. "I did notice some of the hats were out of style. And coming from someone who is woefully out of style herself . . ." Beatrice shrugged to soften the fact that she had happened to notice the latest fashions in hats by looking out the window during the journey from the docks to the store.

In other words: How could Edward miss something so obvious?

"We can't buy new inventory until we sell the old," Edward explained impatiently, as if she were simpleminded. It was, she noted, not unlike how her ex-husband spoke to her. What did she know? She was just a woman. Just a wife. Just some silly society girl.

She'd crossed an ocean to get away from that and the *less than* way it made her feel. She would not tolerate it anymore.

"What about marking it down?" Beatrice inquired. "Move it out quickly, start fresh."

"Our clientele—traditional, respectable men and women—do not want discounted items. We are Goodwin's. We are not cheap."

"So you're just going to sell the whole shop, probably for little more than a song. You are going to give our father's life work, our family's pride and joy, to the highest bidder. You are going to give up."

"Beatrice, that is no way to speak to your brother."

"Never mind, Mother," Edward replied. "If she's so smart, maybe she can present a better idea?"

"Maybe I will," Beatrice snapped.

And just like that, that little fire in her heart that she'd been nurturing flickered and burned a little bigger and brighter. *Maybe you will think of something.* It was a whisper of a mad idea but Beatrice listened. She closed her eyes and shut out the nay-saying of everyone in her life and listened intently for that little voice inside her. *Maybe you will think of something.*

Maybe not. But she could certainly try.

It's not like she had anything else to do.

"I should mention that you don't have much time to do it," Edward said. "The board meets on Friday."

"That doesn't leave much time to save it at all," Beatrice murmured. Her eyes were avoiding her family and staring intently at that last little ember. It wasn't cold outside; otherwise the fire would be stoked to roaring. But she had a hankering to tend to it. She just couldn't let it burn out and fade away. Not the fire. Not the store. Not herself.

So Beatrice stood and made her way to the grate.

"Step aside, Edward."

"Stooping low these days, I see."

"And I see work that needs to be done and no reason not to do it."

"I beg your pardon, *your ladyship*."

That was not the way she was to be properly addressed but that was exactly the point. She was just some lofty lady, out of touch with matters of business and the fast-paced New York life. What did she know about anything? She was just some flighty society girl, some disastrous duchess, some dried-up divorcée.

She was foolish and useless and used up. Or so the duke had said. Roared, really.

She crouched down to tend to the fire.

"Why don't you find a new husband instead?" Edward asked of her backside. Beatrice took a deep breath and let out a slow exhale and concentrated on the fire and not smacking her brother with the poker.

"One of the Schermerhorn boys is said to be looking for a wife," mother said, perking up. "Another marriage would help everyone forget about your failure with the duke."

And just like that Beatrice was eighteen again. Full of hopes and dreams and told to make herself pretty and docile so she could be fobbed off on someone else who would tell her how to style her hair, with whom to associate, and what was appropriate reading material. Someone who would admonish her not to walk too fast or talk so much or laugh so loudly.

Except she wasn't eighteen any longer. She was a grown woman who had endured years of petty slights and outright commands to shrink her body, silence her tongue, stifle her spirit, and otherwise mold herself into a pretty little vessel called Perfect Lady. No longer.

Against all odds, she had escaped.

Every moment now was her second chance.

Beatrice coaxed a little flame out of that last ember. She blew softly upon it and set her mouth in a satisfied smile as it caught into a full-blown flame. The fire, finally, caught flame. It sparked into something bright, hot, and dangerous.

Just like her.

She stood, brushed her hands off on her skirt, ignored her mother's gasp of horror at the ruined dress, and said, "Friday, you say?"

"Yes, but it doesn't matter," Edward said. "We're going to sell and there's nothing you can do about it."

Chapter Three

Dalton's Department Store
Tenth and Broadway
The next day

*G*ood morning, Mr. Dalton."

Wes gave the shopgirl a wink as he passed through her department and onto the next. Like all the others, she was well turned out in her freshly pressed uniform and ready for another busy day to begin.

It was all part of the routine.

At precisely a quarter to nine each morning, he left his office on the top floor and took the long way to the front entrance of the store, passing through every department of his store on his way.

Home furnishings on six, fabrics on five, women's fashions on four, goods for men on three, accessories and seasonal displays on two. He made observations, gave orders, and ensured that everything was in perfect order. He strolled down the sweeping, dramatic staircase to the center aisle which led past a maze of enticing displays—everything from gloves and diamonds—onward to the distinct revolving door that opened onto Broadway.

At precisely nine o'clock he would unlock it.

This morning, Connor caught up with him on the second floor, in the middle of the newly installed soda fountain, a few minutes shy of the opening hour. They kept walking at a brisk pace down to the main sales floor.

"What's the news, Connor?"

Sam Connor was his second in command, the one person in the world whom Dalton could rely on. They had come up together from nothing and succeeded despite all odds stacked against them. Dalton had the vision and the daring; Connor knew how to get things done.

They got plenty done.

Creating the most dazzlingly successful department store in Manhattan, for instance.

Because Dalton knew how to create spectacles that sparked desire and longing in the heart of the beholder. He had a skill, honed over years of practice: how to make women want things they never knew they needed. He knew how to lower the defenses between a woman's better judgment and her purse.

He knew how to spark visions and kindle dreams of the women they *could* be and the beautiful lives they *could* have . . . If only she had the right hat or dress or china on her dining room table.

He hadn't always known how to do this.

A broken heart gave him the motivation to learn and a deal with the devil gave him the opportunity.

Sixteen years later he had earned a fortune from women, specifically the type of society women who had thought nothing of flirting with him but would never consider him for, say, marriage, if they knew who he really was. And so Dalton extracted a fortune from the lot of them, one pair of handmade kidskin gloves at a time. And he laughed all the way to the bank.

"Your duchess has returned to New York," Connor said, which prompted the discovery that even after all these years the mention of her still caused a tightening in his chest that interfered with breathing. "It's all over the papers. It was in the *New York Post*, the *New York Times*, the *New York World* . . ."

Wes knew. Oh, he knew. He'd overheard women talking in the jewelry department yesterday and saw a glimpse of her name in this morning's paper. Both times he'd felt a pang which, being a man, he'd promptly ignored.

"I don't particularly care," Dalton said. "And she's not my duchess."

Connor grinned at him, knowingly. "Oh, I think you do care. She may not be your duchess, but she's definitely the girl who got away. And she's no longer a duchess."

Dalton walked right into a display of perfumes in glass bottles. The whole table rattled precariously and one delicate bottle fell to the marble floor and shattered, assaulting everyone in the vicinity with the strong scent of eau de lilacs.

Shit. Ruthless, seductive, millionaire tycoons did not walk into displays of store merchandise at the mere mention of a woman's name. Even if it was *her*. Not just the one who got away, but the one who ditched him for a duke at the first opportunity. The woman who gave purpose and meaning to his days, just not in a way his younger, idealistic, romantic self had hoped.

But *damn*.

The girl who had picked respectability and security over the promise of his love was now divorced. One had to appreciate the poetic justice in that.

"I don't care that she's back. Or no longer a duchess," Wes said, doing his best to sound bored. "It means nothing to me."

"The gentleman doth protest too much. Shall I tell you why you care that she has returned to Manhattan society?"

"As if I could stop you."

"Because she might complicate things," Connor said, and Wes paused to let his friend explain. He exerted an enormous amount of control to ensure that he outwardly projected calm disinterest even though his heart was pounding wildly. "As you know, Goodwin's is on the verge of bankruptcy."

"All part of my evil plan."

"Easily accomplished because Edward Goodwin doesn't have a head for business. Not like Goodwin Senior, may he rest in peace."

Wes nodded at the known fact. "Maybe if Edward sobered up and applied himself, he would."

It went without saying that he did not.

"The board is meeting Friday. They're going to discuss putting the store up for sale."

Dalton stopped short. They were nearly to the revolving door where a crowd of eager customers were awaiting entry, and mere minutes away from nine o'clock.

"How do you know this?"

"I have my ways. You know that."

"Finally." Wes breathed a slow exhale. "Finally."

"Finally," Connor agreed. This was the moment he had been diligently, ruthlessly working toward for sixteen years. Ever since Estella Goodwin made him an offer he couldn't refuse. Ever since Beatrice revealed that she cared about prestige and fortune more than him.

"But Beatrice might complicate things," Connor continued. "You know how she loved that store. She might put up a fight."

"If I recall correctly, she's not a fighter."

He could vividly recall seeing the notice of her engagement to the duke in the newspaper. The public declaration that she did not love Dalton—not enough anyway. He could also remember the way she laughed, the taste of her kiss, her wit, her smile over her shoulder at him as she slipped out of her bedroom on her way to the duke. The way his heart had felt like it would burst out of his chest. Almost. He could almost forget.

"She divorced a duke. I'd say she's a fighter. Just my two cents," Connor said with a shrug.

"But so am I."

How else would he have gone from Nobody to Somebody? The last time he saw her, she'd left him because he didn't have wealth, power, prestige, or promise. And now he stood in the midst of a retail empire that was so popular and so well-known he didn't even have a sign above the door. He had earned so much money that doors that were previously closed were cracking open for him. Memberships for exclusive clubs; ballrooms of the Four Hundred.

Power. Prestige. Wealth. *Revenge.*

He was so. Damned. Close.

Goodwin's would soon be his. Revenge would soon be his.

Dalton unlocked the door and the women rushed in around him, past him. A fleet of shopgirls moved into position, at the ready to cheerfully divest customers of their money. The air was pitched with the sound of women's chattering voices, exclaiming over the carefully selected and displayed merchandise. What a sensual riot those displays were: a stunning array of colors, scents, and textures. All designed to tempt, to seduce, to conquer. All around him women bought and sold and wanted and craved. Money changed hands.

It was the background noise to his life.

Yet it could not drown out the drumbeat of his heart or the voice in his head repeating: *She's back. She's back. She's back.*

Somewhere on this island. Beatrice was back. Walking on the same earth. Breathing the same air. Just being near. The thought affected him more than he liked. He shoved it aside, repeating instead his all too familiar refrain of the past sixteen years.

My name is Wes Dalton. You stole my love and insulted my honor. I have sworn revenge.

"Friday, my friend. The moment you've been waiting for." Connor clapped his back and made his exit.

Soon, revenge would be his. There was no way he'd allow Beatrice to complicate it. If anything, it only made his inevitable revenge sweeter that she would be here to watch it.

Chapter Four

I have nothing to wear," Beatrice declared.

She stood in the House of Adeline, *the* dressmaker of Manhattan society according to the periodicals lying around the house, mentions in the gossip columns, and the advertisements in the newspapers. The dressmaker, Adeline herself, a petite woman with dark hair and mischievous eyes, appraised her in the mirror that they stood before.

"Nothing?"

"Nothing. I left nearly all of my gowns in England. Now that I'm no longer a duchess, they simply won't suit. I'm no longer a debutante. I need an entirely new wardrobe for the woman I am determined to be."

"And who are you determined to be?" Adeline asked.

"Not a wife, that's for certain," Beatrice answered. "My family wishes for me to find another husband. But I only just escaped the first one and I'm determined not to return to that gilded cage."

"So we are not dressing you to make a match. We're dressing you for *you*."

"Yes. Precisely. Whoever that is. I'm not certain I know anymore. However I do know that I am a divorced duchess returning to society, which is something of a scandal. All eyes will be on me."

"So you must look sensational. Proud. Unapologetic."

"Yes." Beatrice breathed a sigh of relief. For the first time in a very long while, Beatrice felt seen. And taken seriously. "And I want to *feel* sensational. I have spent too many years feeling wrong. I always said the wrong thing, or nothing at all. My ex-husband married me for my money and womb and when I failed to deliver on one of the two, he never ceased to remind me of my failures and flaunt his infidelities. So I have felt lonely and aimless. Invisible and in the way, all at once."

She paused here, feeling the dowager duchess and the duke horrified at the deluge of words she had just shared. And horror, too, that she had unburdened herself to a woman she had only just met.

"I'm so sorry," Beatrice said. "I do not even know you and I am spilling forth my innermost secrets."

"Please don't apologize. There is nothing like the confidence between a woman and her dressmaker," Adeline said. She set down the pale green and light blue fabric swatches she had selected and reached for vibrant reds and pinks instead. "It shall help me craft just the right wardrobe for you. If you are not going to wed, what will you do?"

That was the question.

Beatrice had an *idea.* Ever since Edward had said he was giving up on the store, she'd started dreaming about taking it over herself and proving that she could do better, that she could return it to the magical place it had once been.

Did she dare to say it aloud?

Would Adeline scoff at her the way her mother and Edward did this morning when she broached the subject? The dressmaker was a proprietor of her own establishment, so one had to think she would be amenable to women embarking on a business venture.

So she did.

She said the words.

"I have a mad scheme to take over my family's department store."

And oh, but that gleam in the dressmaker's eye made Beatrice feel like *maybe.* And *maybe* was a new glorious feeling she hadn't felt in a long while. Not since . . . she was twenty years old and young and in love.

"What if I told you that wasn't mad at all?" Adeline asked.

"I'd say that was the reply I'd hoped for. But I need you to convince me of it. You must have heard the store isn't doing well."

"It's not what it used to be," Adeline replied diplomatically.

"My brother wants to sell it as swiftly as possible, but I have thoughts of saving it. I think I could do better. I certainly couldn't do worse. The problem is that I need to convince my brother and the board of directors to allow me to try. And you know . . ."

"Men."

"Exactly."

"You might not have to ask for permission. Goodwin's is a family business, is it not?"

"Yes. My father always said it belonged to all of us."

"Then you might be entitled to have a say. You ought to consult with a lawyer."

Well now, that sounded serious. But she did have experience consulting with lawyers. She'd hoped never to do so again, after going through the process of trying to divorce a duke, but for Goodwin's, and her family's legacy, for her future . . .

It would be worth a try.

But lawyers and legalities and stopping a sale that a boardroom full of men wanted to go through was only the first hurdle. Her stomach dropped into her shoes just thinking about it. All those suits, all those jowls, all those patronizing smiles. They had ways of making even the most confident woman forget her own name and Beatrice was still feeling a little raw and vulnerable.

"Suppose I could stop the sale," she said. "The other problems would still persist—terrible sales figures, the store's reputation for being outdated, to say nothing of my brother whose pride would never allow a woman to succeed where he had failed. It's just so sad that my father's dream, my dream, should be lost forever, at the hands of my wretched brother who would rather blame others than consider how to solve the problem."

The dressmaker was regarding her curiously.

"Have you ever considered that you might be looking right at the solution?"

Beatrice was standing in front of the mirror. Looking right at herself. A woman of a certain age, allegedly past her prime, with faint lines around her eyes. Of course she considered that she was the solution. She *wanted* to be the solution. She wanted it so badly that she was considering facing the roomful of suits and jowls and patronizing smiles. Owning and running the store was her dream.

But the duke and dowager hadn't gotten out of her head yet. Even on another continent she could still hear him.

You? You can barely manage the staff in this household. None of them respect you. How will you run a store? What do you know of business? I thought I told you not to style your hair like that.

"Please consider it," the dressmaker said. "I think you can do it. And should you wish to discuss it further, you can find me and my friends here." Adeline pulled a calling card out of the pocket of her gown and pressed it into Beatrice's palm.

"We take callers on Tuesdays."

Chapter Five

*O*n the first of June in the year 1879, Wes Dalton swore revenge on the Goodwin family.

My name is Wes Dalton. You stole my love and insulted my honor. I have sworn revenge.

First, Beatrice had accepted the duke's proposal, which broke the hell out of Wes's young heart. Because their love had felt so strong, so sure, so all-encompassing that suddenly living without it seemed as impossible as functioning without several vital organs.

Next, Estella Goodwin had offered him money to get lost, in so many words. She hadn't wanted him around, tempting Beatrice. Heartbroken and now humiliated, Wes had done what any poor hopeless bastard would do: he'd taken the money.

Finally, Barney Goodwin—who had plucked him from obscurity and trained him personally—

had fired him when he found out about the whole business. Wes had deceived him by secretly carrying on with his daughter. He had shown himself to be a fortune hunter by taking the money. As such, he was not good enough for Goodwin's.

No, he was better.

He had proven it with the spectacular success of his own store, which was bigger, taller, newer, more stylish, more popular, and much more profitable. But that wasn't enough. He needed to do more.

So revenge. Obviously.

No matter how long it took or what it cost him.

Anything worth doing shouldn't be done halfway.

And now, a mere sixteen years later, vengeance was about to be his. His slow burn of a plan had been in the works ever since that day in June and now, finally, the ultimate success was so close he could almost touch it, taste it. Own it. Claim it.

Dalton had not been invited to the meeting of the board of directors of Goodwin's Department Store, but he still walked in like he already owned the place. Because that was how men like him—self-made millionaires with broken hearts rebuilt with steel and concrete and cash money—moved through the world.

A phalanx of distinguished-looking men in dark suits were seated around a long, highly polished table. The light was dim in the wood-paneled room. The air was thick with the smoke of cigars, the low rumble of male voices, the creak of wooden chairs and leather upholstery as older male flesh settled in and made itself comfortable.

Here was the Old Boys Club.

Edward Goodwin sat at the head of the table.

He was, as he was more often than not, a hell of a mess.

Dalton almost felt a pang of sympathy for him. He'd run his birthright into the ground and was about to sell the store for a pittance and a fraction of what it had once been worth, and to a man he thought beneath him. Even though Dalton had more money, more power, more success.

But Wes did not feel a pang of sympathy, because Edward Goodwin had been born with everything and had lost it due to his own stupidity and sense of entitlement. But that was to be expected when, from the moment of his birth, he'd been told he could do no wrong and that he could have whatever he wanted. As such, Edward never stood a chance against Wes when it came to innovation and competition among their stores.

But the man could have at least *tried*.

The distinguished members of the board all turned their attention to Dalton, the intruder in their midst.

"Gentlemen. I heard you're selling Goodwin's."

A chorus of grumbled voices—How did he know! They had not decided!—conveyed that this was true and they were outraged that he knew it.

Dalton smiled as he said the words Estella had once said to him. "I've come to make you an offer that you can't refuse."

The swift silence indicated that they were indeed of a mind to sell and interested in his offer in spite of themselves.

"Hold your horses, Dalton," Edward said, already letting his pride and ego get in the way of the best deal he was likely to get. "There will be a formal process. We'll entertain bids. Consider our options. Get the best price."

Wes Dalton had not risen to such power and wealth by abiding by formal processes or bidding or waiting while people considered their options.

No, he made the first move. Dazzled. Blinded. Seduced.

It was his first rule of retail: surprise and delight. Never fail to astonish the customer.

"Two million dollars. Right here, right now. It's more than a fair price. We all know that. It will spare you the embarrassment of a formal process of evaluating insultingly low bids that will reveal how few options a creaky old store like this actually has. We all know that Goodwin's is not what it used to be."

On the first of June in 1879, Goodwin's had been *the* premier store in Manhattan.

On the first of June in 1879, the Goodwin family's greatest ambitions had been realized. Through a dash of genius, good luck, and a strategic marriage, Barney Goodwin had made Goodwin's Department Store into a successful retail empire and Estella Goodwin had navigated their entry into high society. The pinnacle of success was their daughter accepting the offer of marriage from an English duke.

Today the store was on the verge of bankruptcy and the daughter was divorced.

Oh, how the mighty had fallen.

Dalton stood, by all appearances, bored to death, while the board of directors grumbled and debated amongst themselves. They were in turns insulted by the presumption of the offer and tempted all the same. Perhaps it would be easier to just accept the offer now and wash their hands of the entire business. Buy a yacht, move on with their lives. That sort of thing.

Dalton checked his timepiece. He did not have all day for them to dither before ultimately accepting. He had no doubt of their acceptance. He always got what he wanted.

Except her.

He told himself that he didn't want her anymore. On the first of June in 1879 he'd wanted her with the heat of a thousand suns. He would have died for her. That was before she accepted the duke, a rebuke to him and what they had shared and who she thought he could become. He had thought she loved him back and believed in him. Clearly not.

Now he only wanted revenge.

He had waited sixteen years; he could wait a few more minutes.

But the moment was interrupted.

By a woman.

For why else would all the men suddenly stand at attention? But for a woman, crashing into a gentlemen's board meeting, strolling in like she owned the place. She did not even bother with hello.

"Gentlemen. There will be no sale."

Wes stiffened. He knew that voice, even if he hadn't heard it in sixteen years, even if it was soft-spoken. Even if her voice trembled. Her voice was inscribed in his soul and haunted his dreams. And if there was any doubt, he knew the way her voice made his heartbeat pick up the pace as if it had somewhere to go, immediately, and that somewhere was in her arms.

You'd think sixteen years would be enough time to forget about it. Apparently not.

My name is Wes Dalton. You stole my love and insulted my honor. I have sworn revenge.

Revenge, he reminded himself. Revenge.

But . . . *she was back.*

It was inevitable that they would meet again once she returned to Manhattan. The island was a big city and a small town all at once.

Truth be told, he'd expected to see her.

Not like this.

Not here.

Wes would never admit it but he had fantasized about seeing her again. But in his fantasies they were in a ballroom, or in his shop, or some other place where he could display his wealth and his power and the fact that despite all efforts to the contrary, they moved in the same circles now. He was *eligible* now.

But he didn't want her anymore. He wanted revenge and he wanted it more than anything.

She might complicate things.

Connor had warned him.

She'd always been the flaw in his plans.

The wrench in his machine.

"There will be no sale," she repeated as she swept into the room in a rush of dark red skirts, a smartly tailored jacket, and a hat perched upon her upswept blond hair. She stood with her spine straight and chin held high like a duchess. She seemed terrified and ferocious all at once.

But it was still *her.* The girl. The one with the soft skin and loud laughter. The one with golden hair and passionate kisses and spark that everyone had always tried to dim. She was the one who made him dare to dream of *more.* She was the reason he was here: rich beyond belief, wildly successful, and about to own the one thing she'd always loved most in the world.

And she was the reason he was lonely.

She was the reason his heart was naught but steel and concrete, like the city she'd left him alone in. He was staring at her—honestly, he couldn't rip his gaze away—so that's how he caught the moment that she saw him for the first time in sixteen years.

Confusion.

Widened blue eyes.

A gasp, from her lips.

Because she recognized him—time had been good to him and they'd meant something to each other, there was no denying that—but she didn't understand what he was doing *here.* Now. She was looking at him like a complicated algebraic equation or a particularly fraught dinner party seating arrangement.

"Dalton," she said softly. She remembered him and her expression hardened. And then she put it together. Where they were, why he was likely there. The look she gave was chilling. "Dalton's."

He swept into a bow. "Your one and only. *Duchess.*"

He watched as she put two and two together. He watched as all the implications dawned on her. The poor nobody she'd left behind was now a very rich somebody who was about to buy her store. Her lips pressed into a firm line.

It felt good. Damned satisfying, in fact.

Then Wes smiled at her. Because this was the moment he had been waiting for. All the sweeter that she was here to witness it. He would buy it, the thing she loved most in the world. And he would close it down. The name *Goodwin* would be a blip on the retail history of this island. While his name and his empire would prevail.

Fortunes reversed.

Beatrice made no move to indicate that they had once known each other. So it would be like *that*. He was enraged all over again.

She turned back to the gentlemen of the board. "As I said, there will be no sale."

Her brother gave a huff of disgust. "Beatrice, what is this nonsense? Dalton here has already made an offer."

"It's not nonsense. It's business. Though they might be one and the same to you, Edward. Otherwise we wouldn't be in this predicament."

Oh, he would *not* quirk a smile. She hadn't lost her spark. Not entirely.

Edward predictably reddened.

"We're going to sell. Dalton here has already made an offer."

"Did he now?"

"He did," Wes said.

"There will be no sale," she said again as if just by repeating it enough she could make it true.

"Dalton made a good offer, Beatrice. I think I speak for the board when I say we all see the merits of a swift and lucrative deal. We can all move on with our lives knowing that Goodwin's is in good hands. It's a win-win situation."

"Not for me it isn't."

The ensuing silence conveyed what no man dared to say aloud: *She didn't really count, did she?*

"With all due respect, your ladyship, this is a complicated matter best left to men with more experience in such matters," one of the men at the table said.

"First of all, it's Beatrice Goodwin Archer, Duchess of Montrose, Marchioness of Hargrove, and Countess of Winslow, and an assortment of other lesser titles. You may address me as 'Duchess' or not at all. And if such matters are best left to you, then could you kindly explain how you have come to run Manhattan's premier shopping emporium into the ground?"

Wes could explain.

Edward could not. Would not.

"I have consulted with my legal counsel and have been apprised that no sale of the company shall occur without my signature," she said. "I am not inclined to sign. Not for anyone, but especially not to *him*. It seems he's only ever wanted the store."

She had thought him a fortune hunter; his acceptance of Estella's offer seemed to prove it years ago. And this moment served to confirm it now.

She turned to face him. And he met her gaze.

He saw love and pain. Years of *what if* and *if only*. The tilt of her chin. The flash of her eyes. The color stealing across her cheeks. A woman, determined. But he also had visions of her walking down the aisle—to someone else. A woman, waving goodbye from a ship. He remembered the hurt like it was yesterday.

Wes had waited sixteen years for the opportunity to buy the thing she loved most in the world and destroy it. He could wait another week or two.

She held his gaze.

She wasn't going to make it easy. But he had no doubt that he would succeed.

"You can consider it all you want," Beatrice went on, "but according to my lawyers you cannot sell Goodwin's without Mother's and my agreement. It's in the terms of Father's will."

She might complicate things, Connor had warned.

She already had.

Chapter Six

$\mathscr{B}$eatrice really would have loved a moment alone to allow her thundering heart to slow, but it was not to be. From the moment she'd pushed open the doors to confront a room full of gray old men in gray suits, her heart had been pounding and hadn't let up. She had been positively shaking under her dress. It had been a battle to hide her nerves, to keep the tremble from her voice, the fidgeting from her hands, as she had tried to project a confidence she didn't quite feel.

She had tried to channel the dowager duchess, that fearsome old dragon.

It was a daring thing to do, storming into business meetings to which one had not been invited, declaring this and insisting on that. She hadn't had practice. She hadn't had the experience which bred unshakable confidence.

Not like Dalton, who apparently made a habit of it. So calm, cool, and collected he had been, offering his millions. The last she had seen him, he'd been begging her to run away with him. Then he'd taken her mother's money to disappear. And now here they were, at odds over the ownership of the store.

Dalton. She hadn't thought of him in years.

Now he was hot on her heels.

They were moving toward the same destination: the elevator at the end of the corridor.

She arrived first, called for the carriage, and stepped back to wait. She tossed a look over her shoulder at him. Ignoring him was impossible.

"Dare I ask if you're following me?"

He barely glanced at her. "I merely have the same destination. Would you rather I take the stairs?"

"Yes, but I should hate to deprive anyone of the joy of modern conveniences."

This was the honest truth. After years in a drafty old castle, it was an understatement to say she was delighted in the newly built Manhattan buildings: hot running water, private water closets, elevators, electric lights.

The elevator dinged its arrival and she stepped in and took a deep, fortifying breath.

She could *do* this. She could stand in close quarters with the man who had only ever wanted one thing: Goodwin's, the store. Not her. Why else would he have taken the money her mother had offered and disappeared when it was made clear that he would never get the store either by marriage to her or by being her father's protégé? Yes, she'd accepted the duke—the pressure upon her to do so had been enormous. At least His Grace had made no bones about marrying her for money.

But Dalton . . . he had made her believe he loved her. He'd been revealed as a fortune hunter all the same.

When Dalton stepped in after her, it felt like all the air in the elevator evaporated.

The elevator attendant nodded at them both in greeting, apparently oblivious to the undercurrent of tension pulsing between them.

"Good afternoon. Which floor may I take you to?"

"The street please."

"The street it is."

Their slow descent began. Silence reigned. The kind of silence that seemed more impossible to break with each passing second of words unspoken. What did one say to one's first love who returned only to possibly ruin one's future plans? At what point has one waited too long to speak and so it was now more awkward to say something than remain quiet? One minute? Two?

One could not broach the topic of the weather. Not after that scene.

Instead, they did the thing where one kept one's eyes focused forward, noting each floor they successfully passed without getting stuck or plummeting to their deaths. A particularly modern demise, that.

It would be swift, at least.

Not like this slow burn of mortification.

It was plain to her now that all he had ever wanted was the store. That explained what he'd done sixteen years ago, and his offer today. Dalton wanted Goodwin's. Full stop. She gave a short exhale. Any lingering doubts she may have nurtured over the years that he'd wanted *her* had now been laid to rest.

How sad.

She had occasionally wondered about him during her long, cold days and nights. Wondered what he was doing, what he had done with the money, or if he had regretted his choice. It was clear now that he had been right here the whole time, turning a windfall into a fortune of his own.

Her mother had never said a word. All the letters they had exchanged and not one word. Then again, Beatrice knew better than to ask.

The elevator came to a slow, merciful stop. She tapped her toes, waiting for the doors to open. Then, finally, the attendant gave them both a nod and opened the door.

Beatrice squared her shoulders, ready to step out and face the world and the rest of her life. Within a few short steps she was out of the building and onto the street without a backward glance.

The air was thick and mildly unpleasant. She was grateful for the din and clamor of the city.

For the rush of activity that swallowed her up and allowed her escape.

Beatrice marched straight to the edge of the street and raised her hand up for a hack.

And waited.

And waited.

Oh, dozens and dozens of vehicles—private carriages, delivery wagons, hacks already full with passengers—passed by her in a crush. Bicyclists whizzed past her and she was jealous. No available hack was to be seen.

"It's a terrible time of day to get a hack." A voice spoke from somewhere in the vicinity of behind her right shoulder. Beatrice didn't need to look to see who it was. To see who would dare to explain Manhattan traffic to her, a born and bred New Yorker. She kept her eyes focused on Broadway.

"There's never a good time of day to get a hack," she replied.

"But this time is particularly unfavorable. The shifts are changing. The horses are eager to get back to their supper. Maybe if you are going uptown someone will take you on their way back to the stables."

"As it happens I am going uptown."

"How is the old Goodwin mansion? Hopefully it's been kept in a better fashion than the store."

That was too rude. And so very unnecessary. Beatrice turned to him.

"Really? Are we really going to do this?"

"What?"

"It's one thing if we are to be in competition with each other for the store which you obviously have wanted from the beginning and *which is mine*. It's another if every conversation is to be trading needlessly petty barbs."

"You're right. I apologize."

"Thank you." She turned back to the business of finding a hack. It *was* a particularly terrible time of day to find one. Especially since, she noted now, the air was thick with the suggestion of a storm. Darkening skies, heavy clouds.

Splendid.

"Make no mistake, Beatrice, there will be a competition."

"A prospect I find thrilling," she said. *Was that a hack up ahead?* She stood tall and firm with her hand raised and prayed hard to The Patron Saint of Quick Escapes and The Goddess of Dramatic Exits. And glory, glory, hallelujah! It rolled to a stop in front of her. Ha! And he said she would not find a hack! The city, bless her, came through in her hour of need. A hack! With an imminent rainstorm!

This was the stuff that made one a true believer in divinity.

She wrenched open the door and climbed in and saw Dalton standing there watching her in disbelief that she had managed to obtain a hack at this time of day, in this uncertain weather. Ha!

Just at that moment, the storm clouds burst open.

In a matter of seconds Dalton was drenched, in his well-tailored suit, hat, and fine shoes. Soaked. Probably ruined. Was it terribly wrong if she found it satisfying? She decided she could be magnanimous in her triumph.

"Would you like a ride somewhere, Dalton? My carriage awaits."

She gestured to the hired hack. It was dark, dirty, and the upholstery was ripped. The smell was somewhat unpleasant, like sweat and spilled things. "And, you know, it's a terrible time of day to get a hack. I doubt you'll find another."

It was raining. He was getting wetter by the second. Comfort and vanity warred with a determination to make a point.

Dalton swore and climbed in.

The driver shouted back, "Where to, lady?"

"One West Thirty-Fourth Street and a second stop for the gentleman."

He gave an address uptown. His own mansion, presumably. She wondered if he had gone for a simple but elegant brownstone or some ornate monstrosity that spanned an entire city block. She would probably never know. The residential situation of Wes Dalton was not her concern.

They both settled in for the ride.

As much as one could in an uncomfortable hired hack with a vaguely unpleasant smell.

He fixed his gaze on hers. His intense blue eyes that hadn't dimmed in reality or her memory. Lashes darkened with rainwater. His black hair had hints of distinguished gray. Drat the man, he looked good soaking wet.

And, she noted, she was at leisure to enjoy the good looks of another man without fearing recriminations and accusations later. *It had been worth it.* The divorce, the scandal, the uncertainty had all been worth it.

"So you want to buy Goodwin's," Beatrice began. Because she felt one ought to make conversation.

"Clearly."

"Why?"

"Why not?"

She gave a huff of annoyance. "Ah. I see. You're going to be broody and inscrutable, perhaps either to dissuade me from further conversation or to entice me by seeming mysterious. Either way, it shall make for an awkward carriage ride. Never mind, then. Don't tell me. It doesn't change anything for me to know why or why not you wish to buy *my* store."

Dalton leaned forward.

"I'm the most successful retailer in New York and therefore the world, probably. I have a fortune to rival Vanderbilt and Rockefeller."

"And so you need a run-down department store across the street . . ."

"You know I could ask the same as you? Why does a divorced woman want a nearly bankrupt business? There are other finer places for you to shop."

"I have to do something all day now that I can't flit about my castle. And don't suggest finding a new husband—I won't do it. It so happens that I am in the curious position of having so thoroughly ruined my reputation that I can do whatever I damned well please. What I have a hankering to do is take my favorite store in the world and return it to its former glory. Even if it means going up against the most successful retailer in New York."

He said nothing. She leaned forward. "Even if it means he'll be bested by a woman."

Beatrice settled back in her seat, which was dreadfully uncomfortable. The smell was appalling. The traffic was awful, of course. Her heart was still racing and she definitely had qualms about what she had done today—and would do tomorrow—but for the moment she was surprised to find she felt *happy* to be exactly here. Doing something. Speaking her mind. She'd never felt so alive.

This feeling is what she'd crawled through the hellfire and agonies of divorcing a duke for.

Dalton looked at her. She looked at him looking at her.

He did not seem to be noticing the faint wrinkles near her eyes, nor did he seem to be eyeing her figure as she'd caught more than one man in the meeting doing today. No, she had the distinct impression he was looking at her as a competitor, trying to discern how much fire and fight she would bring to their competition.

He did not seem to be underestimating her.

That thrilled her. To her dismay. If he'd just looked at her lasciviously as men were wont to do, she could easily dismiss him. But no, he had to look at her like a capable *human* and of course she had to find that . . . intriguing. Arousing.

Was that the word? Was that the feeling? It had been a while.

She gave a sigh. She didn't have time for feelings like that now. Not when she was about to go up against the most successful retailer in Manhattan, who possessed one of the top three great fortunes of the age. Not when she had to quickly plot how to take over from her brother, convince the board to give her time to turn the store around.

And then she had to figure out how to actually turn the store around.

Daunting as the prospect may be, Beatrice would not shy away from it.

She had come too far, braved too much.

She had been too bored. She had sixteen years of living to make up for.

To his credit, Dalton didn't try to dissuade her.

It was unspoken but understood: they were both going to throw themselves headlong into a competition and it was going to be something fierce. Because they grew up in the world of department stores. Of money and desire, tightly intertwined. And it was well-known between them: they were both passionate and determined, perhaps even a little ruthless and practical. She thought of the choice they'd faced years and years ago. How they'd answered. How love and passion only mattered so much.

If he wanted Goodwin's, he would stop at nothing to have it.

The question she ought to ask was, *Why?*

So she did. They had time. They were stuck in traffic.

"Why are you so determined to have it anyway?"

"What if I told you that I've always wanted it?"

"I'd believe you. But still I would ask, why?"

"Let's call it unfinished business. Unsettled debts."

"There you go, being all broody and inscrutable again. I don't know who ever gave the impression that women found it a desirable trait in men."

"Fine. I'll tell you." His eyes flashed. "I want to buy Goodwin's and then I want to shut it down. Because I want revenge for wrongs done to me. For what was stolen from me."

Ah, another man who thought the world owed him something. She nodded and replied soberly. "A noble purpose. Revenge."

"You're mocking me."

His anger flared; she could see it in his eyes and the tightening of his jaw. She'd best remember that she was alone in a carriage with him, and close proximity to an angry man was hardly a desirable place to be, as she knew all too well. Castles weren't *that* big.

But she couldn't just let a declaration of REVENGE go unremarked upon.

They were civilized people in 1895 Manhattan, for Lord's sake.

"And after you have obtained your revenge, hypothetically speaking, what will you do? You are still young enough."

"I'll live my life knowing that I have achieved my purpose."

"You haven't really thought about it, have you?" She lifted one brow. "You have been so fixated on some slight done to you and obtaining satisfaction that you haven't even thought about the rest of your life once you've achieved it."

"Some people would be impressed with my focus."

"I think we both know that I'm not Some People. I suppose this has to do with what happened between us all those years ago."

"What happened all those years ago was this. You and your family—people I loved most in the world, by the way—made clear to me that only one thing mattered. A man's wealth, status, and power. Nothing. Else. So forgive me if I am succeeding—and determined to succeed—at obtaining as much wealth, status, and power as possible. Especially at the expense of the Goodwin family."

To be fair, they had been taught that. Her family had valued a man's wealth, status, and power above all else. That was how she'd ended up married to a duke she'd quickly come to despise, who was only interested in her fortune and not her. It had been a marriage for all the wrong reasons.

"You won't be persuaded to give up the fight, will you?" Beatrice asked him.

"Not a chance."

"Then I shan't try to persuade you. If revenge is what stokes the fire in your belly, gives purpose to your days and warms you on cold nights, then God bless."

"Why are you smirking?"

"Because I know better. I have learned the hard way that wealth, status, and power are a cold comfort." She had learned that what mattered was a sense of purpose. Real love. Companionship. She hadn't had these things herself.

"I find them plenty comforting," he said. "Especially since I remember not ever having them."

He had been poor. A nobody. And she had loved him. Thoroughly. Madly. Passionately. But not fearlessly enough to take the chance of a lifetime, or to buck her parents' wishes and go up against society. And thank goodness. Because all he'd wanted was the store, not her.

It was for the best, she told herself, as he'd quickly shown that he wasn't worth taking a chance on. He had been taught that wealth, status, and power were all that mattered and he had taken the lesson to heart. So she was probably insane to challenge him. But what else was she going to do with the rest of her life?

"Eventually, Dalton, you will either obtain your revenge or you will give up on the quest. You will have to find something else to do."

"Until then, I'm hell-bent on getting Goodwin's."

Chapter Seven

Dalton's Residence
748 Fifth Avenue
Later that afternoon

$\mathcal{D}$owntown, Dalton's store was known as the Marble Palace. His home uptown might as well have been a palace, too. The ornately styled mansion, built of limestone and brick, claimed the city block at the corner of Fifty-Seventh Street before the park. It was the sort of house that people lingered on the sidewalk to openly admire, and the sort of mansion designed to entertain Manhattan society.

The entry hall was five stories high, and from there one accessed the small salon, the grand salon, the library, a two-story ballroom and the dining room, and all the other dozens of rooms.

It had the distinction of being the largest private residence in New York.

Dalton lived there alone with thirty-seven servants.

There were fourteen bedrooms. He slept in one of them.

There were multiple drawing rooms and sitting rooms. He could only occupy one at a time, and currently he waited in the small salon for the caller that his butler had announced. Haynesworth was a genuine English butler, who had spent the better portion of his career serving an earl at his London residence and now had the indignity of serving the household of a new-money immigrant in that new-money city, New York.

But the pay was good. Really good.

The drawing room doors opened. His caller was announced in the low, distinguished tones of the butler's English accent.

It was not Beatrice. The rush of disappointment he felt was . . . interesting.

His caller, Miss Claflin, was one of those new women who were raised in wealth and in all their spare time began to pursue college degrees and public works and charitable endeavors. There were scores of them rushing about the city, improving things.

"Thank you for seeing me, Mr. Dalton."

"The pleasure is all mine, Miss Claflin. Please, take a seat. Haynesworth will bring refreshments shortly."

She sat primly on the edge of one of the upholstered settees, he on a chair opposite. Antiques, from Europe.

It was just the two of them. Alone. In this vast expanse of house. Somewhere, servants hummed with the activity required to keep a house of this magnitude running but one was hardly aware of them. As always, even with a guest, his house felt like a tomb.

"Mr. Dalton, I have heard that you are amenable to receiving certain proposals."

She was nervous, which was to be expected. The decor had been chosen and designed—by his architect and decorator, at his orders—to impress and intimidate anyone who crossed the threshold. It was to be a house worthy of, say, a duchess. But what worked well when entertaining members of the Four Hundred from whom he sought to gain acceptance, seemed overdone and garish when entertaining a caller like Miss Claflin, a young woman who came on her own to solicit funds on behalf of the poor.

He knew all about callers like Miss Claflin. She was not the first to come to him, seeking his support.

"Tell me about your work, Miss Claflin."

"At the Orchard Street Settlement, I work with immigrant women who are down on their luck and whom society has turned its back on. These women are looking for work—honest work—but they often need help finding suitable positions and keeping their families together while getting themselves established."

Women like his mother once had been. Except she hadn't had benefactresses like Miss Claflin with their lofty ideals, society connections, and aspirations to save everyone. Dalton hadn't forgotten; there was not enough marble and gilt in the world to cover up those memories.

"We are based in the Lower East Side," she continued. "Where we are better able to serve our constituents."

Of course they were. The Lower East Side was far downtown. Far away from this palatial spread. Downtown, they slept four to a tiny, dark room, which was probably poorly lit, barely ventilated, and ripe for a disease outbreak. He knew this because he had lived this.

Now Dalton had a city block to himself.

How far he'd come.

This is what he wanted. He had *worked* for this. He had earned it.

He should not feel guilty. And yet . . .

Miss Claflin elaborated upon the services offered, the women the organization had helped, the positive effects upon the neighborhood. She gave him all the information he could need to determine that his money, should he deign to offer it, would go to a worthy cause. And she was every bit as professional as any man he did business with. Perhaps even more so because she was aware that being taken seriously was not a given.

While she projected a calm exterior, he could see the nervous trembling underneath.

In that sense, she reminded him of Beatrice.

Earlier this afternoon she had practically been vibrating with a nervous energy, valiantly struggling to be still. As if perhaps she didn't always go storming into board of director meetings or face down old flames. He couldn't remember the last time he had felt so much like everything was on the line. He was almost jealous.

"Are you nervous, Miss Claflin? Please don't be nervous."

"Forgive me if I am, Mr. Dalton. But so much depends upon me, and you and this interview. Your support would make or break our organization. Lives depend upon the largess of people like you, and people like me trying to convince you to share some of it."

Don't be nervous. It was a stupid thing to say. She was right. People were counting on her braving this gilded palace. People were counting on him—his fortune, really—to save them. And he'd done everything he could to make it hard to ask.

The massive house so far uptown, so far removed from where he had come. The gilt- and marble- and money-drenched walls designed to intimidate. There was a distinct and noticeable lack of a woman's presence or children's laughter that would have softened the mood. But no, he was some lone

rogue bachelor, lording about with his cold and iso-
lated uptown palace, his imported butler, his retail
empire of fine and unaffordable things.

Now he was about to do it again.

Be intimidating. Make her nervous.

"How much?" he asked bluntly. That was why
she was here. But she looked taken aback. "How
much do you need?"

"A thousand dollars."

"No," Dalton said flatly. Her chin quivered
ever so slightly, and it was the only hint of how
much she was counting on success today. "That
is a woefully insufficient number. Ask for more."

Miss Claflin stared at him for a long second.

"Two thousand dollars."

He leaned forward. "More, Miss Claflin."

As Dalton saw it, his store was taking money
from the wealthy. He took a certain perverse
pleasure in giving it back to the people they tried
to keep down. That, and he remembered.

She said an even higher number.

"That's more like it."

Dalton pulled his checkbook from a pocket in
his suit jacket and wrote it out. It was the biggest
number she could bring herself to ask for. And
it was a fairly insignificant amount to him. He
handed the check to her.

"When you call upon the Vanderbilts, Rocke-
fellers, and Astors, tell them I gave you this
amount. They'll match it."

"Are you certain?"

"There is nothing more reliable than male ego's desperate need to impress."

Finally, she smiled. Genuinely smiled. "You don't need to convince me of that."

When she didn't quite move to leave, he asked, "Is there anything else?"

"Thank you, Mr. Dalton. I hope you are not too lonely on your own in this big house."

It was his turn to smile politely, to give no indication of the tumult her words inspired.

While she may have been impressed or intimidated, while she may have gotten the message that he was a Very Impressive Person, she still thought he might be lonely. She might pity him. She insinuated that he did not, in fact, have it all. Or enough. Or the right thing. It was a peculiar feeling he hadn't experienced in years, that of wanting something.

Besides Goodwin's, that is. And revenge.

"After the bustle of the store, I find the quiet uptown a welcome respite."

"Of course. And if you ever do get lonely, please know that you are always welcome to visit us at the Orchard Street Settlement House."

"Thank you for the kind invitation." They both knew he was unlikely to ever do it. She didn't understand that he couldn't bring himself to return to the place he hadn't stopped running from.

Chapter Eight

The Goodwin Residence
One West Thirty-Fourth Street
Later that evening

*B*eatrice returned home, shaking with nerves and excess energy, equal parts exhaustion and exhilaration. She hadn't felt this much in years. The sheer quantity of emotion pulsing through her veins threatened to overwhelm her. She might have to lie down. Except she could not sit still.

It was quite a change from all those endless, empty years at the castle when she had honestly wondered if one could die of boredom.

What a *day*.

Of course Dalton's had to be *the* Wesley Dalton. Her Dalton! Her one and only, once upon a time. Her heart had been full of anguish when she had accepted the duke's proposal because it was The Right Thing To Do and what a Good

Girl would do. She hadn't regretted not running off with Wes—especially when he was revealed to be a fortune hunter—but she had lamented the stark choices she'd been forced into. But it was nothing compared to her heart breaking when she'd learned that all Wes had ever really wanted from her was Goodwin's—why else would he have taken her mother's offer of money to disappear?

Why else would he reappear now, ready to buy it? And he'd been smoldering about it for years, too. It was positively tragic—and terribly inconvenient.

Now he was to be her rival. She had taken a good look in his eyes, blue and stormy as ever, and saw the anger there. He'd been nurturing that anger, holding that grudge, for sixteen years.

He wanted her store.

He had always wanted her store.

He would stop at nothing to make it his.

And it would be her store, if she had anything to do with it *and she did*.

She had summoned every last ounce of her courage and her every last nerve to blaze into that boardroom and declare, in no uncertain terms, that there would be no sale.

It had been *exhilarating*.

And now she had to dress and go down to dinner.

In the dining room, Beatrice had scarcely taken a sip of wine when Edward stumbled in and dropped into his chair. She caught a waft of whiskey; he had already had a drink or two it seemed. Even seated at the head of the table, he didn't look any more commanding here than he had in the boardroom.

A servant immediately and wordlessly placed a glass of spirits on the table.

Edward's hand closed around the glass while he shot her a murderous glare.

"I have never been so humiliated in my life."

"Does that include the time you got so drunk you fell off your horse and wet yourself at the Osgoods' house party in 1881?"

"Beatrice!" her mother exclaimed.

"Do you know what she did today, Mother?"

"This soup is delicious," Estella said. "Try the soup, everyone."

"She interrupted my board meeting and refused a very good offer to buy Goodwin's."

"Beatrice!" her mother gasped again.

"It was a necessary interruption. Did you know, Mother, that our agreement is required for any sale of the company? The gentlemen of the board seemed either ignorant of the fact or unconcerned about upholding the rule of law. It was a good thing I had consulted a lawyer about it," Beatrice said.

No one replied. Silence reigned.

"You're an embarrassment," Edward hissed at her. Beatrice ignored him.

"This soup is delicious, Mother."

"I shall pass our compliments on to the cook."

"Never mind the soup," Edward said impatiently. "Do you honestly think you're going to stop the sale? And then what will you do?"

He smirked and took a long swallow of his drink, draining the glass. His angry gaze never left hers. His expectation that a servant would notice his glass and refill it was met.

"I think I should take over and run the store."

Edward spit out said sip of whiskey.

"Edward!" Mother exclaimed.

"Over my dead body," Edward said.

"Edward, please don't be so dramatic," Beatrice replied.

"Beatrice, running the store will ruin your prospects," her mother said.

"I'm not interested in my prospects."

"You should be. You ought to marry well and marry soon before Edward loses the shop—"

"Mother!" This time Edward shouted. "I'm not *losing* the shop. I'm selling it so I have the funds to invest in Hodsoll's silver mine. I already have an offer from Dalton himself."

And now Estella choked on her wine. A proper lady would choke to death on her wine before she did something as unseemly as spit her drink across the table into this marvelous soup.

A silence fell. And that silence was punctuated by the low, firm, cold voice of Mrs. Estella Goodwin. "You will not sell Goodwin's to that man."

"You don't have a say, Mother."

"I am your mother. Of course I have a say."

"Even the law says she has a say," Beatrice pointed out.

Edward did not take kindly to being reminded of the rule of law. Some men were like that.

"What's wrong with selling to Dalton anyway?" Edward asked.

Beatrice and her mother exchanged A Look across the table.

For various reasons which would not be spoken of, that question would go unanswered. Both mother and daughter knew. Oh, they knew. For Beatrice, the reasons were deeply personal. Estella had her own reasons and she clung to them fiercely.

Make no mistake: Estella would never, ever agree to sell the store to Wes Dalton.

One would be wise to never underestimate two women united in their purpose, especially if it involved thwarting a man. Especially if said man was fixated upon a course of action with which they disagreed.

Nonetheless, Edward persisted in his foolish plans. So really, they were left with no choice but to arrange for his transportation to a sanitarium on Long Island where he might restore his health. The drinking had taken *such* a toll upon his constitution.

And that was how Beatrice, the reigning debutante of 1879 and the scandalously divorced Duchess of Montrose, came to be president of Goodwin's department store.

Chapter Nine

Goodwin's Department Store
Broadway

*B*eatrice pushed open the doors to Goodwin's and stepped inside, feeling both terrified and determined. It was her first day reporting for duty as the president of Goodwin's Department Store. So what if she was a divorced woman with little to no relevant on-paper experience and who was only in this position due to nepotism, ambition, and a nefarious streak?

She squared her shoulders. She could *do* this.

Beatrice strode farther into the store. Her arrival went unremarked upon. As a duchess, she never entered a room without being announced first.

Inexperienced in retail as she might be, she was fairly certain that someone ought to welcome her. The clerks milling around the sales floor might not be aware that she was the new president—did they even know?—but they should at least assume that she was a customer.

She probably ought to . . . announce herself?

Beatrice thought about Dalton and what he would do; he would stroll in like he owned the place and just expect everyone to fall over themselves accommodating his every whim and wish. Except she did own the place, and always had, and so always walked in thusly. She didn't know any other way of walking into a room other than as herself.

Perhaps she needed the authority of an office.

Beatrice made her way to where her father—and she presumed, Edward—had his office. She walked through the main sales floor with tables stacked with gloves and umbrellas and little trinkets, past the pink marble pillars that stretched from ground floor to the ceiling five stories high, up the grand staircase and through a few more departments, and one unmarked door that led to spaces where various functions of the store were done—accounting, for example, and the mail-order business.

It was just like she remembered.

The offices were well lit by large windows, and filled with a smattering of desks and files and men. One in particular she recognized at least.

"Ah, Mr. Stevens! How nice to see a familiar face. It's good to see you."

"Beatrice! Though I suppose we call you duchess now." They both paused awkwardly as they realized one best not. "Anyway, how good of you to visit. I do remember when you were yea high running around the store." He held his hand out waist high to indicate how little she'd been as a girl, how long they'd known each other, and maybe what he still thought of her. "What brings you in today?"

Beatrice blinked. Did he not *know*?

"I'm the president now."

He smiled at her indulgently. The way grandfathers did when children asked for another sweet.

"I did hear a little something to that effect."

And he thought she would not attend to the store?

"Here I am! Reporting for duty!"

Beatrice winced; she went for bright and chipper when she ought to have gone with firm but kind. It was just that Stevens was making her feel "yea high" again. Now she was confirming his worst suspicions about the heiress who fancied herself playing store. And perhaps she *was* but she knew what the store had been once and she knew she could make it so again.

Beatrice took a deep breath. Time to try again.

This time, she would do her best impression of the dowager duchess.

"Please inform everyone that I should like to hold a meeting this morning at ten o'clock. I have a vision for the store that I should like to communicate. Now that I am in charge."

But still she heard her voice creep up at the end of her sentence, twisting her declarations into requests for permission. Dalton probably never spoke thusly.

"Yes, dear," Mr. Stevens said and though he didn't pat her on the head, she felt it all the same.

At ten o'clock a smattering of store employees strolled in—a few clerks, as well as some of the department heads and merchandisers responsible for displaying the wares, and buyers whose job was to acquire things to sell. Beatrice recognized one short young woman with dark hair whom she'd seen rushing around the sales floor just now, and she was the only one who gave Beatrice her full attention. The others stood around, idle and shiftless and clearly there for reasons of morbid curiosity and not an interest in meeting their new president or learning her vision and how to implement it.

Her palms started to sweat.

"Good morning, everyone. I am Mrs. Beatrice Goodwin Archer. As you may have heard, my brother, Mr. Goodwin, has taken a leave of absence from his duties here for his . . . health. In his absence I shall be the president of Goodwin's. Together we will be making some changes."

Bored faces peered back at her.

Not very many bored faces, either.

Except for that one bright young woman.

Surely they employed more people than this?

Of course a few salesgirls were needed to mind the shop, but even so . . .

"We need to unveil a new look in the store, to appeal to a new, modern woman."

"But that's not who our clientele is—" Mr. Stevens interrupted. "The Goodwin's woman is a respectable matron—a wife, a mother—who prizes legacy instead of a flash in the pan."

Beatrice bit the inside of her cheek and tried not to take personally comments about respectable wives and mothers when she was neither respectable, nor a wife, nor a mother, when she had failed at all those things. Nor was she likely to become any of these things.

"Be that as it may," she continued, "I think we should endeavor to attract new clientele. Future wives and mothers, if you will. But to do that we shall have to change our offerings. I suggest that we begin by drastically reducing the price of our merchandise for a limited time—".

"But then we'll lose money. It needs to sell for the price we set otherwise—"

"But it's not earning anything at these prices," she countered. Her voice was rising up into a question again. "We must restock with merchandise that will appeal to a younger clientele that is looking for something new."

Beatrice looked at a sea of bored old white male faces, which were becoming redder old male faces as they started grumbling amongst themselves. Because she was, in effect, some scandalous divorcée with no retail experience other than shopping, telling them that they were bad at their jobs.

But she *did* have experience. She was born and raised in this business, trailing her papa and learning at his knee and listening as he explained a new store policy or one of his guiding principles. She wasn't a complete novice. Until recently, she had also been precisely their ideal customer: a respectable, wealthy woman with nothing to do all day but visit shops and spend her husband's money out of spite.

Besides, it's not like it was surgery.

This was just shopping.

Which was a silly and frivolous thing ladies did to amuse themselves that generated serious and respectable fortunes for men. Yet somehow women were still unqualified for the business of retail.

Beatrice felt herself losing their attention. She would have to hurry now. She did her best impression of the dowager duchess who, despite being a tiny, ancient woman, managed to inspire terror in all whom she met.

"Going forward, I should like to approve all orders," Beatrice declared.

The grumble of male voices intensified.

"What do you know about buying?" some man with slicked-back hair asked hotly.

"I don't see evidence that you know much about it, either," Beatrice replied hotly, without thinking, as she was wont to do.

The man's face reddened with humiliation. He went quiet. His eyes flashed and she felt something like fear quaking through her veins. Yet she had to continue; what option did she have but to continue now?

"I should also like to see a display of bicycles. For women."

This was greeted with laughter.

"But our clientele is old."

"But our clientele are women."

"Frances Willard was fifty-three when she learned to ride a bike," Beatrice pointed out, mentioning the famous suffragist who wrote a bestselling book of her experiences learning to ride. "Bicycling is now all the rage among the younger set. We can sell the bicycles, accessories, the new styles of cycling attire for men and women, Ms. Willard's book. We can offer lessons in the park . . ."

There was some laughter. And some kindly men took to explaining why all of that would never work, why she was misguided, why she ought to leave the running of the business to them. There were some facts and figures that she could not counter. She hadn't proof and experience to support her arguments, just a feeling that other women might be interested in the same things as she, like the feeling of freedom that came from riding one of those steeds of steel.

The employees did not listen to her.

It didn't matter that she had her name above the door.

She was quite certain, fairly certain, that her assessments and plans were sound and that she knew how to appeal to lady shoppers. Perhaps she started too soon, perhaps she ought to have prepared more. Perhaps she never should have embarked on this at all.

Doubts rose up, sticking in her throat.

These men with their mutterings and grumblings and wandering off made her feel like she was back at the castle, inquiring if her husband would be home for a holiday and being told it was none of her business.

The meeting disbanded.

Beatrice promptly went to cry in the ladies' room.

Chapter Ten

The next day

*N*evertheless, she persisted.

Beatrice attended to matters at the store, poring over account books and correspondence, touring every department each day and inserting herself into conversations and decisions, and making a valiant effort to do her job. At every turn, she found it a challenge.

Thank God for Margaret. The salesgirl had been kept occupied with running errands and menial tasks for department heads, and as such she had learned everything about how the store was run. She had ideas how to do it better. Apparently Beatrice was the first and only person who wanted to listen.

As the days went by, Beatrice had the sneaking suspicion that it would be an impossible task to restore Goodwin's to its former glory—and that former glory wouldn't even cut it anymore.

Something drastic and modern and new had to be done to save it from bankruptcy and falling into Dalton's clutches. But what?

But beyond that, Beatrice was at a loss. She spent sleepless nights tossing and turning and considering *how* to change the appearance of the store, the merchandise they sold, the way it was displayed. *How* to convey her vision and inspire the staff, so set in their ways, to make the necessary changes, when they would not even listen to her.

She held the reins—but felt like she didn't know how to drive or where to go.

But the fact remained that *she* held the reins.

So make no mistake, she would have to do something—and soon. One didn't pack off their brother to the sanitarium for no reason. There was a board of directors to answer to, and creditors, and customers, and hundreds of shopgirls and staff members.

The card from the Ladies of Liberty had been resting on her vanity table, next to a silver mirror and brush set from Tiffany and a pretty jar of Dr. Swan's Midnight Miracle cream which she had purchased from an advertisement in the newspaper and which she hoped would do something about the faint lines beginning to appear around her eyes.

We take callers on Tuesdays, the dressmaker had said. The dressmaker, Miss Adeline Black, who had wisely advised her on consulting lawyers and other such businesslike things and it had proved to be invaluable. She had also crafted dresses for Beatrice that made her feel like it was a good idea to storm into a board of directors meeting and make demands.

Today was Tuesday.

Beatrice went downtown to the address on the card and found a plain brick town house. She was shown into the drawing room immediately. The room was sparsely but comfortably furnished, with many upholstered chairs and settees to accommodate a dozen or so women of varying ages, sizes, colors, everything, presenting a full spectrum of the humanity of womankind. They were all very clearly at home with each other, as they sipped tea and ate sandwiches and chatted amongst themselves.

"Duchess, I'm so glad to see you!" Miss Black, the dressmaker, stood to greet her and gave a warm smile. "I think I speak for everyone present when I say that we've been expecting you."

"I'm afraid you all have me at a disadvantage," Beatrice replied nervously. "And please, call me Beatrice."

Another woman stood and stepped forward, hand outstretched, and introduced herself and the group.

"I'm Miss Harriet Burnett and we are the Ladies of Liberty. We are a secret and subversive group dedicated to the professional advancement of women. Ever since we learned of your new position as president of Goodwin's, we have been expecting you. Hoping, rather."

A blonde woman seated nearby said, "For goodness' sake's, Harriet, let the woman sit down and have some tea."

"My apologies. I'm getting ahead of myself. It's just that the possibilities of your position mean that—"

"Please—do sit. Have some tea." The woman gave her a welcoming smile. "I'm Miss Ava Lumley."

She introduced the rest of the women and their various endeavors—writers mingled with physicians and nurses, activists sipped tea with architects, businesswomen spoke in hushed tones with society matrons. All of them women.

Beatrice had never seen a collection of talented, entrepreneurial women assembled all at once, and together they made a simple but stunning show that women could—and did—do more than simper among the draperies. No matter what the newspapers or history books would have one believe.

Beatrice had had some idle awareness of it, deep down, but this made it all clear to her.

Harriet, who could scarcely conceal her delight for Beatrice's presence, launched right in. "Please accept our sincere congratulations on your new role at the store, Beatrice."

She smiled and said "thank you" and was embarrassed because she might have had such an impressive job but she felt woefully inept at it.

"I think I speak for all women present when I say what an accomplishment it is for you to attain such a high-profile position, serving as a beacon to all the other women out there."

Beatrice sipped her tea as the pressure in her chest mounted, because good God she had not thought of *that* on top of everything else. She still hadn't figured out how to handle the staff and now she had to be mindful of all the other women out there, watching her, pinning their hopes and dreams upon her success. It was a different sort of pressure than one felt just being judged by society and coming up wanting—she was accustomed to that. But to fail *and* dash the hearts and hopes of young girls? Well, now she had something else to keep her up at night. Splendid.

"Thank you for your felicitations. I am so glad to know that people are hopeful for my success. But I don't know that I can be a beacon to other women, as you say. I am quite over my head, you see. As you must know, Goodwin's is not what it once was. I have a monumental task ahead of me to make it glorious again." She sipped her tea. What *had* she been thinking? This is what she got for storming into meetings, running her mouth off. This is why she'd always been told to sit still and bite her tongue. To keep herself out of trouble. "To say nothing of the competition."

"Do you doubt yourself?" Harriet asked, as if she could not quite believe it.

"Do not all women doubt themselves?"

"But you were a duchess. You had castles at your command."

"And you grew up in the business of department stores. It is in your blood, surely."

"If nothing else, you are a New Yorker," one woman said with a glimmer in her eye.

"I have spent the past sixteen years in a crumbling old castle, being regularly chastised by the duke and the dowager duchess for breathing too loudly, speaking too much, existing too vibrantly. I am not quite the foolishly ambitious young girl of eighteen I once was," Beatrice said.

She believed in herself but had been told not to a few too many times.

She wanted to succeed wildly, but had been made to feel like a failure more often than she liked.

Of course she burned with ambition and desire to conquer all.

Still, she felt like an imposter.

Nevertheless, she did not want to let them all down. It was important that she manage expectations, especially if these women wished to make an example of her, and wished her to be a role model for countless other women. Beatrice did not need this added pressure to succeed.

"If you are daring, cunning, and ruthless enough to obtain the position, I daresay you have the spirit and stomach to do the job well," Harriet said. "You'll figure it out. You'll learn. You must. Women are looking to you. Counting on you."

"But I don't even know where to begin," Beatrice sighed.

"I should think the first step is obvious," Adeline said with an enviable confidence. "You must go shopping. You must visit every last shop on the Ladies' Mile."

"Yes! You should survey the scene. Take stock of the competition. See what innovations have been done."

"And seek an understanding of what a department store is really providing to its customers," Harriet added sagely. Beatrice understood, in her heart, that it wasn't just the selling of stuff but she didn't know how to express what else it could be.

"Of course you must start at Dalton's," a red-haired woman suggested.

Beatrice smiled tightly. Politely. Under no circumstances could she go to Dalton's.

"Of course she must go to Dalton's. A store so well-known and self-assured that it doesn't even have its name on the building."

"A store that puts all others to shame. Everyone else simply copies what Dalton has done. She needn't visit every shop on the Ladies' Mile at all, just this one."

"Unfortunately I cannot be seen setting foot there," Beatrice said. She sipped her tea and hoped this group of smart women would have another suggestion which they could all discuss. "He is eager to buy Goodwin's. In fact, he had already made an offer which I refused."

"And apparently cajoled the board into refusing, too."

"See, Beatrice, if you have managed that already, surely you can manage a department store."

"My gratitude to Adeline for suggesting that I look into the matter so thoroughly and suggesting professional help."

"We are here to help you in any way we can," Adeline said.

"Can we go back to the part where she refused to sell to Wes Dalton?"

"Can you even imagine?"

More than one woman gave a dreamy sigh. Beatrice was confused; was this a professional women's association or a gathering of women to talk about men?

"If you have refused Wes Dalton you can do anything," one woman said, and Beatrice thought how she didn't even know the half of it. How she'd known him before he was *the* Wes Dalton, the stuff of their daydreams. How she knew him to be a fortune hunter who aspired to nothing more than owning *her* store.

"It's unheard of."

"Unprecedented."

"Who is Wes Dalton and what is so great about him?" asked a young woman who was clearly newly arrived in town.

"Wes Dalton is a legend," Adeline explained. "In a city of unfathomable fortunes he is one of the richest. No one knows where he came from. One day, he's a nobody. The next day he's one of the richest men in New York."

"All the other shops pale in comparison to his. *Shop* is too small a word for the magical space he has created for women."

"You're forgetting the most important part," Harriet said.

"No, I'm getting to it," Adeline said. "He is known to be tremendously supportive of women's charitable endeavors. He gave funds to Miss Van Allen's new Audubon society. And Miss Claflin's settlement house. And a half a dozen other charities supporting women and the poor."

Beatrice had expected them to wax poetical about how handsome he was: those sparkling blue eyes, the distinguished gray in his dark hair, his firm mouth. She hadn't expected him to be so noble. Not when he was so ruthlessly seeking revenge. She felt confused. Worse, she felt intrigued.

"And when he looks at a woman, he looks like he's *really* listening to her."

"Yes, and not scanning the room for someone prettier, thinner, or richer."

And so they went on about how he asked thoughtful questions and listened to the answer, and smelled really good and probably remembered birthdays, too. His store was always a beautiful, brightly lit refuge for women. Beatrice struggled to reconcile this man who'd tried to seduce her for her store and disappeared when her parents paid him off. The one who'd tried to buy her birthright for a song, just so he could shut it down. The one who was hell-bent on revenge.

Drat, now she was intrigued.

"I cannot be seen going into his shop. However, I can certainly take a tour of all the other stores on the Ladies' Mile."

"You really can't miss Dalton's. Not if you want to know who your main competitor is. After all, his department store is right across the street from yours."

A fact of which she was painfully aware. It was there, looming over her when she arrived in the morning and left exhausted each night. It was a six-story marble reminder that she could not fail.

"You said you cannot be *seen* going into his shop," Harriet said shrewdly. "But is there a time he isn't there?"

"Even if there is, he'll certainly have people who will notice her and report back to him that she was there."

"What I'm hearing is that she needs a disguise."

"What, like a pirate?" Beatrice quipped.

"There is a deplorable lack of lady pirates running around the island of Manhattan," Harriet said.

"We can all agree on that," Ava said.

"We do have the power to change that," one woman said, and there were conspiratorial smiles and laughter all around suggesting that when a fleet of lady pirates attacked the docks, Beatrice would know exactly who was behind it.

She imagined it and she laughed.

The other women did, too, all their voices blending together in a roar of mirth.

And something happened: the pressure in her chest eased.

Between the pressures of being a duchess, the strain of trying to obtain her divorce, the uncertainty of her future as a scandalous divorcée, and now the drama surrounding Edward, Dalton, and the store, Beatrice hadn't had a moment to just breathe.

But here was a space that she could just be, where the conversation could flow from professional ambitions to handsome men to lady pirates.

The other women wanted her to succeed. For better or for worse. It was an enormous amount of weight to carry on her shoulders but they would also help her carry it.

This was what Beatrice had been missing in her marriage—support and friendship. The other peeresses had never really welcomed the lowborn, new-money American into their intimate circles. This is what she'd been missing as a debutante; all the other women were in competition with her for husbands.

When the laughter faded out, when the teacups had been refilled, when Beatrice had availed herself of another cookie simply because she wanted one, Ava turned to her and said, "So you must go shopping. And then you'll know what to do."

Just go shopping.

The great advice of this audacious ladies' collective was to "just go shopping." It was not quite offered in the pat-on-the-head, buy-yourself-something-pretty way of patronizing men everywhere.

But still.

Her exhilaration was somewhat diminished. But it seemed rude to convey that, so she said brightly that she should best be on her way. The Ladies' Mile wouldn't walk and shop itself. They said their goodbyes and accepted the invitation to come again and went out to collect their hats.

Harriet caught up with her in the foyer a moment later, before she left.

She clasped her hand.

"I know this may all seem daunting to you, Beatrice. But think of what you can do for womankind from such a lofty position."

If she could just get her employees to listen to her.

"I am considering it, Harriet. That is what makes it all the more daunting."

And just like that, going up against the boy who broke her heart and the man who was the retail king of New York was the least of it. All the girls were watching her. Counting on her.

"But know this, Beatrice. You have us to help you. We are standing behind you, cheering you on and offering our support. You are not one woman alone against the world, even if you may feel thusly."

This made Beatrice think, for a brief shining second, *Maybe*. Maybe she could do this.

All quite overwhelming, really.

And there really was only one thing to do when the circumstances of one's life were tremendously overwhelming: spend some time perusing a selection of shoes. Get lost exploring different fabrics and imagining dresses that she could conquer the world in, wander slowly through a store and let herself forget everything . . . other than darling new hats or new china patterns.

In other words, go shopping.

Chapter Eleven

Dalton's Department Store

Shop was too small a word for Dalton's. *Store* didn't even begin to capture the expansive spectacle. *Department store* gave a hint of what one might expect, but it was woefully insufficient. Maybe that's why they called it the Marble Palace. Six stories of white Tuckahoe marble in the Italianate style, it spanned an entire city block, and was full of beautiful scenes and exquisite things to stoke a woman's desire.

But mostly one only needed to say "Dalton's" and it was understood.

This was not Dalton's first store; he'd started with a small one on Reade Street and over the years had increased the size of his stores as his profits increased. The Marble Palace was his masterpiece. A palace of wonder, desire, a splendor. Anything a woman could possibly want was presented in stunning visual displays that inspired intense yearning for things she didn't even know she wanted yet somehow, suddenly, vitally needed.

He built this.

All of it.

He did it right across the street from Goodwin's. The location was not accidental.

All in the hopes that one day *she* would come back to New York and wander into his shop.

Dalton was well aware that she had married a duke and lived on a vast estate on the far side of the world and owned her own department store across the street, if she was ever in town, and therefore was unlikely to ever cross the threshold of his.

Yet a small part of him had long anticipated the moment that it might happen. And when it did happen, he would impress her with his wealth, power, prestige. He would make her burn with regret, he would inspire her with an intense yearning for the man she thought she didn't need but yet somehow, suddenly, vitally needed.

A foolish dream.

And yet—there she was.

Dalton, dressed in a crisp dark suit, watched from the mezzanine as she pushed through the revolving door—the first and only in Manhattan, thank you very much—and slipped into the shop. It was his habit to spend the better portion of his day on the floor, observing his customers and employees and their intricate dance together.

Beatrice happened to catch his eye.

Dalton was in no rush as he proceeded down the central aisle toward her. He was content to observe the way she traced her fingers along a table of soft, pastel-colored kidskin gloves—a store exclusive, imported from Europe—and linger over a display of diamonds presented on a bed of deep sapphire velvet, locked behind highly polished glass.

He felt no small measure of pride at having orchestrated this moment.

"Of all the department stores in Manhattan, you had to walk into mine," he murmured.

She looked up, hitting him with those blue eyes.

"Oh, hello, Dalton," she said in that way of hers, like they were old friends and nothing more. Yet his heart was thundering with sixteen years of anticipation of This. Exact. Moment.

Look at me now, Beatrice.

Dalton stood in the heart of the marble palace he had built. In an era of obscene fortunes he possessed one of the larger ones. In other words, he was no longer the boy she'd left behind, but a wealthy, powerful, prestigious man to be reckoned with. He had played the game and *won*—almost.

"What brings you into the shop today? Is Goodwin's not to your satisfaction?"

"If you must know, Dalton, I'm here as a spy intent upon stealing your trade secrets."

"Most women come in for perfume, silk, a little trinket."

"I'm not most women."

"I know."

There was a world, a lifetime in that "I know." They both paused subtly in awareness of it, neither of them wanting to make a *thing* of it. They were enemies now and he'd do well to remember it even if the feelings of sixteen years earlier were crashing over him now like time had never passed.

"Would you like a tour?"

"Do you really mean to offer? I am the competition."

"I heard rumors to that effect." After her unapologetic determination to stop the sale of Goodwin's, he'd heard about her brother taking an extended holiday, allegedly for his drinking problem. "How is Edward?"

"He has made the excellent choice to prioritize his heath," she said smoothly. "My mother and I are supportive of his endeavors to get well. He will take all the time he needs."

It was rather curious timing, given the scene he'd witnessed between the siblings at the board meeting. A nearly bankrupt business without its leader only helped his cause. For a moment, Dalton wondered if it would be too easy. For a second, he felt a pang of dismay as if he hungered for a real challenge.

"And who does that leave in charge of the store?" Dalton asked. He noticed a quirk of her brow and upturn of her lips.

"You're looking at her."

He did look at her—fashionably attired, as beautiful as ever—wondering what ruthless streak ran behind that serene expression, that elegant countenance.

"You are the new president of Goodwin's," he said flatly.

"Yes. Someone has to restore it to its former glory. Why not me?"

"So you are not jesting about being the competition."

"Did you doubt me, Dalton?" Beatrice asked with a deceptively sweet smile.

There was no good answer to that question. Instead, he said, "Let me show you around. I'm sure you'll find ideas worth stealing."

She laughed and rolled her eyes. A divorced duchess of a certain age rolled her eyes at him, the merchant prince of Manhattan (or so people said) and one of the city's most eligible bachelors. She rolled her eyes like some young, holier-than-thou girl of sixteen.

Just like that, he remembered young Beatrice, and he remembered working at Goodwin's and finding her . . . distracting. He remembered when she first noticed *him* and all the moments they stole together, young and madly in lust. Running through the housewares department and sales floor after hours. Making eyes over bolts of silk and satin under bright chandeliers. He remembered her laughter. Her enthusiasm. Her inability—or refusal?—to filter her thoughts. He remembered the way she rolled her eyes when her mother told her to soften her laugh or move less exuberantly.

He did not want to remember that version of Beatrice, the version he had once loved.

Instead, he focused on the woman in front of him. His competitor. His rival. His last obstacle before the sweet satisfaction of revenge. She was bright, intelligent, and apparently ruthless. But he had *years* of experience and was equally determined. He could afford to give her a tour; let her steal his secrets, he'd only dream up more.

"Let's start with millinery," he said.

They started with millinery. Dalton explained that he employed his own milliners. He also pointed out the display of the Audobonnet, a hat decorated without feathers, which Miss Van Allen had persuaded him to display prominently, in addition to a donation to her cause, if he would not stop selling feathered hats altogether.

He would not stop selling the popular fashions; he was in business to make money above all.

But only now, as Dalton was explaining this to Beatrice, did it occur to him that he was sacrificing rare and beautiful birds so that he could sell more hats, generate more profits, all to impress a woman who had left him and a society that cared only about him when he had money.

Poor birds.

He moved along, reveling in her gasp of delight at a picnic display. His merchandiser, a gentleman named Mark, excelled at staging beautiful, sensual evocative moments to enchant customers. He instinctively knew one of Dalton's primary rules: always astonish the customer. Sparing no expense, he had painstakingly re-created a clearing in a forest complete with real trees and flowering bushes that had to be watered thrice daily and replaced weekly. On the clearing—with tufts of soft green moss—an elegant blanket had been spread out and upon it a gorgeous picnic had been arranged. Cake. Champagne. Fresh fruit.

Nearby one could purchase the Dalton's Fine Picnic Set—an elegant wicker hamper complete with a crisp linen blanket, a set of four china plates, gold plated cutlery, crystal flutes. And champagne, naturally.

It was *a picnic befitting a duchess.*

"Well, you don't do things by half, do you, Dalton?"

"I don't believe in sacrificing beauty and pleasure," he said, gazing into her eyes. "And one doesn't come to Dalton's for anything less than the best."

"So noted," she murmured.

The words *beauty*, *pleasure*, and *the best* hung in the fragrant air between them.

They were not thinking about picnics. Or merchandizing.

Nearby, a woman was buying one of the hampers and making arrangements for it to be wrapped and delivered to her home later that afternoon.

"I find that ladies don't wish to be encumbered by their purchases, so we offer a delivery service for all packages," he explained. "I've been given the impression that women prefer not to be reminded of their desires and indulgences by carrying their purchases out of the store. They prefer to enjoy them in the privacy of their own homes."

The words *desire* and *indulgence* and *secret* hung in the air between them.

He remembered sneaking into her bedroom and hiding behind the curtains while the duke was shown to the formal parlor.

Dalton gave Beatrice a tour through the other displays in the store, from housewares to women's accessories. Everything was a riot of color and a sensational orgy of textures: the soft whisper of cashmere, the heft of a cut crystal goblet, the gleam of a polished silver brush-and-mirror set, the gorgeous array of silks, satins, and tulles, the heady fragrance from the massive bouquets of fresh-cut blooms that were placed throughout the store.

Dalton had already seen it all. But now he got to watch Beatrice, wide-eyed, drinking it all in. Tracing her fingertips along the soft fabrics, breathing deeply when they passed a bouquet of roses and lilies. She was sinking into that trance of awe and wanting and utterly forgetting *everything* beyond these marble palace walls.

Rule: make women want.

The secret to his success was this: he wasn't merely selling *stuff.* One only needed so much and not more. But that was not what fortunes and legends were made of. Only by constantly stoking a customer's desire, only by constantly offering an ever changing and utterly tantalizing image of what might be if only she bought that necklace, that dress, that pretty china tea set, could a fortune be made.

Dalton knew this.

He was also good at being immune to all this desire and indulgence. *Was.*

It was in home furnishings that things fell apart.

"What is this?" Her eyes lit up as she saw the dramatic swath of red draperies. God save him from Beatrice's eyes when they sparkled with wonder and delight. "I've never seen anything like it."

"This is the Turkish Corner."

"Ooh, that's right! I read about this in the newspaper. You have all the young hearts aflutter and all the old staids in uproar. You have inspired the interior decorating craze of the moment."

"Precisely the reaction I expected when one of my buyers saw it on a recent trip to Turkey and decided to stage a display in the store."

He'd known it would cause a scandal, which is exactly why he brought it to the store. The Turkish Corner was a tentlike affair, with soft fabrics creating an intimate cocoon that was barely lit by an arabesque brass lantern. The interior was strewn with plush cushions. The warmth of light, the comfort of the cushions, the sensation of privacy all conspired for seduction.

Neither of them ventured any closer to the display, even though they could certainly enter and really experience the seclusion, the moody light, the sense of being shut away from the whole world. Just him and her. A long dormant, long forgotten flare of lust struck him. He didn't want to feel that way about her.

My name is Wes Dalton. You stole my love and insulted my honor. I have sworn revenge.

Revenge. Right. That hot burning rage that had driven his every waking moment for years. Sweet, sweet vengeance that was practically his.

Never forget.

But Beatrice, God, Beatrice, was apparently oblivious to his anger and his admittedly awful plans to bankrupt her store, buy it for nothing, burn it to the ground. She looked up at him and flashed a grin as if what happened all those years ago hadn't happened. And then she asked, "Well, shall we?"

Dalton just stared.

No they shall not. It was a terrible idea. They were enemies. Rivals. The last thing they needed to do was ensconce themselves in a den designed for seduction.

"We shall not," he said. "But you go right ahead."

"Don't mind if I do."

And she did. She pushed the drapes aside and disappeared and he wanted to follow her like he would want to breathe air on a sinking ship. He had always known she was impulsive. Unfiltered. Content to flaunt propriety and say yes to temptation. He just thought they would have gotten to her by now. The duke, the whole aristocracy, her mother, all those rule people. They hadn't crushed her yet. And if they hadn't . . .

Who was he to *try*?

She popped her head back out.

"Oh, come on, Dalton! I don't bite. I thought you were a charming, downtown rogue and now you're just another uptight, uptown man. What happened to the wild boy I once knew?"

You broke his heart.

Young Dalton was long gone. That young, romantic, idealistic downtown rogue had received a harsh lesson in hoping beyond one's station. He had learned that money mattered more than love, that power and prestige counted for more than kisses. When the opportunity to have those things presented itself, he took it.

But now he thought about what he'd paid for it.

The girl he gave up.

The empire he gained.

All for this moment when she was here and he could impress her and show her what she had missed. It would make the inevitable revenge burn all the more.

Rule: give women what they want.

"Fine," he said. And he pushed aside the curtains and joined her in the "cozy corner" haven that was the top interior decorating trend of 1895.

He knew, logically and rationally, about the appeal. But he hadn't felt the emotional impact of the space until he was ensconced inside with Beatrice. All of a sudden he couldn't breathe.

They hadn't been this close, nearly touching, for years. All of a sudden he felt twenty-two again. Passionately yearning and desperately uncertain all at once, with an intensity that was paralyzing.

"It's just like old times, and yet not at all, all at once," she said softly.

"That makes no sense and yet I know exactly what you mean," he replied.

This, this was like old times. Just the two of them, the department store as their playground, a world within a world where nothing mattered as much as catching one of her quick smiles, or sparking her laugh. It was coming back to him now: the heady rush of first love, the first hot flares of lust. It made a man think *maybe* about everything and anything—like a high society heiress marrying an assistant store manager.

He didn't want the memories.

Memories got in the way of revenge.

He didn't want the tension of competitors to morph into the tension of desire.

But there it all was, in the air between them, a feeling of fierce competition, unbelievable hurt, uncertainty. And still, after all the years of heartache and anger, in this moment he wanted nothing more than to kiss her.

He didn't want the feelings.

Feelings got in the way of revenge.

"I should think you've seen enough," he said, standing and making his escape. "Good day, Beatrice, and good luck."

Chapter Twelve

The Ladies of Liberty Club
25 West Tenth Street
One week later

$\mathscr{B}$eatrice sank into the settee in a state of utter despair. Ava pressed a cup of tea into her hand. She hadn't been aware how *trying* things had been until she arrived at the weekly meeting of the Ladies of Liberty. Though many of the women were only recent acquaintances, Beatrice still felt safe enough to relax.

Harriet, who had devoted her time to the Ladies of Liberty and opened her home to the members, had created a magical space in her drawing room.

"How goes your adventures in commerce?" Harriet asked, obviously hoping for word of success.

"Not well, I'm afraid."

The women made sounds of commiseration, urging her to tell them everything, to share her burdens with them.

"I have managed to obtain this position," Beatrice began. "I have done my research on the other department stores and their innovations in pricing, merchandizing, and service offerings. I even braved Dalton's and an encounter with the man himself." Here, she paused, still a little shaken from the experience. "I believe I know what needs to be done for Goodwin's to become competitive again. Yet I can't seem to command the staff to do it. I speak, and it is like I have not even spoken."

Once she began, she felt the tension in her chest ease, as if she'd loosened her corset at the end of a long day. Chasing that feeling, Beatrice continued. "But I am the president. Or perhaps they don't listen because I haven't much experience? And yet how is any woman supposed to get sufficient experience to lead if she's expected to marry and stay home? I simply don't know what I need to do."

"It is because you are a woman," Harriet said sagely. "I have noticed that some men seem unable to hear our voices."

"You can say that again."

"And again and again, if a man's listening," Daisy said and they all laughed.

"We need an invention that makes our voices sound like men's."

"Someone tell Mr. Edison," Adeline quipped.

"But will he even listen if a woman tells him the idea?"

"Perhaps we ought to have a man follow us around, repeating everything in a loud, booming male voice so that other men will listen. Like a human microphone," Ava suggested.

"A male translator."

The ladies were laughing now, so hard that teacups rattled in their saucers and women drew handkerchiefs from their pockets to dab at the tears in their eyes.

Some women paused to consider it.

"I daresay it has potential," Harriet said. "Think of what we could accomplish if we had men to announce our ideas as their own?"

"Yes, imagine if we had men declaring that women ought to have the vote or equal wages."

"Oh, but a man is so high maintenance," Ava said. "A man must be fed and watered. And like a horse you must provide for it. They cannot seem to manage it on their own."

"My own husband can scarcely find his own shoes without assistance from myself and the maid," one woman said.

"Maybe I ought to dress as a man," Beatrice mused. She started to envision herself in trousers, started to wonder how it would feel to have that much freedom of movement. It would certainly make riding her bicycle to work a much easier task.

"I highly recommend it," Eunice said. She wore trousers. Unapologetically. But then again, she worked in the theater and they were a bit more tolerant than the rest of society.

"It would certainly make riding a bike easier."

"An excellent idea if you want to have everyone in town talking about you. We saw what happened when women wore bloomers," Ava said, sounding glum at the truth of it. But this made Beatrice smile.

"The thing about being a divorced duchess who openly displays the ambition to run a department store is that there is nothing more scandalous that I can do. Dressing in male attire and riding a bicycle to work will be the least of it. So perhaps I ought to do all of it."

"Well, bicycle riding is all the rage. And it is becoming less scandalous by the day!"

"Now, if only we had fashionable cycling attire . . ." Adeline, the dressmaker, said with a gleam in her eye.

"Did you know I asked them to create a display of bicycles made for women, in order to sell the bicycles themselves and appropriate ladies cycling attire?" Beatrice said. "At first they told me it was impossible, then they said they could not manage it, and then they simply did not do it."

"I would love a friendly store where I might inquire about a bicycle. I dream of riding one but getting one is another matter entirely."

"The problem is that I cannot implement my

improvements if the people who work with me won't listen."

"Did they listen to your brother when he was in charge?"

"It's hard to say. I don't think he ever asked anything of them, other than to show up and do what has always been done. Honestly, I wish to just fire them all."

It was an audacious, tyrannical thing to hear coming from the mouth of a woman. Why, she ought to have just suggested burning the whole building to the ground and starting all over.

And then Harriet, daring Harriet, surprised her. "Why don't you?"

She had reasons.

"I think of the families that they must all support," Beatrice said. "And their loyalty. Some have been employees since I was a girl. Mr. Roger Stevens, in particular. He has been there since I was 'yea high.'"

Harriet was having none of it.

"I bet their wives would do a better job *and* be loyal to the person who hired them. Which is to say *you*."

"There are so many women in the city who would excel at retail work," Adeline added. "And do they not deserve a clean, safe, well-paying, and honorable job, such as the ones you would provide?"

There it was again. Be the beacon for all the girls. Be the one to rescue them all. Be the one to blaze the path and set an example and change the world. She was supposed to do all that yet she could not get her own employees to listen to her.

Beatrice sighed, exhausted from the prospect of it, and sipped her tea.

"I would love to but . . ." She did not intend to finish that sentence, just let it hang there and let the others explain why not. But then she realized that would make her no better than Mr. Stevens, dismissing women's ideas out of hand.

So Beatrice thought for a moment why not, and instead ended up thinking why she *should*.

She could hire wives and women, dozens of them. Scores of young women were leaving farms and small towns and coming to the city to find work and, perhaps, independence and time to find true love rather than marrying the richest man who would have them. Could Goodwin's give them the chance she had never had?

She could hire people who shared her vision and wanted to work with her rather than resist her at every turn. And they, too, had families to support or lives to live.

She had no good reason *why not*.

"I would love to. Full stop."

Harriet beamed at her. "A store by women, for women. Imagine that."

"There would be decent *facilities*, if you know what I mean," Daisy declared. "And I'm not just talking a private place to reapply their lip paint."

"That was the first thing on my list!" Beatrice exclaimed. She got the idea after Dalton's was the only store to provide clean, sufficient space for women. It grudgingly earned her respect and, if she were another shopper, her endless devotion. "But Mr. Stevens told me that ladies should not stay out long enough to need them or better yet, they ought to stay home."

"Outrageous!"

"You really must fire him, Beatrice."

"He inadvertently has an excellent business point, though," Ava mused. "If you are going to provide facilities, then women can stay awhile longer. It would afford them more time to shop."

"You could have a restaurant or tearoom. A place for women to go and enjoy being served by someone else for once."

"And delivery of packages so she might buy more than she can carry, of course."

"A place to leave the children so a mother might shop in peace for Lord's sake," another woman said.

"Perhaps a space to just be. For a moment."

The ideas were coming fast and furious by women who had never been asked what kind of experience they wanted to have from the world. Being a woman at large meant always adapting to a world built for men, which meant always contorting themselves to fit. But what if they had a space that was built for them to enjoy? Someplace safe, clean, elegant, and built for them to linger in comfort. None of these suggestions were incredibly novel or particularly impossible, but taken all together—and with the right merchandise—she could create something new and wonderful. Something more than a department store, a destination store.

Or she could fail spectacularly in front of everyone in New York City—especially all the girls watching her ascent with bated breath.

That was if she could even bring herself to do what she knew needed to be done.

Chapter Thirteen

$\mathscr{B}$eatrice knew what she had to do. But . . . oh, she was not looking forward to it. There would be greener pastures on the other side, just as soon as she traveled through hellfire and agonies to get there.

It was not unlike how she'd felt when she'd decided to pursue a divorce from a duke. But that was a testament to how bad things had become; she would rather crawl through hellfire and agonies on the chance that she *might* survive rather than remain for the all but assured death of her spirit.

So she had summoned her courage with the last spark she had left.

She had succeeded.

So she could *do* this.

Beatrice approached Mr. Roger Stevens, a man who had helped her father run the store, who had known her since she was yea high, who had attended her wedding, who had loyally served her brother, and who had simply always been there.

"Mr. Stevens, if I might have a word with you."

"I'm busy at the moment, sweetheart."

Sweetheart. Like she was a mere barmaid or secretary and not the president of the establishment that employed him.

Her confidence faltered. Slightly.

But then she remembered she had survived the hellfire and agonies before. She had taken on a duke and won; this man was one she could certainly manage.

"Now," she said firmly.

And then, involuntarily the words "If you please" fell out of her mouth and drifted into the air. Worse, they came out softly when she needed to sound firm. If she had to say them at all, then it must be in the voice of the dowager duchess which made *if you please* sound like *if you care to keep your head attached to your body.*

Beatrice took a deep breath and summoned her inner dowager; in other words, her inner woman who was too old and too rich to care what any man thought.

"Mr. Stevens."

Finally, he looked up. She turned and went into her office and waited at the open door for him to hastily join her. He did.

She shut the door.

They were alone.

Her nerves were on edge.

They both took seats on opposite sides of the desk.

"Mr. Stevens, things I have requested have not been done. Why?"

He smiled at her. Patiently. As if she were a simpleton and he had to explain the basics.

"They have not been done because I have not ordered them to be done. Because that is not the way things have been done here. I wouldn't expect you to understand that since you're . . . new."

New. He was going to go with *new*.

She nodded.

"So you have *deliberately* not implemented my orders."

"For your own good. And for the good of Goodwin's. I didn't want you to have regrets when it was too late." He didn't say the words "you're welcome" but the meaning was plain in his expression and his voice: she was a woman, and as such she was silly and frivolous and had to be protected from herself.

Beatrice swallowed her anger and said, "You think I don't know my own mind."

"Well, you are very . . . new."

On the marriage mart, she was too old. But in this position she was too new. It seemed she would always be the wrong age for whatever she wanted to do. What traps the world had set for women! She gave a harrumph of laughter, which had the effect of startling him and sparking a fire in her.

Of course. He expected her to wilt like a delicate flower on a hot day.

"You seem very firm in your opinions."

"Yes," he boasted because a man ought to be firm in his opinions.

"Very set in your ways."

"Yes." He said this less firmly now because "set in one's way" implied old and unyielding and unyielding things often broke.

Beatrice summoned the memory of the dowager duchess, particularly the way she held her shoulders back, her spine rigid. She held her head high, like she had the entire hardbound collection of Shakespeare's works, both the comedies and tragedies, upon her head and it was no burden upon her movements whatsoever.

"Well, Mr. Stevens, we must do things differently around here." She sat tall, spine straight and rigid, her hands folded in a ladylike way on her desk. Her heart was thundering like the horses at Ascot. "Since you are, admittedly, firm in your opinions and set in your ways and unwilling to change, I think it's best that you explore other opportunities for employment."

"I'm quite comfortable here at Goodwin's."

"I'm not asking you, Mr. Stevens."

He could be hired by another department store. Or perhaps he might retire. Either way *this* he had managed to hear. She watched his cheeks flush with shame and his eyes flash with anger, the particular look of a man who could not tolerate being challenged by a woman. She knew it well. Her heart began to race. It took all of her training to keep her hands clasped on the desk and not fidgeting with her skirts.

"Are you saying what I understand you to be saying?" Mr. Steven replied hotly.

"Yes. Thank you for your years of service to Goodwin's but—"

Now her heart was thundering like the horses at Ascot during the final stretch of the race, all while an earthquake was happening. Nothing like being alone with an angry man to get one's pulse racing. And he was angry. Red faced, nostrils flaring, deathly calm voice.

"You cannot fire me. I worked for your father. Your brother. They trusted me to execute their orders."

"All true. But I cannot trust you to execute my orders. And I can fire you."

Her instinct was to storm out, make a dramatic exit. Then she remembered this was *her* office and she had asked—no, ordered—him to leave. Every nerve in her body was twitching for escape but she would not give him the satisfaction. She'd have to try another tactic instead.

Beatrice rose to her feet, a ruthlessly simple demonstration of her power. By anyone's definition of etiquette, a man ought to stand when a lady did, and Mr. Stevens, out of habit, stood, as well. Ha! She was now halfway to elegantly ejecting him from her office.

She remained standing behind the desk making every effort to project an unwavering courage of her convictions. She did know she was right. She was just terrified and exhilarated at the same time.

He did not move.

Neither did she.

But Mr. Stevens did not know that if there is one thing women are trained to do, it is to stand still and quiet and let the world rage around them, regardless of the hellfire and agonies they endured. Discomfort was nothing new.

She had lived in discomfort for years; she could wait a few more minutes.

Finally, Mr. Stevens realized that she was firm. Unyielding.

He gave her a withering look that would have made tigers roll over and roses drop their thorns.

"I won't forget this, *sweetheart*. And make no mistake, I will make you regret this." And then he muttered, "Bitch," on his way out.

The door slammed behind him. It rattled the door frame, it rattled her bones. He rattled her carefully constructed equilibrium.

Beatrice promptly sat down and cried.

These hot tears were not of sadness or fear, but relief. Because she had gone to battle and won. Because she had stood firm and now could be at ease for a moment. She let the tears fall.

She was alone.

After crawling through hellfire and agonies again.

This was the other side.

And here, she sat down and cried.

Beatrice hadn't cried like this since she stole away from London to meet with solicitors who gave her the news she had desperately hoped to hear: she had a chance in hell of obtaining her divorce. Her freedom. Her future.

That was all she needed, a chance in hell. A long shot was still a shot.

Victory was wet cheeks, heaving sobs. When she was done, she felt lighter and a hell of a lot stronger.

Chapter Fourteen

A ballroom uptown
The following evening

Wes Dalton had waited his entire life for a moment like this, to be on the inside of a ballroom when Beatrice arrived. To be sure, he was still considered "new money" but at least he was in the damned room.

What an impressive room it was, with Old Masters and society portraits clinging to the walls, and crystal chandeliers dripping from the ceiling. The room was full of women dripping in diamonds and ropes of pearls, gossiping with one another and jockeying for social prominence. Men in stark black-and-white evening clothes stepped onto the terrace to trade stock tips and light imported cigars with flaming hundred-dollar bills.

People were starving in the streets.

Dalton had once been one of them.

He wouldn't be in this ballroom at all if it weren't for a little windfall, once upon a time. That, and his hard work and high risks and his ruthless determination to succeed meant he was here. Which meant he was finally worthy of her.

Beatrice.

It was only a matter of time before they came face-to-face near the windows leading out to the terrace.

It felt like he'd waited his whole life for this moment.

"Good evening, Beatrice."

"Oh, hello, Dalton."

God, she had a way of saying "oh, hello, Dalton" that somehow belied all they were to each other—former lovers, present competitors, shared owners of a secret history.

"I heard a rumor that you have fired your entire staff," he said. "Shocking news. One would think it smart to keep the more experienced staff and yet I don't doubt your intelligence."

"I haven't fired the *entire* staff," she replied. "Some of the women I have promoted."

"So it's essentially true," he said. "You're either reckless or ruthless."

"I'm playing to win. Let that sink in." She took a sip of champagne and defiantly met his gaze. She was resolute. He was intrigued, in spite of himself. "I would think you'd be rejoicing at what everyone is calling a foolish thing to do, but perhaps you think I've made a shrewd move?"

"You might have done something smart," Dalton replied. "Women do tend to work harder than men and for half the wages."

"Do you really pay the women in your employ less than the men?"

"How do you think I got to be one of the richest men in Manhattan?" Dalton remarked.

She did not laugh. A man would have laughed.

"Are you actually *proud* of having earned your fortune off the backs of hardworking, underpaid people? *You* should know better."

He felt his temperature flare at the mention of his humble origins, which he had taken care to conceal from most of the people in this room. People who were watching them avidly. The rivalry between them had graced the gossip pages.

"What I'm proud of is learning the rules of the game, playing to win, and succeeding."

Almost.

Beatrice did not seem impressed.

He thought again of the beautiful rare birds that were slaughtered so he could sell feathered hats. *Give the women what they want*. He thought of the shopgirls deprived of higher wages in the name of market rates. *Give the women what they want?* Birds and women sacrificed so he could stand in a ballroom, sip champagne, and feel important.

The flash of insight was inconvenient and uncomfortable, so he ignored it.

"Without staff, you do realize you'll have to shut down the store," he pointed out. "For days. Weeks. It'll take that long until you fill all the positions and get everyone trained up. In the meantime you'll lose money and I'll make more. So much more that you won't have a prayer of bringing Goodwin's back to life."

He would buy it for some throwaway sum. Destroy it.

This is what he wanted.

My name is Wes Dalton. You stole my love and insulted my honor. I have sworn revenge.

But she was smirking at him.

"I should think that would be good news for you. So why, Dalton, do you sound like you're trying to talk me out of it?"

"I'm not trying to talk you out of it. I've been waiting sixteen years for the Goodwin siblings to run the store into the ground. But it wouldn't be very sporting of me to win by letting you make some egregious and disastrous mistakes."

"What a hollow victory that would be," she replied.

"Exactly."

"It would make your revenge just that less sweet," she teased.

"Indeed."

"Or are you procrastinating because you haven't made your plans for *after*?" That hint of a smile again. Like she was teasing him. Another man might have felt angry. He felt the thrill of a challenge.

"I'm more interested in your plans. Are you certain you know what you're doing? Are you certain you don't wish to sell? I'll strike a deal with you, right here. Right now."

"Dalton, this is hardly proper ballroom conversation," she chided him. "If you really want to make a serious offer, you'll make an appointment to speak with me in my office. Privately."

He had visions of her in an office.

Up against a desk. Lips tilted up to his. Soft laughter, not the mocking kind.

No, he would not make an appointment to speak privately with her in her office.

"But then again, it took a lot for us to both get here," she mused. "To have inappropriate ballroom conversation."

And just like that, things took a turn for the personal.

"All I had to do was earn a fortune from nothing."

"Not *nothing*, Dalton," she said pointedly. "There was that three thousand dollars that my parents gave you not to marry me. Hardly an insignificant amount of money."

"That old news? You had already accepted the duke and you wanted me to stay in town and watch it all unfold?"

"My mother thought you were such a temptation to me that she had to pay you to leave town. Doesn't that tell you something?"

"It does now. Much too late."

"Much too late, indeed. You have already revealed that all you ever wanted was Goodwin's. Your obsession with buying it now only confirms it. You never wanted me, just the store."

"And the duke was not after your fortune?"

"He never pretended to love me."

Her words landed like a slap across the face.

"Is that what you think? That my feelings had just been an act? That I bared my body and soul to you with an ulterior motive? It was never pretend, Beatrice."

She tilted her head curiously. "Then why did you take it?"

"Why did you say yes to him?"

"A marriage proposal from a duke was an offer I wasn't allowed to refuse. Tell me, Dalton, how a young girl is supposed to reject the one thing she was born and bred to do, especially when she had no other options?"

"Tell me, Beatrice, how a young man with few opportunities is supposed to say no to a life-changing windfall?"

"Well you certainly didn't squander it. There is that, at least. You may have even gotten the better end of the deal."

No, he had not squandered it. But he wondered what she meant by "the better end of the deal."

For the first time since her return to New York, Dalton stopped to think about what she must have endured to get back *here* to this ballroom. Divorce wasn't unheard of, but it was still rare, especially among the sort of people in this ballroom. For a woman to refuse a duke was nearly unheard of. He wondered what life was like that she became so desperate to risk such a great scandal.

What she must have suffered through to prove she deserved it.

His heart suffered a pang for what the girl he once loved had lived through.

If only she'd chosen me instead.

But it was too late for thoughts like that.

"I know everyone thinks I'm a scandalous failure of a woman," she said with a shrug. "But I actually find it quite liberating. I have lived too long trying to please other people, I now wish only to please myself."

"I've been underestimating you, haven't I?" Dalton said.

"You and the rest of the world."

"I'll admit I'm curious to see what you'll do next."

She smiled, a wicked smile, and he felt it like an arrow to his heart. Somehow, they had moved close together—pressed close by the crowds, drawn together. So close he could feel the heat of her, breathe in the faint scent of her perfume.

"Are you saying you've got your eyes on me, Dalton?"

"As a matter of fact, I do," he murmured.

And his gaze locked with hers and for a second it felt like they were eighteen again, which is to say a yearning so intense that the rest of the world could have fallen away and he wouldn't have noticed. All of a sudden, all at once, it felt like the years hadn't happened. And he could, maybe, reach out and tuck a wayward strand of hair behind her ear, whisper a secret, press his lips to hers, laugh about something funny only to them. How could she have ever doubted him?

"But you won't give up on your plans for revenge, will you?"

"Not when I'm so. Damned. Close."

Chapter Fifteen

*O*ne did not expect to have callers at breakfast, especially when one dined as early as Beatrice did. As a duchess, she lolled in bed, reading newspapers. As president of a struggling department store, she glanced at them over tea and toast at what her mother termed an ungodly early hour.

Nevertheless she had a caller at breakfast.

Wes Dalton himself.

For all the hours they'd spent together in their youth, it had never been in the dining room. They stole moments together in back rooms and broom closets, stockrooms and secret stairways. Later, when their love had blossomed and desire couldn't be constrained, he'd snuck into her bedroom after hours.

Now he had come calling and she was about to entertain him in the dining room. *Unchaperoned.* And it would be acceptable.

The perks of being a divorcée.

It was curious, though, that he should come calling. Any business they might have could be conducted at their respective offices. She couldn't imagine that they had personal business to discuss at home. They certainly hadn't ceded any ground to each other at the ball last night, though she might have felt something like temptation. Being so near to him brought the memories back. They were not unpleasant. Quite the contrary.

And Dalton did cut a fine figure in his evening attire, and his focused gaze on her made her feel like the only woman in the world and that was something. When she teased and provoked him, he didn't get angry and storm off. She was herself with him, for better or for worse and he didn't disparage her for it.

Now that was the stuff of romance and seduction.

Therein lay danger and temptation. Worse yet: distraction.

She could not afford distraction.

She had ideas about the store that she had begun to implement, especially now that she'd gotten Mr. Stevens out of the way. Things were proceeding at pace once she had removed him and the other naysayers and staffed their positions with spirited men and women who did not even know The Way Things Were Always Done and who were keen to do something new. There were renovations to embark on, new merchandise to select and stock, dazzling displays to dream up and make real.

Which is to say, she was excited to get to work.

But first, Dalton.

"Hello, Dalton. Twice in one week. Making up for lost time I suppose."

"Hello, Beatrice."

She sat at the head of the dining table and he took the chair to her right. For a brief second she was struck with the impression of him and her as man and wife. At home, breakfasting together. It was so intimate, that.

She offered him tea. He accepted.

Business, she reminded herself.

In a low voice she asked, "Are you here for revenge? Shall I hide the knives?"

She gestured to a lone butter knife on the table between them.

He smiled wryly. "I deserve that."

"Yes. You do. Are you? Or perhaps you are here to confess your nefarious plans just before you expire, in the way of all storybook villains."

"I'm young, in good health, and have no aspirations to be a villain."

"I could have poisoned the tea," she said. "I'm not saying I did. Just that I could have."

"Maybe we ought to have a chaperone after all. To protect myself."

"You're safe. It's one thing for me to be a divorcée, a murderess would be going a touch too far, don't you think?"

"One hopes. As it happens I'm here in a somewhat professional capacity."

"Oh? If you've come to talk me out of the store or make me an offer for sale, you can take it and yourself right back downtown."

"And miss the spectacle? Prodigal daughter returns home, disbands with drunken brother, and attempts to bring faded department store back to life? I wouldn't dream of missing that. I've come to even the playing field."

Beatrice eyed him suspiciously.

He appeared to be earnest. It was a good look on him. Drat the man.

"I've come to give you this," he said as he reached into his jacket pocket for a slip of paper that he offered to her.

Beatrice took it. Looked at it. Her anger flared. Instantly.

"This is a check for three thousand dollars."

"It is."

"If you think you can just buy me off—" she said hotly. If he had to make her an insulting overture he could at least give her a decent sum that recognized her worth. Three thousand dollars! From the man who had the third greatest fortune in New York. Why she ought to have poisoned the tea or resorted to some violence—

"Three thousand dollars is the amount of money your parents gave me to disappear. The amount of money they gave me which I used to start my first business selling imported Irish linens and lace. This—along with hard work and a decent amount of luck—was what I made my fortune out of. I thought it only fair you get the same."

"Oh." She felt herself deflate. She took a moment to make sense of it. Her rival was here to be fair?

"But I'm also giving it back because I have not disappeared and I have no intention of doing so."

"Ah, I see. You are no longer going to abide by the original terms. This is to be a fight, but a fair one. You have no other motive."

"None. See what you can do with it. Make no mistake, this is not an attempt to woo you."

"Good."

"I am compelled by honor. Notions of fair play."

"How noble of you."

"I have no intentions of resuming any intimacies or feelings we might have once had," he said, and her vanity had thoughts about that.

"I, as well."

"So please, don't romanticize it too much. It will make my inevitable revenge all the more sweet to know that it was something of a fair fight."

His gaze connected with hers. Blue eyes hot and fixed on hers. She understood. He loved the fight. He loved the challenge. He loved the fire of fury and that was what kept him up at night and powered him through the day. Maybe he was after revenge, or maybe he just wanted to be the best. This was not an attempt to woo; she would not be wooed. This was not meant to insult her, either. He was raising the stakes.

Well. Two could play at that game.

Beatrice handed the check back to him.

"My parents gave you three thousand dollars sixteen years ago. If one adjusts for inflation this should be more."

His eyes flashed.

She didn't try to hide her smile.

"Not just a pretty face, am I? But do go on thinking so. It will make my work so much easier."

Dalton stood just then and Beatrice turned to see that her mother had swept into the dining room. Her lips were pinched together and her eyes asked what the devil the likes of him was doing sipping tea at her dining table at this hour.

"He's here on business, Mother. He's paying us back. I do believe you and Papa gave him three thousand dollars to go away. As you can see, he has not. So he has come to return the money."

The tension in the room was thick. Because while Manhattan might not know his past, or not care about it, Mrs. Goodwin knew. She had not forgotten.

"It was a trifling sum to prove my point that he was just a fortune hunter and, as such, beneath your matrimonial considerations. I've spent more on forks for dinner parties," Mrs. Goodwin said. "By accepting the money he proved that he was unsuitable."

Beatrice didn't miss the flash of anger in his eyes.

"One might argue it has made me into a suitable candidate. I have wealth, a fine home, a lucrative and reliable income, prestige. Was it just the fortune I was lacking, Mrs. Goodwin, or did you take issue with something else?"

Beatrice waited for her mother to explain *something else* but Estella swept out of the room, as if she could not endure such discomfort in the morning. It didn't escape her notice that her mother still did not approve of him, which was just as well; Beatrice had no notion of anything more than this with Dalton. Business, only.

But the way he looked at her didn't make her think of just business.

The private parlor

THE MINUTE THE door closed on Dalton, Beatrice rushed off to find her mother in the parlor where she was sipping tea and sorting through a stack of invitations and correspondence.

"What was that all about?"

"I could ask you the same thing, Beatrice."

"It was a business matter. Though it felt personal. I'm not sure what to make of it." She peeked out the window. "He's gone now, and he's taken his check with him."

"Edward was too blind with drink to see it, but I wasn't. Your father was too distracted with other work matters to see it, but I wasn't. And you . . . you had stars in your eyes that blinded you all the same. Dalton only ever wanted one thing and one thing only—our store. I hate to see how he used you to get it."

"I won't let him."

"But that is all you'll be able to do. Fight and resist him at every turn. It will take all of your time and focus. You'll have little time for anything else. Until Edward returns."

"How is my darling brother? Any word?"

"Remarkably he is not inclined to write us

long letters detailing how he spends his days," her mother said drily.

"It's not like he has much else to do," Beatrice muttered in the manner of a petulant fourteen-year-old girl and not a grown woman of six and thirty.

"He must focus on getting well, Beatrice," her mother said gently, with motherly concern.

"I do wish him the best."

Edward had not gone enthusiastically or even entirely willingly to Dr. Barnacle's Restorative Home. But he'd been too ill with drink to put up much of a resistance, which in Beatrice's opinion meant he definitely ought to stay for an extended visit under the doctor's care and guidance.

She did not wish him ill; she wasn't a monster. But as she dug into the details of the business, pored over the account books, learned the origins and reasons for foolish decisions, the more she realized what an *idiot* he was. Their father's lifework was being run into the ground, in a series of poor choices and missed opportunities and a stubborn refusal to change. His laziness and arrogance were his downfall. And thus, the store's.

If she hadn't arrived in time, he would have sold a former empire for a song and that's all it would have been worth. Three generations of labor and love, gone.

If she hadn't gathered her nerve to seek her divorce . . .

If she hadn't gathered the nerve to seize control . . .

"Beatrice, I didn't do this just to help you get him out of the way so you could play store and tangle with Dalton. I did it because he also needed help."

"What happens when he comes back, Mother?"

"We'll see."

"We'll see" was mother-speak for *you're not going to like what I have to say.*

Beatrice understood this to mean that her mother would take sides and Beatrice might not like it.

"You don't mean to give it back to him when he returns?"

Her mother just said, "Hmm." Which was mother-speak for *don't make me say it, please.*

"But he'll just turn around and sell it to Dalton! Edward just wants the money."

"He can't sell it to Dalton if Dalton cannot afford to buy it. And if you are there to provide assistance to your brother . . ."

"You'll let me fix everything and then hand it back to Edward to ruin?" There was no hiding the outrage in her voice.

"I don't know, Beatrice!" She tossed down the letters in her hand. "I don't know what to do. This whole situation is unseemly and unusual.

Women running department stores." Here she gave a bitter laugh. "I've been told the world isn't ready for it."

No. Intolerable. Beatrice would not allow it. She would not hand it over to a stupid boy who would only wreck things. She would *not* go back to living in the shadows, existing at the whim of a man who didn't deserve her.

She couldn't lose it all again. Not now, when things were coming along, when she finally had an idea of what to do and people to help her do it.

Well, that "we'll see" and that "hmmm" were all the more reason to get herself positively entrenched. She had to ensure that when anyone in Manhattan thought of Goodwin's, they thought of *her.* Beatrice. She had to make herself the name, the face, the One.

The beacon.

She had to create something so successful, so unabashedly female, so distinctly *hers* that Edward couldn't—or wouldn't—lay claim to it.

"Besides, Beatrice, you might even be married by the time he returns and you'll want him to resume his duties so you can feather your new nest. You're not too old yet. Mr. Wallace is no longer in mourning, and Mr. Fisk has yet to settle down."

"Unlikely, Mother. And by unlikely I mean absolutely not."

"So Dalton's call this morning was simply . . . business. Not anything else?"

Ah, interesting. Beatrice regarded her mother thoughtfully. She had never liked him, even when he was merely an associate her father had taken notice of and given special training to. Her father always used to say *he reminds me of myself at that age* with a jovial laugh, and for some reason that didn't soothe Estella Goodwin's misgivings about him.

"Why don't you like him?"

"I don't know him well enough to form an opinion."

That was society-lady-speak for *utterly beneath my notice.*

"Allow me to rephrase the question. Why don't you like him for me?"

"He was a fortune hunter, Beatrice."

"Fair. But so was the duke."

"Nakedly so. Dalton wooed you into a foolish, girlish infatuation that would inevitably end with you brokenhearted and destitute."

"He seems to have done well for himself though. Better than the duke." Montrose had blown through her fortune. When no more was forthcoming from the Goodwin family—and she had yet to deliver him an heir—he was suddenly more amenable to a divorce. It would allow him to start again with a younger, richer bride.

"So it was only my heart that you were concerned with," Beatrice said.

"Beatrice, be sensible. He was an impoverished Irish immigrant who worked at the store arranging boxes and things. He had aspirations for more and he would have used you to get it. But had you run off with him you would have been cut off from the society you grew up with, you would be poor, you would be an outcast, you would have been nothing."

"I would have been loved." Her mother pursed her lips. "And he did manage to earn the third greatest fortune in New York, if that's so important."

"Yes, with money he took *not* to marry you. Is that love, Beatrice? Is that stronger than what I feel for you and Edward? I only want success for my children. Security. Their futures assured."

"Then you'll want me to succeed. You'll want *me* to make a success of the store. We both know Edward cannot or will not do it. But I need *your* help to do so, Mother."

"Beatrice . . ."

"Mother, I'm wondering if you'll help me throw a party."

Her mother lifted one brow and it was society-lady-speak for *I am intrigued in spite of myself.*

"I need you to organize a debut party."

"Aren't you a little old for that, darling? That ship has sailed."

"A debut party for the store. We are reopening soon and I want the whole world to know it. I want the grand opening to make a statement, an indelible impression. And I want to get people talking. So I need a debut party. A guest list, flowers, champagne, music, spectacle . . ."

"I do know what goes into throwing a party," Estella murmured, and Beatrice's heart beat a little faster with hope. If her mother could work with her, instead of against her. If she could just show her mother how she and the store belonged together, if she could just get her mother on her side . . .

Chapter Sixteen

Dalton's Department Store
A few days later

*I*t was a gray day with the feeling of storm in the air, when Dalton stood at the window of his office, looking down at the spectacle across the street. The windows of Goodwin's had been darkened and boarded over, upon which notices had been posted advertising for available positions.

In blazing red letters on a soft pink background were the words WANTED: Women Who Want More. And then, in smaller print:

> *GOODWIN'S IS HIRING CLERKS.*
> *FAIR WAGES. OPPORTUNITIES FOR*
> *ADVANCEMENT. CHILDCARE PROVIDED.*
> *INQUIRE WITHIN.*

This was the fourth day in a row in which women formed a long line, snaking around the block, to inquire within. The newspapers were certain this spelled doom for Manhattan's most prestigious department store—his. Dalton would never admit it but he was starting to feel something like trepidation.

A knock at the door diverted his attentions. He turned.

"Do you have a moment, Mr. Dalton?"

"Good morning, Miss Baldwin. Do come in."

He always had time for Clara Baldwin, one of his best shopgirls and department managers who was especially adept at training new hires. She hardly ever troubled him; she simply performed her job expertly and efficiently while he raked in the money.

Today she stood nervously before his desk.

"What can I help you with, Miss Baldwin?"

"I'm very sorry, Mr. Dalton, but I have come to give my resignation."

"You'll have to repeat that, Miss Baldwin. It sounded like you said you were offering your resignation."

"I did. I am."

"That is unexpected to say the least. May I inquire as to your reason? Good news, I hope."

It was expected that women would resign when they were married or found themselves with child. Dalton racked his brain for facts about Clara that might explain this. Did she have a sweetheart who might have proposed marriage? Was she already secretly married and expecting?

Perhaps she was moving home, wherever that might be.

"Oh, I have not been unhappy here, Mr. Dalton. However, I did learn of an opportunity for advancement . . ."

He refused to turn around and look at that damned line, that sign, that store.

WANTED: Women Who Want More.

"Goodwin's?" he asked.

"Yes," she said, relieved.

"How much?"

"Ten dollars a week."

He gave a low whistle.

"Exactly. And I am to be given a very prestigious title—*vice president of training.* I shall be training all the new hires." She laughed nervously. "I do have my work cut out for me."

"I didn't realize you were unhappy with your position here."

"I didn't, either. But then I saw the signs and made some inquiries. I wanted to see what I was worth, Mr. Dalton. Then she gave me an offer I could not refuse."

"I understand," he said. And he did. Miss Baldwin was no different from him: she was not content with *fine*. She hungered for more and would seize opportunities that would afford her higher wages or a chance for professional advancement. He would have done the same thing in her position.

The mistake he'd made was thinking that women didn't burn with the same ambition, that they would be content with five dollars a week, sixteen-hour days, and the title of shopgirl.

By that afternoon, it proved to be a costly mistake. Miss Baldwin was not the only employee to leave his store for the one across the street. Seven—seven!—other shopgirls gave notice, as well. Connor had come up to his office to give him the grim news.

"A few more and it'll be a certified exodus," Connor said darkly. "And then what will people say?"

The publicity would be unfavorable. The gossip would be unpleasant. If this exodus continued, service would suffer and customers would flee. Dalton's was a place where a woman could come to have all her needs met right down to a porter to follow her through the store, carrying her purchases. Without such caring, attentive service, they'd go elsewhere. Say, across the street. Then he'd be in no position to exact his revenge.

He did not come so far to come up so short.

It was not to be borne.

He was going to have a word with her.

"They're not going to say anything because they're not going to know. This is going to stop. Now."

"GOOD AFTERNOON, MR. DALTON!" The shopgirls chirped their usual greeting as he strode determinedly through the store on his way to the revolving door. This time there were no friendly winks as he passed by. Anger had sharpened his focus.

He pushed through the heavy glass doors, stepped out onto the sidewalk, strode across the street. He stormed into Goodwin's on the heels of some laborers carrying in supplies, like lumber and tools and things he didn't recognize.

Dalton barely registered the disruption. He paused and noted that the Goodwin's he had once known was gone. Much of the store was deep in the throes of dusty, intensive renovations. But still, enough remained to remind him.

Memories had a way of tugging on the heart and whispering, *Remember?* when you were only trying to forget.

He remembered being a mere delivery boy who never wanted anything as much as he wanted to belong in that store.

He remembered falling in love here. And never wanting anything as much as he wanted to be with Beatrice.

He remembered being cast out of paradise.

In this moment he wanted to torch the place as much as he had on the first of June in 1879.

Beatrice turned, caught sight of him, strolled over.

"Oh, hello, Dalton." She smiled like she knew exactly why he was here. He nearly lost his temper on the spot.

"You're stealing my shopgirls and you greet me with a cheerful 'hello, Dalton'? I don't think so."

"They are freeborn human beings, Dalton, I'm not stealing them. I simply posted notices that I was hiring. Didn't you see them?"

"I saw the notices," he said tightly. "It's not like one could miss them, the way you plastered them all over the front of the store."

"Well, you know that I fired the previous staff," she explained calmly, which only angered him more. "You didn't think I was going to run a store of this size without clerks, did you?"

"Of course not. I just didn't think you would hire *my* salespeople. There are enough people looking for work in this city that I thought you'd get—and train—your own. I thought you would have some notion of fair play."

But no.

They were going to fight and the gloves were off. *Fine.* He'd been too close to satisfying his revenge to start losing ground now. But he was. First it was seven salesclerks, and then more would inevitably follow. He could and would hire more, but as he sacrificed the time to train them, Dalton's renowned and impeccable service would slowly falter.

Rule: please a woman and she'll be yours. Keep her waiting and she's gone forever.

It wasn't just seven salesgirls.

Dalton, seething, took a step closer and looked down at her. It was, admittedly, a move designed to intimidate and one he'd employed when necessary in conversations with other businessmen. But this, oh, this, was not the same. His heart was thundering and he became acutely aware of the rise and fall of his own chest as he breathed. If he weren't so angry it would have felt like desire.

But it was rage, certainly.

Pure molten rage that had no other feelings mixed in.

Yet Beatrice tilted her chin up stubbornly and refused to step back. She held her ground. In fact she stepped closer.

"A very qualified bunch of candidates applied. I hired them."

"I know they are a very qualified bunch of candidates, Beatrice. I know it because I'm the one who trained them."

"And I'm the one paying them more."

Dalton and Beatrice were toe to toe now. Tempers flaring, heat rising. He imagined he could feel the heat from her body, drawing him closer. But he could not allow himself to think of her body now.

"You have poached them. You could at least apologize."

"They're my employees now. And there is no point in quibbling over them. They are humans with free will to make choices. Such as the choice to work for a woman who understands their circumstances and offers them a higher wage. And who gives them a break during the long workday."

"A higher wage? What are you paying them?"

There was a beat of silence.

"What they're worth."

He gave a short bark of laughter. "You'll never turn a profit like that."

Beatrice wasn't intimidated in the slightest.

"Best not let Josephine Shaw Lowell hear you say that. She's putting together a list of stores that treat their female employees with decency so the women of Manhattan know where to best spend their money. I know Goodwin's will be on The White List. But will Dalton's?"

She lifted one brow.

He felt another surge of anger.

Because this was the first time he was hearing of Josephine Shaw Lowell and her White List. Who the devil was she and did he really have to care?

Beatrice was fighting back. Dalton was not about to argue any of her points. He was going to learn how much she was paying and give all his employees a raise accordingly. It would cut into his profits but he had plenty of profits. Or he could wait it out. Wait until Goodwin's went bankrupt, then hire back all those employees at their former rate when her great experiment failed.

And he really had to put someone on the case of Josephine Shaw Lowell and her White List.

Standing where he was, in the wreckage of the store and memories, it seemed impossible that she would make a success out of this dusty mess of wood, glass, and mirror. And toilets. And . . . the strangest-looking chair contraption that he had ever seen. It reclined, and there was an odd space indented for the neck, presumably. Two burly men were carrying it past him, toward a newly installed elevator.

They looked at Beatrice for instruction. "Where do you want these, Mrs. Archer?"

"What the devil are those?" Dalton inquired.

Everyone ignored him.

"Upstairs, please. In the section for Martha."

"Who is Martha? What are those for?"

"I can't tell you, Dalton. We're competitors, remember?"

"Oh, I remember. And it seems we're playing dirty."

"If that's how you want to play, Dalton," she replied, and if he didn't know better he'd say she sounded flirtatious. But this was no flirting matter. She gave him that smile again. It did things to his insides. It made him feel like he was falling from the very top of the New York World Building. Falling and flailing and anxiously reaching out for something to hold on to. His instinct was to reach out to her.

He was mad. Furious. That was why his heart was pounding. All the dust was the reason his chest felt tight and his breathing fast and shallow.

It certainly wasn't desire.

It couldn't be.

That was a complication he didn't want or need.

"You're upset," she said calmly which did nothing to calm him. "You're upset that I'm not selling you the store. You're upset that I'm not just going to add floral arrangements and hope for the best. You're upset that I'm not going to let you have your revenge so easily. You're upset that you have nothing else to occupy your mind other than business and stupid ideas of revenge."

Every word landed like a sniper's shot.

"Upset? Men do not become upset. I am righteously enraged."

"Perhaps you need to take a walk around the block. Breathe deeply. Count backward from a thousand."

"You don't know what I need."

She stopped and whirled around, nearly colliding with his chest. She pushed him. Her palms thumping against the wool of his suit jacket.

"*I* don't care what *you* need. In case you hadn't noticed, I am trying to do something here and it doesn't concern you. No matter how much you stomp about trying to make yourself the center of attention. Look at me, Dalton. I'm not the girl who broke your heart. I'm a woman trying to run a business."

Fine. He looked at her, really looked at her.

Upswept hair with flecks of dust. Deep blue eyes, bright and fiery. He saw faint lines around them, but that didn't make them look any less beautiful. It suggested that she had seen things, that she could really see him if he'd let her.

He dropped his gaze to her mouth, full and sensuous and firm. He could just picture those lips telling him what to do and damn if the orders she gave in his fantasy weren't ones he wanted to follow.

She wore a dark, stylish yet serviceable shirt-waist, skirt, and jacket. It hadn't escaped his notice the way she moved confidently through this wreckage of a store. The way she stood before him, unapologetic and defiant.

He didn't see the girl who broke his heart. He saw a woman trying to run a business.

And she was magnificent.

"What is that look, Dalton? If I didn't know any better I'd think you wanted to kiss me."

"Don't tempt me," he said sharply.

"Or what?" Beatrice challenged.

"Or I just might."

"Oooh," she breathed. "Oh I am so . . ."

"So what, Beatrice?"

Dalton took a step close, too close. There were mere inches separating their thundering hearts. He either wanted to kiss her or throttle her and it took all of his self-control to keep himself in check.

This was not usually how he conducted business. He would never stand so close.

He would never feel so much.

He would never think of kissing.

That's what this felt like. A prelude to a kiss. An up-against-the-wall, cannot-even-breathe, about-to-explode, scorching kiss. One long overdue.

He noticed the quick rise and fall of her chest, the darkening of her eyes, her refusal to step back and relinquish even an inch of ground.

One thing was clear to him now: this wasn't just about vengeance or employees. It was about the unfinished business between them.

Dalton's Department Store
Moments later

DALTON SLAMMED THE door to his office behind him. Connor followed a moment later.

"Let me guess. She complicated things," Connor said. His voice conveyed a distinct lack of shock. His eyes betrayed a glimmer of amusement though.

Dalton was not amused.

The whole situation was no laughing matter. Everything he'd worked toward for his entire life was under threat and all he could think about was wanting to kiss her.

"I almost kissed her." Dalton said the words out loud as if it might make the unbelievable more believable. But he was practically vibrating with unsatisfied wanting and his heart was still racing, so it must have been true.

"Circumstances?"

"In the throes of a fight about her poaching our employees."

"So you almost kissed her during the heat of an argument. Interesting strategy." Connor nodded. "You know, it happens. Particularly when discussing business. I mean, think of all the times you almost kissed Macy, Fields, Wanamaker . . ."

It wasn't a strategy.

"It's her," Dalton admitted as he poured himself a whiskey. "And it wasn't entirely about business."

She wasn't a business problem, much as he may wish to relegate her to one. She was so much more; a *personal* problem. The crash and burn of young love, his wounded heart and bruised feelings. She was foolish dreams crashing into reality. She was messy feelings and complicated desires. She was a choice between what he wanted and what he had once upon a time sworn to do.

She was a challenge. It was her voice he imagined, asking him the most provoking questions: *Oh hello, Dalton what do you really want?*

He wanted power, prestige, and a fortune.

Why do you want that?

He wanted her to choose him. He never wanted to be cast out of paradise again.

But can you admit that?

No.

Dalton took a swallow of whiskey.

"I told you she would complicate things," Connor said.

"If you're such a know-it-all fortune-teller, maybe you can tell me what I should do?"

"You should probably apologize."

"Flowers?"

Connor rubbed his eyes, weary. He took the bottle and poured a small amount for himself.

"Are you trying to woo her or destroy her life's work and the thing that brings her joy? Because I'm confused."

"That makes two of us."

"You should probably decide. Do you want her, or her store?"

"I'm curious to see what she does. But I cannot let her wreck my life's work, either."

"Is your life's work revenge? Or has it always been to amass enough of a fortune so that you feel worthy of her?"

They went way back, him and Connor. They had grown up in the tenements together, stealing every chance and seizing every opportunity that came their way. The empire Dalton built was his—his risk, his vision—but he never would have accomplished it without Connor by his side.

But sometimes such good friends were annoying. Like when they distilled a lifetime into one neat little question.

Did he really want the store? Or had he always just wanted her?

In trying to be worthy of her he was putting them at odds. It made them together an impossibility.

She was impossible.

Since when did duchesses get divorced? Since when did they sail back into a man's life and start competing with him for his place in the world?

"I don't know," Dalton said, a rare admission.

"Well, either way, you can't go around kissing your business competitors or colleagues. It's a recipe for disaster," Connor said. "You should apologize—without flowers. And then you have to decide. Give it all up for the girl or go all out and try to win it all—but at the expense of the girl."

Chapter Seventeen

*I*n the wreckage of one of Manhattan's once great department stores, two women stood with heads bowed together, surveying the laborers, consulting the architectural plans, and reviewing the handwritten lists of things to do. Beatrice's divorce settlement, family money, and an investment from the Ladies of Liberty had provided the capital to make some strategic improvements to the store. There were pages and pages of lists in hand, most of them in Beatrice's elegant writing.

Nothing soothed her like making lists and after yesterday's *encounter* with Dalton she was in need of soothing. She was also resolved to fight for her store, even if that meant fighting him.

"My mother is threatening to send the invitations on Thursday," Beatrice said. "She is determined for the debut party to take place in three weeks' time."

"We're not ready," Margaret replied, eyes wide in horror. In Beatrice's reorganization, Margaret had gone from underappreciated shopgirl to Beatrice's right-hand woman. She had a gift for numbers which she applied to bookkeeping, a patient demeanor that helped manage the shopgirls, and a knack for keeping everyone and everything organized. "We won't be ready. Unless we want to sell dust and half-built dreams."

"We have to be ready. She has already scheduled the delivery of a ridiculous number of flowers. I have never seen someone so enthusiastically embark on a task—other than you and I remodeling Goodwin's."

Inviting her mother to help with the store had been a lucky stroke of genius. With something to do, Estella was less interested in Beatrice's matrimonial prospects (or lack of) and she also spoke less of Edward's involvement once he returned. Hopefully she would see that the store belonged in her daughter's capable hands and not her son's.

"Can you get her to delay a week at least?" Margaret asked.

"Have you met my mother?"

"If she's anything like I'm imagining based on my experience with society women and managing mothers, I'd rather not."

"Scared?"

"Terrified."

"We can do it. I'm sure everything looks worse than it is."

"It's possible. As long as we don't pause to eat or sleep for the next three weeks."

And with that, the two lady bosses went back to their lists and status updates and plans and projections. Not for the first time did Beatrice offer up a silent prayer of thanks for Margaret, who knew everything about how the store was run, and had ideas about how it could be better.

Beatrice had vision. She had lofty ideals and grand ambitions and the audacity to go for it. Margaret knew how to make it real.

"How is the training and hiring going?" Beatrice asked. This was an area that Margaret had claimed management over.

"I am relieved to say that it's going well. Only because we persuaded Clara to leave The Store Across the Street." By mutual unspoken agreement they did not whisper the name of their competitor's store across the street. "She's running the show and seems to have it all under control."

Beatrice was about to remark on all the talented women she'd persuaded to work for her with nothing more than a promise of a good wage, autonomy and opportunity to do more. But she and Margaret were interrupted.

A hulking man stood nearby, a stack of boxes and crates at his back.

"I have a shipment for John Washington."

"Who is that—?" Beatrice began but Margaret shushed her and turned to the deliveryman.

"Yes, thank you. I will accept that for him. He's our vice president of operational considerations. He is currently in a very important meeting and cannot be interrupted."

"Who are you? Are you sure you can accept it?"

"Oh, I'm his secretary," Margaret said breezily. "I just accept deliveries, serve coffee, and remember his wife's birthday."

"Whatever you say, lady," he replied warily, eager to be on his way.

Beatrice had questions. She turned and peered curiously at Margaret.

"Who is John Washington? And since when do we have a vice president of operational considerations? What would that role even do? And why are we not invited to this very important meeting?"

Margaret grinned.

"John Washington is a wonderful creation of my own imagination. He's a tremendously useful fellow. When I would call on places to place orders for the store, something in my voice caused people to be skeptical that I had the authority to make the purchase or arrange the delivery. But I have no problems when I'm working on behalf of John Washington, vice president of operational considerations."

Beatrice's mouth had parted in surprise, but had turned up into a wicked grin at Margaret's explanation.

"We'll have to get him some calling cards," she said.

"You should add him to the guest list for the party."

"I'll let my mother know. I did promise her a list of names."

Then Margaret nodded at something—someone—behind her.

"Irate male, two o'clock. He's heading your way."

"Which one is it?" Beatrice asked, in what she thought was an admirably neutral voice. Margaret just gave her A Look.

"The one."

"Again?"

Beatrice took a deep breath, pasted a smile on her face, and spun around to see the one irate male that she had expected to see.

"Oh, hello, Dalton."

"Hello, Beatrice." He paused for a beat and her heart paused for a beat.

He had better not still be upset about the employee situation. He had better not expect her to apologize, either. She stood by what she offered her employees and if he couldn't compete, then he could go argue with John Washington about it. But Dalton said something she hadn't expected to hear from his lips *at all*. "I have come to apologize."

Margaret muttered some excuses and went to see about something urgent, critical, and vitally important.

"I am terribly busy but this might be something I have time for."

"I'm sorry that I lost my temper yesterday," he said.

"Thank you for your apology. Dalton, it's just business."

"Is it?"

His eyes dropped to her lips and they both knew he was thinking about and apologizing for that furiously charged almost-kiss—not the argument about the exodus of employees. Yesterday she'd had overwhelming *How Dare He!* feelings about that almost-kiss. And also *If only* feelings. And the kind of unnamed feelings when thinking about kissing and Dalton that lead to thinking about more than just kissing with Dalton.

As a rival businessperson, she didn't want her thoughts to go there. Beatrice was acutely aware that she was setting an example to all the other women looking up to her, whether she wanted to or not. Beatrice the Beacon could not lose her wits and let one irate male get her flustered. She

could not kiss her way out of problems or into
them. The least she could do was not get stupid
over a man.

But the long-lost part of her that had been
nearly smothered to death in her loveless marriage liked the sparks. She wanted the fire.

As a gracious human, there was only one thing
to say.

"Apology accepted. Thank you."

Dalton grinned. "I would have brought flowers
but that seems inappropriate, given that I would
not have brought flowers had you been a man."

"You mean to say that you're not bringing
bouquets and chocolates to Mr. Fields and Mr.
Wanamaker?"

"I'm not in the habit of it, no."

She lifted her eyes to find him gazing at her.
Those blue eyes had once been so full of love and
fire for her. And now she dared to think she still
saw some sparks.

How inconvenient that would be.

What a distraction, too.

She could not afford distractions.

She also could not be sure that any attempt
at seduction was not just a means to an end—
Goodwin's. Revenge. The ultimate betrayal.

She had time for none of that—not when her
mother was planning to send out invitations to
celebrate the opening of a store that was currently a mess of dust and debris and hope.

"I think we find ourselves in a situation for which there is no established etiquette," he said.

"If you mean working with women—"

"I mean working with *you*. Given what we once were to each other."

"And what's that?" She wanted to know what he thought of it. Them. Their past. That something between them that somehow hadn't quite gone away.

"Greatest love, greatest regret. One of the two," he said with a shrug.

"Something like that I suppose," she replied softly. "What has made you suddenly so introspective and considerate?"

"It doesn't take a miracle or a dramatic turn of events for a man's temper to cool and for him to see an apology is in order. It's not exactly one of the great mysteries of the universe to know. Also, my friend Connor told me in no uncertain terms that an apology was in order."

She was about to make some flippant comment about his smart friends when Margaret interrupted.

"Beatrice? I think you want to come see this."

"What is it?"

"Probably nothing but . . . there is a chance it's dangerous, threatening, and totally nefarious."

"Well, now I'm intrigued," Beatrice said but her heartbeat had quickened and it wasn't because of Dalton. Margaret was not one for dramatics so if she said something was possibly dangerous, threatening, and nefarious it probably was.

She followed Margaret, and Dalton followed her, and a moment later they were standing in the newly constructed space designed as a luxurious ladies' retiring room. It would be a space where they might freshen up, have a good cry and pull themselves together, look in the mirror and daringly reapply their lipstick.

Mirrors which had just been installed only yesterday. And which were now smashed.

"I would think it's an accident but I'm not that charitable in my thoughts," Margaret said and Beatrice concurred.

"You're not wrong," Dalton said. "It looks like someone took a hammer to each one in the center. It definitely looks deliberate."

Beatrice gazed at the damage and beyond that, her reflection, which was fractured into a dozen tiny pieces instead of showing a whole woman.

Dalton swore under his breath.

"My thoughts exactly."

"This wasn't an accident," Margaret said. She and Beatrice exchanged A Look that Dalton missed as he was examining the damage up close. Which was just as well since it was A Look that asked, *Who wants to thwart our success?*

And A Look that answered, *The man standing right next to you.*

And another look that said, *This will not be tolerated.*

"I'm going to call the police," Beatrice said. "We can't have anything interfere with my mother's party. As scary as this is, there's nothing I fear more than the thwarted ambitions of my mother. Nothing."

Chapter Eighteen

Goodwin's Debut Ball
Three weeks later

*O*bviously Dalton avoided Beatrice until he could not avoid her any longer. And then the invitation arrived and Dalton could not avoid her any longer.

The occasion was the debut ball celebrating the relaunch of Goodwin's. A "grand reopening" sounded desperate and old, but a debut party sounded like a fresh, bright young thing was about to be unleashed upon the world. Smart. New York society would be besides themselves to attend.

It was essential that *he* attend, for professional reasons.

But he was just one guest in a big crowd.

The sidewalk was mobbed with hordes of people who had come to gawk at the building, which had finally been unveiled and lit up, to say nothing of the party guests arriving in all their finery. But even the famous faces from Broadway and the fashionably dressed, jewel-bedecked members of the Four Hundred could hardly compete with the display in the windows.

He didn't *want* to push through the crowds, like some newcomer to the city. But it was in his best professional interests to take a close look. So he did and he felt something twist in his gut because what she created was *good*. Maybe even great.

The windows had been enlarged to take advantage of large plates of glass which, thanks to advances in technology, could now be made. The scene within was newly illuminated with electric lights that would likely stay on through the night, a beacon in the darkest hours.

The scene in the windows took his breath away.

Real women and men rode bicycles that somehow remained stationary, while painstakingly painted backgrounds on some sort of mechanical device gave the impression that they were moving through a forest, the seaside, the city. As they pedaled away, these real models laughed and chatted and gave the appearance of living their very best lives.

They wore the latest, most daring fashions.

He saw ankle.

He saw red lips.

He saw women having fun.

And damn, if he didn't want to join in. Damn if he wasn't ready to buy a bicycle right on the spot.

He pushed his way into the store, where a waiter handed him a flute of champagne. He took a sip and let himself get swept farther into the store, where crowds marveled at the shiny new version of a Manhattan legend. They *oohed* and *ahhed* at the light, the airy space, the arresting and colorful displays of scarves and gloves and perfumes and a million other things.

Dalton had just one thought: *Fuck.*

She had mastered another one of his inviolable rules: *surprise and delight. Astonish the customer.*

He who had invented the rules, who had created retail as the world knew it, found himself taking a longer look, surprised by the way she had counters of cosmetics openly on display, allowing women to sample them under the supervision of trained technicians in white coats, lending an air of respectability to the still slightly scandalous product. He saw color everywhere, from the wall of spinning umbrellas to tables of gloves and cascades of silks and tulles. The space she had created was exactly what he had expected but completely novel, all at the same time.

And just like that he was drawn deeper into the store.

Familiar landmarks were noted—those distinctive pink marble pillars—but they were polished, brighter, and finally allowed to let their beauty shine. Heavy wood had given way to delicate glass, mirrors, all of which reflected the warm glow of massive, electric crystal chandeliers. Massive bouquets of flowers adorned the space and scented the air.

In the center of it all, on the grand central staircase, Beatrice stood like a queen.

She wore red.

A red dress that simply stated, *Look at me.* On her mouth, red lip paint. He wondered what it would be like to kiss her red, arresting mouth. Once upon a time he had known.

Behind her on the mezzanine was another dazzling display of bicycles, an array of shiny black steel steeds hanging from the ceiling like they were in flight. Nearby mannequins modeled the new styles of cycling attire. Upon a table was an artfully arranged stack of books—*How I Learned To Ride the Bicycle* by the famous Frances Willard, and a stylish notice promoting private lessons for ladies in the park, free with purchase of a bicycle.

Somewhere an orchestra played.

Everywhere, people mingled, sipping champagne, delighting over every new thing.

There was only one thing to do: drink a second

glass of champagne while taking a turn about the store, thoroughly spying on his competition, and then getting the hell out and start plotting ways to compete.

Because this lit a fire inside. This was a challenge. A dare.

Beatrice was gunning for his retail crown and he would have to fight to keep it.

Connor found him, as he was halfway through his tour of the second floor.

"There you are. I knew I would find you here."

"I'm here in a purely professional capacity."

"Market research. Competitive analysis. Of course." Connor nodded seriously with a gleam in his eye suggesting that they both knew better. "I think we can conclude that she is going to give you a run for your money."

Dalton couldn't agree out loud, but he did not protest, either. Because everywhere they turned, there was something to catch the eye, or some novel innovation to make him mutter softly under his breath, "Damn."

They stopped in front of a hair salon.

"Have you ever even heard of a hair salon?" Dalton asked.

He and Connor had paused in front of a section of the store designated as Martha Matilda Harper's Salon, where apparently women could come to have their hair washed, cut, and styled as per The Harper Method, while seated in those curious chairs he'd seen carried in during the day they fought over employee poaching.

Hair styling was one of those things he understood that ladies did, but he'd never considered the logistics of. It was not within his purview. Perhaps it ought to have been. Maybe if he'd had a wife or daughters he would have an idea of these things.

And all at once a sort of loneliness snuck up on him.

"Do you have any questions I can help you with, gentlemen?"

Dalton turned at the familiar voice. Clara, one of his best salesgirls who had defected.

"Clara Baldwin."

"Hello, Mr. Dalton. I'm not sure if I'm surprised or dismayed to see you here."

"Wouldn't miss the opportunity to spy on the competition. Tell me, Miss Baldwin, what does Goodwin's have that Dalton's doesn't?" Connor asked. "Dalton is too proud to ask but he's desperate to know."

"If you must know . . ." She gave a conspiratorial smile and leaned in to confide in them. "Childcare."

"For sale?"

"She provides childcare to customers and staff alike."

As a lifelong confirmed bachelor, he had never given a thought to childcare. His clientele all had nannies and people and private boarding schools for that. And if one could not afford such things, one could not afford to shop in his store. Or so he had assumed. It seemed Beatrice knew better.

"And what about that chair?" Connor asked. "It looks like some instrument of torture."

"Of course. It's a reclining chair for shampooing. Martha Matilda Harper designed it herself to make it more convenient for ladies to have their hair washed without interfering with their attire, before it is cut and styled. Would you like to try it?"

"Another time, perhaps."

Dalton and Connor kept strolling along until they came to a set of doors guarded by two women in uniform. Ladies were entering and exiting but the doors remained firmly shut when Dalton and Connor approached.

"My apologies, gentlemen, but this space is for ladies only."

"Well, now I'm curious," Dalton drawled. "What is in there?"

"A reading room. For ladies. Only."

The shopgirl standing guard smiled. It was the smile of someone who was not at all sorry to tell gentlemen that they were not permitted to enter. It was the smile of someone experiencing the heady rush of power for the first time.

Everywhere Dalton turned and looked in this store, he saw the New Woman. From the gowns on display, to the services offered, to the refuge provided. Even the guests at this "debut" party weren't entirely the usual suspects of the Four Hundred, but a mix of society wives, professional women, and young girls with starry eyes.

Everywhere he looked, Dalton saw his plans for revenge fading into nothing, an impossible dream that had its moment and was now gone forever. It was one thing to buy an outdated store on the cheap and reduce it to rubble for his private satisfaction.

It was another matter entirely to pay a fortune for this shiny, newly polished jewel only to destroy it. He still could, if he wanted to. It would be more expensive but he was a ruthless millionaire merchant prince with the third greatest fortune of the Gilded Age. It was not impossible.

If that's what he really wanted . . .

My name is Wes Dalton . . .

The familiar refrain faltered. He was on the verge of becoming ridiculous. Blowing a fortune on something so petty as revenge. Blowing up a store like this and all it represented. He was not that kind of man.

And so Dalton had to decide, right there in the middle of the ladies accessories department, what kind of man he would be. One hell-bent on revenge, still nurturing a heartache. Or would he rise to the challenge Beatrice presented? He thought he'd nearly conquered Manhattan but maybe he was only just getting started.

And then.

A voice.

A jocular had-too-much-to-drink man's voice emerging above the chatter of the crowd.

"It's just shopping, isn't it? It's just a shop. All you need to do is run in, pick a scarf, buy it, and leave. All this does is slow down the process."

Dalton was not the only one to overhear the old man and take issue with his foolish opinions. Beatrice was nearby; her eyes narrowed and then her gaze connected with his.

They were sworn rivals and bitter enemies, but in this they were of one mind. It was a slight that would not go unchecked.

In unison they turned and faced the drunk know-it-all man. Dalton recognized him; his name was McConnell, and his wife spent hours in his store. She didn't necessarily spend a fortune though. One was given to understand that the store provided an escape from the duties of home and her overbearing bore of a husband.

"Just shopping?" Beatrice queried in the politely lethal tones of a woman about to slay.

"My good man, it is not just shopping," Dalton repeated, in case his male voice would better make the point.

"It's just a bunch of stuff for sale, though, innit?" McConnell, silver-haired and red-faced, was definitely on the verge of falling into his cups.

"Shopping, especially in a store like mine or Dalton's, is a meditation upon who we are and who we wish to be," Beatrice explained. "It is a pleasant and sensual experience that engages both present and future thinking simultaneously. To be shopping is to be thinking of something as lofty as one's aspirations and something as practical as mathematics. All while one's senses are engaged. Where else can you feel something as soft as cashmere, breathe in the heady fragrance of flowers, imagine who you want to be and buy the things to make that dream into a reality?"

"Some men are not up for pleasant, sensual, and immersive experiences," Dalton remarked to Beatrice, in a way that suggested he was not one of those men. Her eyes flashed, understanding.

"Let us not forget that people are so very terrified of women enjoying themselves," Beatrice said.

"We should not be afraid of women's desires or women's pleasure," Dalton said. "For it is the engine that drives the world. What we do," he nodded to Beatrice, "is stoke a woman's desire, satisfy her desire and transform it into money and power."

Her gaze locked with his and he felt himself stand taller. She nodded at him to continue, so he did.

"We make a woman *want*—whether it's a dress or gloves or a reticule. She makes the purchase, which provides jobs to women at the mills and factories, and it keeps the shopgirls employed."

"The dressmakers and her seamstresses," Beatrice added. "The milliners, the cleaners."

"The delivery boys, the boys in the mailroom, those in accounting," he added. "All those people earn their bread by a woman's desire. By a woman's determination to dream and make it real. Whether it's a dress, a place setting, or a whole life."

The man was redder now. They had an audience now. Dalton was really feeling what he was saying. They made magic, him and Beatrice, and he wasn't going to give up.

"And this is not *just* a store," Beatrice added. "It is not a place for errands or mere acquisitions. This store is a space for women to live and thrive outside of the home. For where else can we safely go outside of the house to gather, to talk, to live, to dream, to do?"

All at once Dalton understood the reading room.

The childcare.

The hair salon.

What she'd created was not just a department store, it was a destination. Perhaps even a revolution.

"So as you can see, it is not *just shopping*. But I wonder if you instinctively understand what we do—empowering women through their own desires and pleasures—is precisely what one objects to."

"What she said," Dalton said.

The man was walking off in a huff without even trying to drop the last word. The crowd dispersed. Dalton and Beatrice turned to each other once the spectacle was over.

"I thought we were rivals," she said, lifting one brow. "But now I'm not so sure."

Chapter Nineteen

$\mathcal{B}$eatrice turned toward Dalton, her heart still racing as it always did when she was shooting her mouth off again, and now Dalton was near and these two things together had her in quite a state.

"Congratulations," Dalton said, gazing at her. "I will admit that I'm impressed."

"Well, if *you* are impressed then I must have done something spectacular," she quipped but really, truly his compliment meant more than anyone else's. He knew. He saw. "Thank you."

"I know what it takes to make something in your head become real. To say nothing of hiring and training staff, stocking the merchandise, dreaming up displays, and orchestrating a fleet of shopgirls, errand boys, and all the others. To launch a store is no small feat. But you have done something more than that."

"Thank you, Dalton," she said and she felt seen, truly seen, in a way she hadn't from the others in her life.

He smiled wryly.

"In building something so remarkable, you have also ruined my plans for revenge. Probably."

"May have or definitely have?" Beatrice teased. "Or will you just have to try harder?"

Of course she and her mouth had to go and essentially dare him to try to ruin her. All of a sudden she felt like the champagne had gone to her head. Or maybe that feeling was just from the way Dalton was looking at her. His eyes were just so blue and they were fixed only on her, even though there was a marvelous spectacle all around her.

"Make no mistake, we're still rivals," he murmured. "But you have inspired me."

"Be still my beating heart."

She said it for a laugh but her overexcited heart really needed to calm down. Between the rush of confrontation with that man and now Dalton so close at her side, there was much to set her heart racing.

Because somehow they had wandered off from the crowds and they were alone and the chatter was quiet, the orchestra far away, and the lights were dim.

"This is dangerous territory. Us. Alone. You no longer hell-bent on destroying me."

"I didn't say that," he replied. "My store closes at eight. I need a hobby for after hours."

"You really know how to make a woman swoon," she said.

Speaking of swooning—they had unintentionally wandered into the home furnishings department. It was never the most popular and it was sparsely attended by party guests at present.

Miss Lumley and Margaret had worked together to stage little rooms—a parlor here, a dining table set with the finest new styles of china and silver, a bedroom there. Miss Lumley had an eye for interior decoration and she orchestrated a new style of furnishings, lighter and newer than all the heavy old Victorian stuff.

Dalton wandered over to it, Beatrice, too.

"So you're on the side of twin beds," he said, referring to the debate currently raging among doctors, theologians, and interior decorators about whether a married couple ought to sleep in one bed or two. They stood side by side, looking at the beds in question, piled high with soft white linens.

"Unapologetically. It's more hygienic, among other reasons."

She didn't want to remember the other reasons right now, reasons like unfeeling husbands and marital rights. Thank God she'd had her own suite of rooms at the castle, but she could imagine for those who didn't a twin bed of one's own would be the next best thing.

Or not being married to an unfeeling man one didn't love at all.

Beatrice did not want to think of any of that now.

Now when her old flame, Wes Dalton, was here looking like he was thinking of kissing her. She realized she wanted to kiss him, too. She was supposed to be old and dried up; she'd been told she was cold and unfeeling. But she did not feel any of those things now. She felt eighteen again, heart racing because she was close to maybe kissing Wes Dalton.

"What about on a cold night, Beatrice? What about newlyweds, young and in love? What about on a night like this, when two consenting adults are alone after drinking champagne? And looking at me the way you are."

"Like how, Dalton?"

"Like it's been a long time."

"Well, it has been a long time," she said and her voice came out huskier than she would have liked. All of a sudden she was keenly aware that it had been a while since she had a good kiss. Years.

"And like you're thinking of kissing me," he murmured.

He stood close enough to do so now. There was an electric hum in the air and she rather thought it was from the two of them, sparking as they got close together, and not the electrified chandeliers above on a dim setting.

"Maybe I am."

Dalton stepped closer to her. She leaned back against a heavy wooden chest of drawers, lending her much-needed support. Her knees were weakening, for God's sake, like she was some idealistic young girl and not a divorcée of a certain age.

"But a kiss would complicate things," he murmured.

"All the best kisses do," she whispered.

All of a sudden she cared little for complications.

He was thinking about it, she could tell. Leaning in. Hesitating. Despite all his vows of revenge and ruination his lips were mere inches from hers. He knew, as well as she, that a kiss now would complicate things tremendously. She didn't entirely believe him when he said he was no longer hell-bent on revenge. One didn't just give it up, on the spot.

Not after the years of what they had suffered.

Was a kiss—and what might come after—another way of obtaining what he wanted from her? She could see how he could play it: *make her want, make her desire, propose marriage, and what is hers becomes his.*

It was entirely possible.

This was the man who had made her love and then took money to disappear. This was a man who had never hidden his intent to own her store.

Her gaze dropped to his mouth and she saw it was set in a half hint of a smile, the smile of a millionaire rogue intent on seduction, and who was accustomed to getting what he wanted.

And the slow burn began in her core and roared through the rest of her like a forest fire. It had been so damned long since she'd had a good, really good kiss. Years. A lifetime even.

She hadn't forgotten how good it had once been.

She was done playing it safe.

Beatrice was no longer some eager-to-please debutante, wearing white and doing what was expected. Tonight she wore red. She spoke up instead of biting her tongue. And, she impulsively decided, kissed a man if she wanted to. Even if it was a terrible idea.

A kiss would complicate things. Of course. That was half the fun of it.

"What's stopping you, Dalton?"

"Besides the crowds of people just downstairs? The ball in full swing?"

"It's just like old times. My debut party. Remember?"

"I wasn't invited to that one."

"But you snuck up to my room after. And look at us now. Competitors in a compromising position."

He was so close that she could feel his body against hers and the rise and fall of his chest with each slow and steady breath. She breathed him in. Pressed one palm on his chest to steady herself, but she felt how wildly his heart was beating.

There was no hiding how much this was affecting him, too. His obvious desire for her made her own wanting more intense.

So Beatrice slid her hands on his chest, then grabbed a fistful of his black satin lapel and kissed him. His mouth claimed hers, or hers claimed his. They kissed, with the pent-up longing of sixteen years of hurt and yearning, anger and desire. It was slow and tentative and hesitant for exactly one second.

Two strong forces colliding and surrendering upon impact.

All at once, it was just like old times, better than she remembered and everything she ever wanted.

The strong planes of his chest, hot to the touch, heart pounding underneath the layers of wool and whatever. She'd been so cold for so long and so she didn't give a thought to burning alive by the pressure of his body against hers.

This. She survived and crawled through hellfire and agonies for this and it was worth it. Dalton's fingers sank into her hair, holding her as he drank her in. Like he'd been dying for her the whole time they'd been apart.

She kissed him back and thought, *Same.*

She kissed him back and thought, *What a waste.* All those years of cold and longing when they could have had this. But any thoughts of *what if* and *why not* and *what had she been thinking* vanished like items on sale. In a frenzied rush. Here one moment and just gone the next.

Dalton's hands slid down, tugging the sleeves of her dress down in a slow caress of his bare palms against her bare skin, then skimming over her breasts, and she thought, *Stay,* and then they finally settled on her waist and held her against him. She felt his arousal for her. The promise of it. The warning of it.

He wasn't here to play.

Neither was she.

Beatrice wrapped her arms around his neck and let her head fall back as they kissed and kissed and the world was reduced to nothing but him and her and this long-overdue kiss tasting of desire and regrets and no promises whatsoever, but this was definitely not enough.

"I thought I remembered." She gasped. Breathing. What was breathing and how did one do it?

"This is better."

"You remember."

"Kissing you, Beatrice, is not something a man forgets."

"Stop. I might swoon." He pressed a kiss against the soft skin of her neck, his fingers urging the strap of her gown off its perch on her shoulder. "Truly. I might faint."

"No. You won't. Because you don't want to miss a thing. And I'm only just getting started."

Oh, hell yes, this was going to complicate everything.

Chapter Twenty

Dalton's Department Store
The next day

*D*o you think we can get an automobile up here?" Dalton asked Connor, whose immediate expression was not one of enthusiasm for Dalton's latest mad idea. "Up here" was the roof of the department store.

It offered an impressive, bird's-eye view of the line wrapped around the block—for Goodwin's.

Dalton was not surprised at Beatrice's obvious success; he saw the store, he understood what she was building, and he knew women. He knew how they would show up in droves for what she was selling—and what she was selling wasn't just gloves.

It was a damned shame he hadn't anticipated this and done it first. But he'd been distracted by ideas of revenge and seeing Goodwin's suffer, not making Dalton's even better. He sure as hell wasn't going to sit back and let her remake

Goodwin's into a bigger, better, more successful department store, either. Not without some competition.

The ruthless, competitive streak that had made him a millionaire didn't just end because she made a brilliant move in their battle.

Not even if she kissed him like he was the only man in the world she wanted.

"Why do we need an automobile on the roof?" Connor asked. "They're just noisy, smoky death traps. And they go on roads not roofs."

"The noisy, smoky death traps *of the future*, yes," Dalton corrected, stepping back from the ledge and prowling around the expanse of roof. Presently, automobiles were an unreliable novelty that only the richest of the rich would consider having and only then as a toy. "We'll put it on display. We'll let people get up close. Touch it. Experience it. It will get everyone talking about the hot new thing of the future and Dalton's."

"The roof though?"

"They put on entire theatrical productions on the roof of the Casino, so why can't I put an automobile on the roof of my store?" Dalton was getting excited now. "Can't you just see it, Connor? One of those gleaming black automobiles parked up here, so one could get the sense of this new, dangerous creature out in the wild. To help them imagine the wind in their hair, the sun on their faces. It's perfect—customers will have to go through the entire store to get to it. I bet they'll buy something on the way in. And out."

Dalton grinned, imaging the spectacle. And all the souvenirs and carefully curated and stunningly displayed merchandise. He imagined the sales, the profits, the rush of people crowded into the space because of his vision. He imagined Beatrice watching the lines around his store from her office window.

Connor turned from looking out at the city to his friend.

"I haven't seen you on fire like this since you launched this store. I'm going to conclude it's her."

"It's not her. But it's her. Completely. But only somewhat."

"We need drinks for this," Connor muttered, pushing his fingers through his hair.

"Perhaps we should serve refreshments up here, as well . . ." Dalton continued. Honestly, the possibilities were endless. He was rich and not afraid of risk—so why not?

Connor dropped his face into his hands.

"She's competition, Connor. Serious competition. We need to *win*. She has bicycles. Ergo, we have a car. Bigger, better, stronger, faster."

"Are you still drunk from the party? She doesn't just have bicycles, she has what bicycles represent. She has that reading room."

"It's a smart statement she's making, I'll grant you that. But at the end of the day, it's a room. With chairs. And books. She's not even selling anything in there! We could do the same, though, and make it a membership or subscription service. We charge money just to breathe air and sit in our chairs. Brilliant!" Dalton was off and running now, the ideas spinning. God, he hadn't felt this excited for a store display in ages. He could almost kiss her he was so thankful for the spark of inspiration. Or cutthroat competition—one of the two. "I know! We'll launch the Dalton's Membership with exclusive access and benefits. Anyone with a membership will always turn to Dalton's first."

"Now that might be an idea. The car on display I'm not so sure of. It's not like you're going to take orders for them and run them down to the factory."

"Why not?"

"You sell *things*, Dalton. Things that a woman can pick out that morning, have delivered that afternoon, and wear out that evening. And then you send the bills to their fathers and husbands and slowly and steadily siphon your fortune from theirs."

"I don't just sell *things*," Dalton said, really warming to his topic now. "I sell spectacle. Promise. Exclusivity. The future. What better than an automobile? The promise of freedom, of sights unseen, of adventure waiting to happen. And yes, totally possibly completely lethal. Ruinous. Dangerous. But that's half the fun of it."

Like her. She was spectacle and promise. She was adventure waiting to happen, she was dangerous, she was possibly the death of him and his ambitions but . . . he'd had one hell of a time kissing her last night. Years of pent-up passions and frustrations and longings for *her* finally had their moment.

It was a moment he couldn't stop thinking about. Couldn't stop wanting more of. Which was why he had to avoid her. He couldn't concentrate otherwise. He couldn't compete if he couldn't concentrate.

"This is about your plans for revenge, isn't it?" Connor asked.

Dalton motioned for Connor to join him at the edge. He pointed to the spectacle.

"Look at that."

They both took a long look, from the vantage point of the roof, where no one could see them looking. They saw a gleaming, restored storefront wrapped up in a line of women, and some men, stretching around the block. Officers had arrived on horseback to help manage the energy of the crowds.

And there was a steady flow of people exiting with distinctive Goodwin's bags on their arms, in a world where practically all purchases were delivered discreetly.

Women don't want to be reminded of their desires or their indulgences.

Unless they did? Unless they refused to feel shame about it? Dalton saw in an instant what she had achieved: all those distinctive bags, all those conversation points, all those moments where a friend would recommend Goodwin's to another friend. All those women owning what they wanted.

He was going to need more than a car on display.

"Ah. I see." Connor nodded. "Revenge would be nice but survival will be better. You're going up against a girl, Dalton. You better not miss or then what will everyone say?"

"So you see that I need the automobile. Dangerous, powerful, adventurous, the way of the future."

What Wes Dalton wanted, Wes Dalton got.

25 West Tenth Street
One week later

IN A DRAWING room down the street from the great stores of Dalton's and Goodwin's, a group of select ladies were laughing at Wes Dalton. That great merchant prince of Manhattan, that forever most eligible bachelor women sought after, had made one great mistake. His latest display was a sensation—and a possibly fatal misstep all the same.

"An automobile!"

The Ladies of Liberty laughed uproariously. They had seen the advertisements in the newspapers, and a few had braved the crowds of men to go see it themselves. They'd also heard the men in their lives discussing it earnestly, at length.

"Shh. We are supposed to be impressed with his big, powerful, hulking . . . machinery," Ava said with a strained seriousness that devolved into giggles and blushes.

They were not talking about the car. Or were they?

"The display of the automobile shows that he does not understand what we have created," Beatrice said. "And as such, what he is truly competing with."

The automobile was a spectacle that drew massive crowds; she saw the lines around the block from her corner office. At first, she felt panicked. But upon closer look, she noticed something: those waiting in line were mostly men with the occasional woman accompanying them. When she strolled around the sales floor in Goodwin's, she heard her female customers chattering about the serene space her store provided, the escape from all those men who wanted to stand around and talk about horsepower and throbbing engines and combustion and whatnot.

There was no sign at Goodwin's that said Ladies Only but the space had that effect of welcoming women and warding off men.

So no, she was not threatened by the power of his automobile, the thrust of his horsepower engine, or the long lines of men.

"So you're not worried about the competition, Beatrice?"

"In a case of compacts versus cars, I think I know what our clientele wants," she said with a smile.

"Compacts, I'm delighted to say," Daisy replied. Her Dr. Swan's product line of night creams and lip paints was flying off the shelves. It so happened the department store was the perfect venue for her oh so scandalous product—women could go into Goodwin's to purchase something else and just happen to sample the product with assistance from specially trained salesgirls and carry it out in a Goodwin's bag, with no one any wiser.

"Confirmed," Beatrice said proudly. "Everything is flying off the shelves. The relaunch of the store is a smashing success. It's been running Margaret and myself ragged, so I haven't had a moment to look at that automobile but I do hear women glad to find a respite from the men and the crowds in our ladies-only reading room."

"I love the reading room," sighed one woman. "It's the only space where I can sit down for a moment without anyone crawling on me and asking me for something."

"Well, I would be interested in the automobile if they let ladies drive it," Harriet said. "I wouldn't mind having such power under my command. I don't believe for a second that the fairer sex cannot handle it."

"That's what they say now," Adeline replied. "Give it time. Ladies will be driving all over the world."

Beatrice sipped her tea and listened to her friends talk about driving and power and escape and the wind in their hair. It was the feeling she had when riding her bicycle to work each morning and home each night. It was the feeling that she could go anywhere in the world that she wanted.

Such a glorious feeling, that.

And if she could go anywhere in the world?

Why she would come right here, in the company of these women where she at once felt safer and yet more daring, all at once.

But she also had a hankering to wander a few blocks east, toward Broadway.

To Dalton's.

Because they had kissed. A hot, take-no-prisoners kiss.

It had been sixteen years since she'd had a kiss that made her want to throw caution to the wind and indulge in all sorts of wickedness. Her desire had been asleep all these years and that kiss had woken it up. It was roaring back to life, making demands.

Then Dalton had proceeded to ignore her.

There was no note, no personal call, no hello on the street.

Which was maddening because he was *right there* on Broadway in his marble palace and she was *right there* across the street, also on Broadway in her own castle of commerce. It would have been easy enough to make their paths cross, if one should be so inclined.

One had to conclude that he was avoiding her. Or was an utter, absolute cad.

This was a problem because she wanted to kiss him again. And she could, if she wanted. If he was amenable. He had felt very . . . amenable.

True fact.

Thank God she had other things on her mind so thoughts of kissing him didn't occupy her *every* waking hour. Important things, like the status of a shipment of cashmere shawls, or disputes between shopgirls in different departments, or dreaming up a new spectacle that would rival his automobile and keep people talking about *her* store, not his.

That kiss though. It had awoken a sleeping dragon inside of her. And now that dragon was hungry.

And he had disappeared, which made her consider that he was not trying to seduce her to destroy her. Which only made her want him more.

But Dalton was too busy with his car. With a big, hulking, powerful machine. Well, if he were really interested in powerful forces then he should be so lucky as to feel the constant thrum of desire she was feeling now. She had spent her youth keeping her wanton feelings (mostly) in check. She had . . . survived . . . her marriage. And now no forces of shame or scandal could compel her to keep her feelings to herself.

She wanted him. The man she had once loved and who knew how to make her burn.

"Beatrice?"

She blinked to attention at the sound of her name.

The conversation had already moved on to other things, such as the series of lectures that Harriet was organizing for the store on things like domestic hygiene, literature, scientific cooking, and public speaking. All topics which drew women into the store in droves. But Beatrice had been left behind.

"Apologies. I am distracted."

"Is it the car?" Harriet asked with a smirk, knowing full well it was not the car.

"Yes. It is the car. I feel like I ought to see it. For professional purposes," Beatrice replied, which was a lie that everyone understood the truth of but was kind enough not to say. The man himself was far more compelling than any hunk of metal.

"If you go now you can catch a glimpse of *the car* before closing time," Ava said with that smile she got when she sensed an opportunity for matchmaking.

Beatrice decided she would go. She would go flirt with danger, risk a little scandal, seek her share of pleasure. Just because she could.

Chapter Twenty-one

Dalton's Department Store

*D*alton noted with no small amount of satisfaction that the lines were wrapped around *his* store once again, all thanks to that automobile display and the extensive newspaper advertising he had done for it.

The people came in droves. The problem was that it was mostly men who were willing to line up and look at the car up close. Oh, the men brought their entire families with them. But it was the men who lingered, talked garrulously, and held up the line, which left women to chase after children and keep them from touching the display and generally running amok.

Nobody shopped.

Nobody could, with their attentions fixed upon ogling a car or wrangling a child or standing by their man.

Nevertheless, it *looked* like a success.

There were crowds of people clamoring for their turn to view the automobile, the press was raving about it, and everywhere he turned at his club or parties or in the park, people were talking about it.

Of all the people who streamed in to see the car, one did not.

It felt as if none of it mattered—not the spectacle he'd created, the dreams he'd conjured in crowds of people, the sales he'd made—if Beatrice didn't see it.

Dalton hated that he noticed her absence. He had spent the better part of a decade not noticing her absence. But then again, he'd kissed her last week and the memory was still strong, and he swore he could still taste her. He refused to lose to her, and since he wasn't certain he could resist her, he stayed away.

Besides, he was busy.

Running Manhattan's premier department store and assuring it stayed that way wasn't something one did part-time.

And then he caught sight of Beatrice pushing through the revolving door at three minutes to closing time.

"I've come to see that car," she said by way of hello when she saw him. "The famous, fancy car."

"The store is closing in . . ." Dalton made a show of checking his timepiece. "Three minutes."

"I know." She flashed him a smile and strolled past him as if she owned the place and as if the rules did not apply to her. What was he to do but follow? He couldn't have his competitor running wild in his store, unchaperoned, after hours. A few salesclerks glanced at her and then him warily as they were eager to complete their closing tasks for the day.

He followed her.

He followed her and reluctantly admired the sway of her hips in that dress, the tendrils of curls that escaped her coiffure and suggested she'd been so busy, running around all day, doing important things.

What? he wondered. *What was she up to next?*

If he were her lover and not her rival she might tell him . . .

She fought the crowds, all moving toward the exit while she was moving deeper into the store, up the stairs, until she arrived on the roof, in front of the display. A gleaming black open-top automobile on a pedestal. A velvet rope encircled it, keeping the crowds at bay.

Dalton stopped beside her. "She's a beauty, isn't she?"

"Are you talking about me or the car, Dalton?"

Only Beatrice—impetuous, dangerous Beatrice— could *flirt* with him when everything was on the line.

She flashed him a smile and all he said was, "Yes."

Beatrice began a slow circle around the automobile, examining it from every angle. Yet he didn't miss how her gaze strayed more often to him than the car. He couldn't miss how her gaze affected him, either. It turned out ruthless millionaire tycoons weren't immune to seductive glances.

"What are you doing here, Beatrice? Why do I suspect that you're not here to gawk at a horseless carriage?"

"We kissed," she said, matter-of-factly.

"It happened."

"Excellent. I just wished to confirm that it wasn't my imagination. Especially since I haven't heard a word from you since." She gave him a pointed, heated look which he understood to mean that he was a cad for his silence but she was considering forgiving him. All at once he felt a rush of a feeling—shame—for his silence and for the reasons for it. He'd thrown himself headlong into this car and showing everyone that he was still their merchant prince, as if it mattered what all of Manhattan thought of him more than what she did.

Did it?

"You could see how I feared I might imagine it," she continued.

"You did not imagine it."

"Good." She'd done a full circle around the car now and was standing right in front of him. "Because I would like for it to happen again."

Heart. Stop. Keep. Distance.

"We're rivals, remember? I'm very busy plotting my revenge," he said.

"And making plans for after. Or at least a hobby, Dalton. Honestly."

"One thing at a time," he said. But she was stepping over the velvet rope designed to keep people out and climbing into the car. "What are you doing?"

"Some people might be content just to look. I'm not." Her gaze connected with his. He felt electrified. "I want to know how it feels, Dalton, to be on the inside."

"This is not fair, Beatrice." His voice was rough. God, she was getting to him. With those tendrils and the sway of her hips and those heated gazes.

Between her and the car and the New York sky at night, he was going to be wrecked.

"I'm not playing a game, Dalton."

"What is this about, then?"

"Get in. I'll tell you."

Dalton paused because this felt like one of those moments where things shifted. He tried, he really did, to think of her only as his rival. As his one and only obstacle to success and revenge and something like happiness. But she was all skirts and pretty hair, and climbing into the front seat of an open-top car after hours and saying "get in with me," and honestly what human man could say no?

Dalton climbed in beside her. He had ideas about keeping his distance but that was impossible in a little car like this. On a roof. In the middle of Manhattan.

"This is ridiculous," he said. "We can't go anywhere."

"Are you speaking literally or metaphorically?"

"Yes," he said. Then he made the mistake of breathing her in. "Yes."

The rest of the world faded away. It was all so very out there and they were right here. Just the two of them in the front seat of the car, parked on a roof, under a rapidly setting sun. Darkness was falling. The city was lighting up. It was still such a novel and arresting sight—an electrified, towering New York—but it paled in comparison to looking at Beatrice.

The store was closed. They had all night.

"My wedding night was fine, I suppose," she began, apropos of nothing and he suddenly found it hard to breathe. They were going to *talk* and he was trapped. And they were going to talk as if they were . . . friends, not rivals. Or rather, she was going to talk and he was going to sit very still and listen and try to remember about his plans for vengeance and dominance. He was going to keep telling himself that he cared only for his business and winning and nothing for her.

My name is Wes Dalton. You stole my . . .

His constant refrain was no match for what she said next.

"I knew what I was supposed to do in the sense that I knew I was supposed to do whatever the duke wanted. Allow him whatever liberty. That sort of thing."

She spoke very matter-of-factly.

Something twisted in Dalton's gut.

"I didn't particularly enjoy it and I tried not to let it upset me too much. He wasn't you, Dalton. He didn't do the things you knew—or cared—to do."

Dalton sat very still and willed himself to keep inhaling and exhaling. Breathing. That was something he could do when he felt so damned powerless and cowardly. This was old news, he protested silently to himself. It was none of his business. It was the way of the world. She had *chosen* the duke and all that over him.

She deserved it, he told himself.

No one deserved it, or what she described next.

"It was after the second or third time that I started to think I might have made a mistake. He wanted an heir and a spare, of course, to go along with my astronomical dowry. And all I had to do was endure. Submit. Endure. Submit. Endure. Because what other option did I have?"

Leave, he thought.

Fight, he thought.

But these were things more easily said than done. Especially by twenty-year-old debutantes in a world dominated by men.

"It's very trying on one's soul, all that submitting and enduring. Until finally he gave up. Thank God."

"Good." His voice was rough.

"It was better. But . . ." Here, she paused. Dalton was aware of her turning to him, lifting her lashes, and settling her gaze on him. "But I still wanted to be touched in the way that you had touched me once upon a time. And duchesses locked in castles are not touched. They are politely tolerated until they have the graciousness to expire and make way for a new, younger, dewier duchess."

Fools. Because he knew no one compared to Beatrice. This woman had a light of her own. She outshone New York City at nightfall.

"And despite all the submitting and enduring, tedious days and torturous nights, after years of purgatory in an old drafty castle still . . . my fire hadn't gone out." Her eyes flashed with the wonder of it. Could he believe it? She could not. It was a miracle, that, and she spoke of it as reverentially as a miracle. *"My fire hadn't gone out."*

He nodded, speechless.

"They couldn't snuff me out of existence and once I realized that, I came roaring back to life.

So here I am," she said, arms wide to the night sky and New York.

They sat side by side in the darkness.

Beatrice reached for his hand.

My name is Wes Dalton. You stole my—

She didn't steal anything. She'd made a choice and lived with the consequences of it until she could not. During all those years apart, he had imagined her flitting around the castle, duke on her arm. That was not what she had described.

All these years Dalton had been so consumed by his own heartache and fixation on how he'd been wronged that he hadn't once paused to consider that perhaps she wasn't flitting about the castle. She was submitting and enduring.

Now he knew.

Since he knew, he would have to rearrange his understanding of him and her in the world.

"Why are you telling me this, Beatrice?"

She turned to face him. "I'm telling you so that you know why I'm about to kiss you. Because I have years of deprivation to make up for. I am telling you, Dalton, why I'm going to kiss you right now even though I am going to ruthlessly compete with you for customers. All. Day. Long."

"Rivals by day, lovers by night?"

"You can say no," she said and he had to laugh. Because Beatrice was not someone a man said no to. Not when she was offering the deal of a lifetime.

He could say no.

He could also say yes.

He could suggest that they discuss this more.

Dalton didn't say anything as he cradled her face in his hands.

What a waste of time and heart and years.

What the world had missed. What she could have done if she hadn't been all caged up. What they might have done together.

Now she was free to do whatever she damned well pleased and she wanted to kiss him.

A man didn't say no to that.

Not when he felt the same way.

Her mouth found his, and all that pent-up passion became his to revel in. And he did, oh, he did. Dalton was helpless to resist the pressure of her lips against his, the way she leaned into him, soft and warm and tasting sweet. He sank his fingertips into her hair and held her close and kissed her deeply.

He realized he, too, had been lonely.

This wasn't like when they'd kissed all those years before, when they'd foolishly thought they would have forever and a day and the world wouldn't make them choose between love and money. When they hadn't known better.

He knew better now.

He knew to seize the moment and hold on because it might not last.

Dalton tugged her into his lap and she tumbled over in a mass of skirts of laughter, and something in his heart clenched because wasn't this everything he ever wanted? Beatrice in his arms, looking up at him with blue eyes full of unconcealed wanting. She was in his arms, in his castle now.

He felt a surge of accomplishment so strong that he had to wonder if maybe this was what he really wanted all along.

"Kiss me, Dalton. We have lost time to make up for."

And he did. Under the darkening night sky, under the light of the moon, in the ever brightening nighttime glow of New York, he kissed her. And he didn't stop at her mouth, either.

He found the hollow of her throat.

He unbuttoned her jacket, her skirt and did away with all the things standing between her bare skin and his lips. There was unfortunately all the layers of skirts and petticoats and trousers between his rock-hard arousal and her most intimate spot.

Before he could let his thoughts spiral, wondering what it all meant, she murmured, "I missed you, Wes," as she shrugged out of her jacket and unbuttoned the rest of her shirt and treated him to the exquisite sight of her breasts peeking above the lace edge of her corset. She writhed above him and he groaned. She was definitely going to destroy him.

He held on for dear life, holding on to bunches of skirts, his hands skimming around her waist, feeling her up and down and learning once again all the secret details of her body. The curve of her breasts, the flare of her hips. These things were no longer fantasies but known to him now. Again.

Buttons, undone.

His restraint, gone.

It was all happening so fast. Her hair tumbling down around her shoulders, bare under his palms. A little bite of her lower lip. A kiss on the lobe of her ear. His strong hands and her lovely breasts.

He had missed her with such a frightening intensity that he couldn't get the words out. So he kissed her instead, letting himself get lost in the pleasure of her body, the soft sounds of her sighs and moans. He kissed her until the hour grew late, darkness had fallen in earnest, and he forgot all about revenge.

Chapter Twenty-two

Goodwin's Department Store
The next day

*I*t was not strictly for professional reasons that Dalton exited his own store and crossed Broadway and strolled into his competitor's store near to closing time, when the shops were emptying of customers and the streets were full of people rushing home. The note had arrived earlier that afternoon, her exquisite handwriting requesting his presence on the third floor at the closing hour.

Business? Not at this hour.

Rivals by day, lovers by night.

Pleasure. Definitely pleasure.

Something like anticipation dulled his attention to the displays he walked by; it was hard to concentrate on how her fleet of employees had arranged parasols and reticules and whatnot when he was about to see Beatrice. See *more* of Beatrice than he'd glimpsed in the moonlight and city light last night.

He found the third floor, and found it was home to the ladies lingerie department, which brought a wry smile to his mouth. Beatrice had a wicked sense of humor.

A lesser man might have hesitated among the delicate, intimate garments and among the shop-girls tidying up after the last of the customers had left. Dalton strolled right in.

He didn't see her at first, and while he waited, he considered the merchandise. Corsets and other underthings, all in soft, neutral shades. He found something about it wanting.

And then there she was: Beatrice. A vision in a blue dress, the color of the Newport ocean, to match her eyes. She strolled through like she owned the place. Which she did.

"Oh, hello, Dalton," she said. She had to acknowledge him for the sake of the shopgirls finishing up, though after being on their feet since opening hours, they were more eager to depart than to gossip. He watched as they cast intrigued glances over their shoulders on the way out. A moment later, the lights dimmed all around the store.

"Have you come to spy on us?" Beatrice asked coyly.

"Perhaps I've come to buy something," he said.

"The store still isn't for sale," she said.

"You know that's not why I'm here."

"Is it?"

"Let me prove it to you."

"Well, if you insist," she murmured. Then she turned and sauntered off with an inviting glance. He followed her as she weaved her way through tables and displays of all the secret delicate things women wore next to their bare skin. He didn't miss the inviting glance she gave him.

What was she wearing under that dress?

He would soon find out.

It was just her and him, alone in this great big department store after hours. There was nothing like having an empty public palace to oneself at night. They might have been the only two people in New York who knew the feeling.

He found her in the fitting rooms, in a small chamber enclosed with thick plum-colored velvet curtains that shut out the low hum of closing sounds in the store. Electric lights glowed softly above. And out of the corner of his eye, he caught a glance of her and him in a full-length mirror.

"Of all the places in Manhattan and *this* is where you abscond with me?"

"Maybe it's a particular fantasy of mine," she murmured, and he remembered the younger version of themselves taking this particular risk, sneaking off to steal a kiss in whichever darkened corner was available. *Unfinished business.* But then Beatrice pulled him close and tilted her lips up to meet his.

They were not wasting time, then.

His mouth found hers and in an instant, all the events of the day melted away. The conversations and problems and matters of business that usually drained him were just forgotten. There was only her and him—her tall, luscious body pressing against his.

There was only this kiss.

And *more*.

He watched with darkened eyes as she shrugged out of her jacket and he was mesmerized by the arch of her back and the way her breasts strained against her shirt. That little action, like something she might do alone at the end of the day, excited him. Because it was the sort of little intimate action that he'd never gotten to witness with her. And it was one that suggested certain things were about to happen.

He wanted those things.

His heart was racing for those things.

And then the shirt. God, she was undoing the buttons on her crisp white shirt.

"Beatrice, are you sure?"

His heart was pounding now. Blood roaring and rushing and there was nothing else in the world, nothing else at all except for this moment that once upon a time was all he had ever wanted. Beatrice, free and offering herself up to him.

He'd thought he would die when he'd learned she'd said yes to the duke. He still remembered the blackness and bleakness that had settled over his existence when he'd lost her because he hadn't been *enough*. But now here she was. Her arms around him, her lips teasing his, leading him unto temptation. There was no question of resistance.

"What part of sixteen years of a cold, loveless marriage—" But he didn't hear the rest, because he was transfixed by the sight of her standing with her shirt half-unbuttoned, revealing a peach pink silk corset. Her breasts swelled above it.

"I'm very, very sure," she said.

And then all his restraint was gone.

His mouth crashed down on hers for a kiss that was all pent-up frustration and years of longing. She pressed her body up against his, and he sank against her, and the wall. A tangle of skirt and shirts and velvet curtains and damask wallpaper. His eyes were closed, his body on high alert to her every writhe and moan, and they just . . . kissed.

Her lips.

The exposed hollow of her throat.

He drank her in. Breathed her in.

"Yes," she sighed. "*Yes*."

A few more buttons were let go. But that was slow, fumbled going.

"Just rip it off," she murmured. So he did the thing, the rakish impetuous thing of just ripping her shirtwaist apart. It was no feat of strength, all that delicate cotton and little pearl buttons shredded like paper and littered the dressing room floor.

"Terribly sorry about your shirt," he said softly and he only somewhat meant it. He drank in the gorgeous image of her exposed skin and pale corset and the swell of her breasts.

That faint peachy pink got to him. It was so almost white, so virginal and missish and shy and it hardly seemed right for the woman passionately kissing him in the dressing room of a department store that she owned and ran. Her lips were red. Her eyes mischievous, unapologetic. Her cheeks flushed with arousal.

"Don't worry about it. I carry an extensive selection of buttons and other trimmings on the second floor," she gasped as he was teasing the dusky centers of her breasts.

"Of course you do," he murmured. "At my store—"

"Shut up, Dalton. I don't care about your store. Keep kissing me."

Dalton kissed her.

And he dared to touch her. Tracing a finger along her bare shoulder, slipping off the sleeves, revealing more and more of her bare skin.

"I want to touch you," she whispered, and soon enough his jacket and shirt were just fabric on the floor, relics of the day, and she was gazing at his bare chest with heated longing that she couldn't hide if she even tried.

She didn't seem to be trying.

So he didn't hide how much he wanted her, either.

She bit her lip and skimmed her bare palms across the planes of his chest, the muscles of his shoulder, the bulge of his biceps. Then she leaned over and teased his nipple with her mouth, and he hissed her name and murmured, "Oh, God," as her fingers toyed with the waistband of his trousers.

Gazes locked. She smiled mischievously. She had ideas, his Beatrice. She was no longer some enthusiastic innocent, but a woman who knew what she wanted and would take it.

"Beatrice."

"Dalton."

"Ladies first."

"If you insist."

"I do."

A rush of fabric. A soft gasp. His hand skimmed along her silk stockings. She closed her eyes and moaned with the pleasure of his touch in the soft folds of her sex. It wasn't their first time but it had been a long time and things had changed and it felt like they were new to each other all over again. She dug into his shoulder with her nails, clinging to him as he stroked harder, slipped one then two fingers inside.

"Oh, God." She sighed and she moved against his hand. She knew what she wanted; he gave it to her.

He ached to be inside her. She seemed to know. Beatrice reached for him, and took his cock in hand and began to stroke the hot, hard length of it. He forgot about his store. And hers. He forget they were competitors. In this moment he was just a man at her mercy and he wouldn't have traded places with anyone.

"Oh, God." The invocation was drawn from his lips. It wasn't just her touch—although she knew just the right speed, just the right pressure to swiftly bring him to the brink—it was *her*. The woman he felt so many tortured and twisty and complicated feelings for.

He captured her soft moans with kisses. He groaned into her hair.

When she cried out at her climax, he caught that sound, too. A moment later he, too, was biting back a shout and was spent. She sagged against him. He turned and leaned against the dressing room wall for support. He began to take note of his surroundings. A dressing room. In a department store. After hours.

God, it was like they were eighteen all over again.

"Dalton," she gasped, when she had caught her breath.

Her pressed a kiss on her lips and said, "Next time we'll do that in a bed."

Chapter Twenty-three

Goodwin's Department Store
The next morning

*W*ell, Beatrice was never going to look at that fitting room the same way again. Or any dressing room, for that matter. Not after last night, when she'd disregarded a number of rules on proper behavior, with Dalton as her willing partner in delicious crime.

She had lost her mind, like a lovestruck young girl, but without fear of the consequences.

It was *glorious*.

But now she must pay attention to matters of business, not matters of pleasure. It was the start of a new day at work and she began it like any other, with a tour of each department to confer with all department heads to ensure that all was right and ready for another busy day with customers.

In the trimmings department on the second floor, she discreetly acquired a packet of buttons.

In women's undergarments on three, she did her best not to blush as she was flooded by memories of last night. The firm pressure of his mouth on hers, the way he held her, the way he touched her—strong and sure and reverentially all the same, until she was completely undone in his arms. In housewares, she reconsidered the twin beds.

Outside the reading room, everything had gone wrong.

Beatrice arrived to see a group of women standing in a huddle near the entryway, their faces drawn, their fists anxiously gripping their dark skirts. She quickened her steps.

"What is it?"

"Take a look," Margaret said grimly and the rest of the women stepped aside.

Beatrice looked into the room and uttered some choice words that a society debutante and duchess had no business knowing.

"Who and what and how?" Beatrice sputtered.

Nearly all the books had been swiped from the shelves to land on a jumbled heap on the floor. All the periodicals—newspapers and issues of *Mme. Demorest's Mirror of Fashions* and *Mrs. Frank Leslie's Illustrated Newspaper* were slashed, shredded, and strewn about the room. It looked like a storm had hit, or a tantrum. But this was no accident. It was very clearly intentional.

What Beatrice was looking at through narrowed eyes was busy work. Hours and hours of busy work to put the room to rights. It was the sort of mischief that didn't cause lasting damage—other than a feeling of vague unease—but it would result in hours of tedious work for women who had better things to do than reshelve a library full of books.

"It happened sometime between closing hour last night and this morning," Margaret explained.

Beatrice felt her temperature drop.

"Do we have any idea who did this?"

She assumed it was a man who had done this—along with the smashed mirrors a few weeks earlier. Women didn't usually have the combination of free time and lack of empathy that such vandalism required. But which man? Any number of them would be out of sorts enough with her—Mr. Stevens, or any of the other men she had fired? Maybe even Dalton?

She did her best to sound normal but her heart was racing because she had been here late last night. And so had Dalton. She racked her brain searching for a moment when he might have been able to do this. Would he have done it? He certainly didn't want to see her store succeed.

"No one saw anything or anyone," Margaret said. "Do you have any idea, Beatrice?"

Beatrice peered at all the women looking at her anxiously and expectantly for an answer and assurance. She so badly wanted to give it to them but what could she say?

Perhaps it was Dalton because I was here with him after hours?

Consider me your fearless leader while I consort with the enemy?

There are so many men I have angered with my ambition and now we are all in danger because of it?

"No," she said finally. "I don't know who might have done this. But I do know that we cannot let it stop us."

Chapter Twenty-four

Dalton's Department Store
The next night

$\mathcal{T}$he note Dalton sent to Beatrice that afternoon simply read "Your store or mine?" Her reply was immediate: "Yours, tonight." Thus he began counting down to closing time.

It was an hour that Dalton usually approached with dread. After the hustle and bustle of his store, the quiet solitude of his mansion was an uncomfortable weight on his chest. It was a feeling that, for all he had attained and accomplished, something was missing.

He did not, in fact, have it all. Whatever it was.

He was fairly certain it wasn't just a wife, any wife. He hadn't been a monk and he hadn't avoided courtship, either. But something was still missing.

One might have called it loneliness, yet he was a rich, powerful, connected man about town who never wanted for company or people surrounding him.

So he went to his club to avoid thinking about it. He spent evenings at the opera, he dined out and attended balls.

But just like that, the promise of Beatrice had him begging for closing time. He was ready and waiting when she strolled through the revolving door a minute shy of eight o'clock. He met her at the bottom of the grand staircase and led her up, up, up to the housewares department. They arrived just as the last employees left the sales floor and the doors were locked to the outside world.

They were alone.

Like Goodwin's, the department was full of little staged domestic scenes. A dining room here, set for twelve with the finest crystal, silver, and china with fresh flowers and candles. Over there, a parlor set up, complete with a faux mantel. There were plush velvet upholstered settees and chairs, with a low table between them that he'd set with chilled champagne, crystal flutes, more candles, and fresh flowers.

"Oh, Dalton, everything is so romantic. And here I thought we were just having a secret, illicit affair. This is much more than just a romp in the dressing rooms."

He grabbed her hand and pulled her close, and she laughed as he wrapped his arms around her and claimed her mouth with his. They kissed with all the passion of two people making up for lost time.

Flowers and champagne were forgotten.

"I feel like we should be catching up," Dalton murmured in between kisses. "The last time I saw you, you were waving from the deck of a ship, on your way to England." Dalton had gone down to the docks to watch the famous New York duchess leave. He knew that he needed to see her sail off, otherwise he feared wandering the city, anticipating a chance encounter. "What have you been doing all this time?"

"Nothing," she sighed.

"No, really. It's been sixteen years, Beatrice. How did you spend your days?"

He already knew about her nights.

She undid his tie and let it fall to the floor.

His jacket was shrugged off and tossed aside.

"Literally nothing. The dowager duchess did not trust me to execute the tasks of a duchess— menu planning, correspondence, hostessing, that sort of thing—as I was some lowborn, new-money *American* with no knowledge of how English society worked. So I languished in various rooms, took epically long strolls through the countryside, and considered flinging myself off a turret."

He fixed his attentions on the process of removing her hat and jacket and tossing them on the settee, just like they were at home together, the thought of which caused a sharp pang in his chest.

"What have you been doing all this time, Dalton?"

"Working."

"And?"

"I attended some parties, the opera, a few society events. But working, mostly."

"Women?"

"Some."

"Sounds like you haven't had much fun at all. It sounds lonely."

Lonely. That word again. He stepped back and poured her a glass of champagne, one for himself, and they sat upon the settee.

"It wasn't the worst of times. I never considered flinging myself off, say, the top of the World Building."

"Of course not. It was only recently built," she replied. Her eyes sparkled. "Sounds like we have some lost time to make up for."

"Excellent plan. As long as you aren't too busy with your lecture series, typing demonstrations, and musicals."

Beatrice sipped her champagne. "You read my newspaper profile! Or rather, one of them. It's been so hard to keep up with the press. It pays to be friends with all the female reporters in town. And to be living a story they want to cover."

"I'll be honest, I have someone read the newspapers for me. They provide me with all the necessary clippings. Especially with regards to my competition."

"Too busy launching an art gallery? Or is that new department dedicated to women's ready-made attire and children's toys taking up all your time?"

"How did you know?"

"I have spies. I have to keep up with what my chief competitor is up to."

"We launch on Tuesday."

She leaned in. Stroked his chest. Played with the buttons on his shirt. "Can a woman get a preview?"

"I might need to be persuaded," he murmured. But it was a lie. He needed no persuasion. Which made him tremendously vulnerable to her. But in this moment—so intimate and perfect, lounging on the settee, sipping champagne, speaking about their day, the promise of pleasure later—he couldn't remember why that would be so terrible.

He raised his glass.

"Your new window display is causing quite the sensation," he said. "The crowds on the sidewalk are making it difficult to walk past. Who knew that dressing cats up in baby clothes and letting them roll around in bassinets would be so appealing?"

"Margaret knew," Beatrice said, laughing. "The display was her idea. I foresee a great future in dressing cats up in adorable outfits. People can't seem to get enough of it."

She raised her glass to his for another toast.

"Cheers, by the way, to Dalton's making The White List. I love that we both claimed top spots." A local woman on a crusade to better the world, Josephine Shaw Lowell had recently published a pamphlet detailing the department stores that offered the best treatment for their female employees with the noble goal of encouraging shoppers to patronize these shops. The effect was already being seen. Female employees received higher wages and breaks where they might rest their feet. And there were dire repercussions for stores that failed to meet her criteria.

"If it weren't for you, I never would have made it. You saved me, Beatrice."

"I was never worried," she said.

"If I hadn't had to raise wages to meet the ones you were offering, I'd be suffering the same fate as the other low-ranking stores. Shopgirls in revolt. Customers fleeing and protesting at the entrance."

"You're welcome," she said with a laugh.

"Let me thank you personally."

"Yes, please. Especially if we move to that large bed over there."

He didn't need to look to know that she was referring to a massive four-poster bed topped with a feather mattress and mounds of pillows, all of which were made up in the finest, softest linens with silk-lined cashmere blankets. He'd been acutely aware.

"You did say that next time we should be in a bed," she said softly. The words *next time* from Beatrice's lips made him feel things.

"As you wish."

And then before he knew it, they were trying to kiss and walk and undress and tumbling down on the bed, a tangle of bare skin and fabric and wanting.

His shirt was gone, lost somewhere on the floor. Her dress was a heap on the floor, her corset, too. Dalton lowered himself over her, sinking into the pleasure of her body beneath his and whispered, "I missed you, Bea," before he could remind himself that they were just lovers by night, that she had broken his heart once, that he was supposed to be . . .

He couldn't remember what he was supposed to be.

Because Beatrice was wrapping her arms around him, stealing kisses from his lips, and murmuring, "Touch me, Wes, it's been so damned long. We have a lot of lost time to make up for."

So they did.

His mouth on hers. His hands upon her full breasts. Her fingers threading through his hair. His mouth pressing kisses along her neck, the hollow of her throat and lower still. She lay upon the mattress, her hair spilling across the pillows, arching up to him, offering herself to him. His mouth closing around the dusky centers of her breasts. Her low moan of pleasure.

They were a tangle of limbs and kisses and bedding. Touching all the soft parts of her, tasting her bare skin, exploring what made her sigh. Remembering and rediscovering all the things they once knew about each other. Beatrice still laughed nervously when his hot trail of kisses on her belly went lower and lower still. And then she wasn't laughing but her breath was shallow and quick and wanting.

"Let me please you, Bea," he said quietly, hovering slightly above her and desperately wanting nothing more than to make her forget all that submitting and enduring and to chase away the cold she'd told him about. And she said yes.

She sighed, "Yes," as her soft thighs opened to him.

Dalton felt another, sharper pang in his chest as she lay herself bare to him. She was making herself *vulnerable*. That word again. *Trusting* that he was going to be worth it. *Forgiving*. This was a second chance and he wasn't going to waste it.

She moaned when his lips touched the delicate skin of her inner thighs before moving slowly to the soft folds of her sex. He breathed her in and teased her, gentle at first, before he found the rhythm of his mouth and tongue that had her breathing hard and fast. She threaded her fingers through his hair, guiding him. He lost himself in the moment, aware of nothing but the exquisite taste of her and the sound of her breathing and how she was writhing now, moaning and demanding more because she was closer and closer to the brink.

He didn't stop. No, he intensified everything until he felt the climax rocket through her.

When she cried out in pleasure, the sound echoed through all six stories of this marble palace.

In an instant he realized he had done it all for her.

Not for revenge.

But to be worthy.

And that took his breath away.

"Hold me," she said. He did, sinking into the soft, warm haven of her arms. His cock was hard and throbbing and feeling how she was wet and ready for him. Her lips claimed his for a deep kiss and he felt her hands press him closer to her.

He wanted to be inside her. Be one with her. Surrender to this driving need to connect.

But not even Beatrice in his arms and eager for him could make him forget where they were—a store, for God's sake, where thousands of people passed through every day. He couldn't forget that they weren't just rivals or just lovers. Once upon a time, he thought she'd been the love of his life.

And now?

Maybe.

"I want more of you, Wes." She arched up to him, she pulled him closer. There was no mistaking what she wanted. "I want you inside me, Wes."

He wanted that, too. Desperately. Achingly. He was hard and throbbing for her and she was ready and willing.

"I can't," he said, rolling to the side but still holding her. She was breathing hard in the silence.

"Cannot or will not?" Beatrice asked in a small voice because they could both feel that he certainly could. If he wanted.

Dalton turned to face her. He gently pushed a strand of hair away from her face and let his hand rest possessively on her waist.

"When we do this, I want it to mean something, Beatrice."

"Oh," she replied in a small voice that slayed him.

He was laying himself bare to her. Removing his armor. Setting down his sword. And she only said "oh."

He felt that pang in his chest again, only this time it felt more like a knife than an extra hard beat of his heart.

"I can't promise you daytime things," she said. "I can't promise you lifetime things. But at night . . . Dalton, I can be yours."

"Can't promise me or can't promise anyone?"

"If there's anyone it's you. But I want my freedom. I won't be owned again."

He understood. This thing between them was too fragile and tenuous to be speaking of forever bonds. But something had been missing from his life and he had a hunch it was her and what they could possibly share together if things between them went a little further than an after-hours romp in a department store display bed.

"Can I try to change your mind?"

"You can try," she said, and he saw her smile in the dim light. "I hope you do. Especially if it involves more of what we just did."

He pressed a kiss on her lips and said, "Challenge accepted."

Chapter Twenty-five

Dalton's Department Store

*T*onight they were in his office. Beatrice was perched upon his desk, looking remarkably at home in the space. They had nicked a bottle of champagne from the wine department, along with two crystal flutes from housewares.

"I brought you a gift," Dalton said, extending a box wrapped in a gorgeous pink ribbon. Wooing meant gifts. Flowers. Trinkets. Tokens of affection. But what did a man get for the woman who had everything, and could have anything she wanted?

The one thing she couldn't buy. Yet.

"I am not opposed to gifts," she said with a smile that did things to his heart.

She eagerly unwrapped the package and breathed a soft *ooooh* when she saw what was inside: a few yards of a spectacular pink silk. It was soft to the touch, strong and light all the same. And it was a shade of pink like a woman's secrets or like the flush of a woman's skin after her climax. Strong and subtle all at once.

It was a pink that he'd had invented and made just for her, with her in mind. All the peachy pink underthings in her shop hadn't been vibrant enough to match her spirit.

"Dalton, it's lovely," she sighed, clutching it to her chest. "I've never seen anything like this."

"Make it up into whatever you want. Right now you're the only woman in Manhattan who has it."

"Where did you find this?"

"It's a secret."

"A secret? We'll see about that," she murmured, setting the silk aside and pulling him close for a kiss.

"It's exclusive to Dalton's," he admitted.

Her body stilled. She pushed him away.

"Exclusive? You know I cannot wear this if it's exclusive to *your* store. As the president of Goodwin's, your chief rival, I cannot waltz around New York wearing the exclusive wares of my competitor. I'm not going to be a walking advertisement for you."

"For me or for us?" Dalton asked softly, but seriously.

"Yes. Both. It's impossible that I should be seen wearing it."

"Afraid of scandal?"

"I'm afraid of being seen as yours. All the progress I have made to make the world see me as my own woman—not a debutante, not a duchess, not just a divorcée—will be undone. And I'll just be Dalton's woman and nothing more."

"So don't wear it," he murmured, pressing his lips to that spot on her neck that drove her wild. "Don't wear anything at all."

He kissed her, like it was another one of their rendezvous and he hadn't just asked her to do two appalling things with one gift of pink silk.

His fingers found the edge of her dress, slid underneath to caress her skin and oh, she still yearned for his touch but . . .

"Stop. I am too mad at you right now."

"Because of a little pink silk? It's supposed to be a gift, from a man to his lover."

"It's more than that and you know it. You are asking me to parade around in your *flag* like I've been conquered. I won't be conquered."

"What happened to rivals by day, lovers by night?"

"You blurred the lines. I have to go."

"Beatrice, wait—"

She was gone. And she took the damned silk with her.

25 West Tenth Street
Two days later

THE LADIES OF LIBERTY were meeting and sipping tea and plotting world domination as ladies were wont to do, when Beatrice stormed in late, skirts rustling and hat askew. She had the worst news.

"Ladies we have a problem. A pink silk problem."

Beatrice pulled a swatch of the most gorgeous pink silk that had ever been imagined and woven to life from her pocket and tossed it to their outstretched hands, like one might toss breadcrumbs to a goose.

Ava caught it first.

"Oh, that is gorgeous," she cooed. "This is like spun sugar and a maiden's blush and cherry blossoms."

"It would make the prettiest ball gown," Adeline added, reaching for it hungrily. "God what I would give to design with this."

"It's so soft and delicate, too. It'd be a dream next to my skin."

"Or tea gown! Or underthings. Can you just imagine? Oh, I now want to commission an entirely new wardrobe with this pink silk."

They could indeed just imagine all sorts of garments made with this particularly gorgeous silk. The shade of pink was like flowers in spring, the inside of a conch shell, like a woman's cheeks after a man whispered all the wicked and wonderful things he wanted to do with her.

It was a universally flattering shade of pink, as one could see as each woman passed it around and held it up to her face and somehow it made everyone look younger and happier and healthier. Daisy Prescott was giving it particular consideration, likely using her scientific brain to distill the what and how and why of this particular shade. Probably so she could invent a shade of lip paint or rouge to match.

"Anything made with this would be a delight," Harriet said. "And I hate pink."

"No!" Beatrice cried, her cheeks a shade of this very pink, though perhaps with a shade more fury. "We cannot make anything with it!"

"What's the problem? It's lovely."

"That is the problem. It is loveliness in fabric form. I want to remake my wardrobe and reupholster all the furniture in my house with it. I want to make flags to fly from every flagpole in the city with it. But it is exclusive to Dalton's."

Oh. A sudden cold hush swept over the women. What dreadful news. Because if it was exclusive to Dalton's that meant they could not buy it, not without jeopardizing the investment they'd all made in Goodwin's, and their commitment to Beatrice's store and the sisterhood. Not without making their fearless leader wear this public display of submission.

"Oh, that is a problem," Ava said. As she looked longingly at the swatch.

In an effort to have their pink and wear it, too, one woman suggested a possible solution. "Perhaps you can go to the mill and negotiate your own purchase! Perhaps you could even get it for less than Dalton's."

"Margaret and I first sent word from John Washington. And when even he couldn't close the deal, I made the journey myself to the mill upstate only to learn that it is exclusively made for Dalton because he owns the factory."

"Oh, that's very clever," Harriet said. The rest of the women murmured their concern.

"It is, isn't it? Which makes it all the more enraging."

Beatrice flopped back on the settee. Someone handed her a fortifying cup of tea and someone else handed her an entire plate of pastries, bless her. This might just get her through the afternoon.

She was at once exhilarated and exhausted from the day-to-day business of running the store. There was so much to manage! The ledgers and the orders and the rivalries between salesgirls and departments and establishing new displays. It was a far cry from all those days she swanned about the castle, trying to find something to do.

And now this!

She was about to be undone by pink silk.

It would be the death of her business, her dreams, her.

Beatrice had gotten used to success. And there

was no denying she was a success—the store was busy, the sales were brisk, the chatter among women was favorable, the press was good. Success suited her and she was not ready to relinquish it. This was possibly how Dalton had felt, too, when she'd come to town and taken over the store.

Elizabeth was longingly caressing the silk with a faraway look in her eyes, clearly imagining herself in gowns and corsets and parasols made of it, living her best life in this pink silk. Finding love, personal fulfillment, saving orphans, and being declared the best-dressed woman in all of New York, in this silk.

Maybe Dalton did understand women and what they wanted after all.

Didn't that just make her feel . . . Oh, that made her feel all sorts of violently conflicting things. Mainly, though, it made her feel hot and bothered. Because he wanted to love her and make love to her and dress her in beautiful pink silks and she . . . couldn't. The price was more than she was willing to pay.

"No, Ava. Put down Dalton's Wild Rose," she said, sharing the name of the shade of pink.

"Oh, it has a name!" Ava cried.

"I know. I know."

"Could you do your own version? Perhaps even slightly cheaper?"

"It's possible. But it would be a second-best version and people will see that we are copying

Dalton's, which is to say that we are just following what the man does, which means that they will see we are second best," Beatrice replied. "I'm not ready to be second best just yet. Though I suppose it's bound to happen. This fabric will be a sensation, it will draw in all the customers who will buy other things while they're already there, and they'll have no reason to go across the street into Goodwin's and we'll be ruined. My apologies, ladies, I tried."

"No, we're not ruined," Adeline, the dressmaker, declared in no uncertain terms. The room fell silent. But it was the glimmer in her eye that had them on tenterhooks because Adeline clearly had an idea of what to do. "We're not ruined. We will simply make it unfashionable."

And didn't that inspire some curious expressions and refills of teacups.

"Do go on."

"Adeline, I am intrigued."

"Does this mean we cannot wear it?"

"We cannot wear it," Adeline said firmly. "We won't even want to wear it. No one will. If we do this correctly."

"Sad!"

"But how do we make it unfashionable?"

At this, Adeline's eyes lit up. "This we are uniquely suited to do. And if we work together we can all pull it off. Ladies who write for the papers—Fanny, Nelly, Jane—you shall have to pick another color to champion. You will have to write disparaging things about pink. Harriet, Susan, perhaps you might give lectures on the frivolity of the color. And as for myself, I should of course refuse to make anything with it. Better yet, my dressmaking establishment is soon to be launched at Goodwin's. And . . . we'll have a fashion show."

"What is a fashion show?"

"I have no idea. I just invented it. But it will be something that will display our rival color and fabric, something that all the newspapers will cover, something that women will clamor to witness and will tell their friends about."

Was this fluttering feeling . . . hope? Perhaps not all was lost after all. Perhaps this team of women might save everything. All they had to do was sacrifice the joy and pleasure of wearing the most delectable pink silk that had ever been invented.

"But this means we will have to deprive ourselves of gorgeous pink gowns and everything pink."

"Yes," Adeline said sadly. "None of us can wear it."

"It might not have worked with your complexion anyway."

"That's going too far. It's clearly universally flattering."

"I suppose but . . ."

"We must make sacrifices for the sake of what we are building with Goodwin's," Harriet said. "Think of what is on the line here . . . All the jobs we have created for women."

"To say nothing of all the female entrepreneurs who tied their businesses to it," Adeline said. Such as herself. She exchanged a glance with Daisy and Martha and Madame CJ Walker, who had all opened outposts of their popular cosmetics stores and salons within Goodwin's.

"All the women we have made feel good about themselves by offering them a safe space to be inspired by beautiful things," Daisy said.

"And the safe space we have created for women to develop dreams and friendships and purchase the things they need without hassle."

"Think of what a beacon we are to other women the world over," Beatrice said, tripping slightly over the word *beacon*, but aware as always that this was never just about her. It was all of these women who were finding professional success and personal fulfillment because of what they'd built together.

"All right, for all that, I will sacrifice the Wild Rose pink," Ava said mournfully. "But I want front row seats at this fashion show, whatever it is."

Chapter Twenty-six

Dalton's Department Store
One week later

𝒯he tantalizing advertisements had appeared in all the New York City papers, so everybody who possibly cared about this sort of thing—people who liked stylish attire, not a small number—knew that Dalton's was launching a newly invented, totally exclusive shade of silk called *Wild Rose*. In addition to the advertisements, brilliantly designed and executed with the assistance of a new firm established by Theodore Prescott the Third, there was dramatic advertising throughout his store so that the legions of Dalton's shoppers would know there was something coming.

A massive pink silk bow hung on the exterior, over the revolving door, a bright spot on the gray stone of Broadway. Inside huge swathes of it draped the walls and the ceiling, enveloping the store in a soft, delicate glow of pink. It was like being inside of a kiss, or something even a little more intimate.

In other words, Dalton went all in.

On pink silk.

He had learned from the automobile debacle. Spectacle in and of itself was pointless if it appealed to the wrong clientele. Asserting the power of his engine, trying to impress with a hunk of metal was not what would bring women into the store, their hearts pounding and purses open. The truth was plain, in black and white and numbers in the store account ledgers: he was sunk without women.

He had known this instinctively—harnessing their power was how he'd built his empire—but this rivalry with Beatrice had made him forget this inviolable truth.

Women were the real engine who made everything else possible.

And so, he had bought a mill and staffed it with well-paid girls eager to escape a life of housewifery and drudgery on farms all over New England and out West. They came by train in droves.

And so, he'd invented this Wild Rose Pink and designed it with a woman's pleasure in mind. The color that flattered all complexions, the pleasingly soft caress of it against bare skin. It was designed to appeal to all senses, to be wearable at all hours of the day whether a corset, a tea dress, or a ball gown.

And he Made It Known.

The silk would be available on the first Saturday of the month.

Exclusively at Dalton's.

But when the appointed day and the appointed hour arrived, there were no more than the usual number of customers milling about in the usual way, purchasing the usual things. He experienced a slight pang of concern.

Some of the silk sold. But not nearly enough considering how much he had spent on acquiring the massive inventory. Excess inventory could be lethal to a retail establishment.

By midday, when the anticipated hordes of women had failed to appear, Dalton started to fear that he would die, smothered to death by an absurd amount of stupid pink silk. He would be mummified in the stuff. Future generations would find him wrapped up in a cocoon of pink silk failure and question his soundness of mind, his mastery of his domain, his understanding of women.

At two o'clock the crowds he had anticipated still had not arrived.

Under his custom-tailored suit he began to sweat that this gamble would not pay off. It felt like failing to sell water to people in the desert, lifeboats to people on sinking ships, or give candy to children. It was mortifying.

But the calculations! The projections! He had done MATH! He had sixteen years of retail experience and extensive knowledge of his customers; such could not lead him so far astray. Dalton was not one to doubt himself, not on retail, in which he had made himself an expert at the expense of the rest of his life. He could not be wrong.

There must be something else at play.

"Something is afoot," Dalton said to Connor. They were hovering anxiously in the mezzanine, awaiting the anticipated crowds and striving to appear utterly nonchalant at the nonevent happening in their store.

"Certainly not customers," Connor replied drily.

"Where did we go wrong?" Dalton mused. "It's pink silk. Women love pink and silk."

"I generally like to avoid blanket statements of what women like and don't like," Connor replied. "But yes, it should be an easy sell and it's not. And I reckon this ought to have been your first clue."

Connor pointed to something in the newspaper he pulled out of his jacket pocket— a large advertisement for something called a "fashion demonstration." At Goodwin's. At two o'clock. Seating was limited and first come, first served which meant especially motivated fashion-forward customers would have spent all day in Goodwin's.

They could pass the time in that damned reading room. Have a nice luncheon and tea service in the ladies-only restaurant. Freshen up in the ladies retiring room. All before gathering on the fifth floor for a fashion demonstration, whatever the hell that was.

"Wait, it gets worse," Connor said.

"I don't want to hear about worse."

"Of course you do. It's cohosted by the House of Adeline."

Dalton issued a swear word. The House of Adeline was the favorite of the fashion-forward women in the city. Something about dresses with pockets. He had approached her about a line of dresses for his store, but failed to close a deal with her, and so he hired someone else to design exclusively for his store—indeed there was an entire floor full of seamstresses sewing pockets into shirtwaists on the top floor, and forgot all about it.

"And there's even more bad news."

"Splendid."

"There aren't just advertisements but articles about the new spring trends and ready-made styles."

"Why are you reading the ladies section of the newspaper?"

"I think the better question is why you aren't.

Seems like maybe you should have. Then you might have known that floral patterns were the new anticipated style for spring. And you would know that only Goodwin's is giving an exclusive, live preview to the new ready-made styles designed by The House of Adeline, just in for spring."

Dalton stood very still, considering.

"Florals for spring. Groundbreaking. And Miss Black had previously refused a deal with us, but she's apparently struck one with Beatrice. It's almost enough to make one think it's all one giant conspiracy."

"I know women talk among themselves but do you really think they organized all this just to spite you? The newspaper articles, advertisements, the fashion demonstration, the clashing style for spring . . . all just to best you?"

Yes, he did. Which was madness. There couldn't possibly be some secret lady cabal, manipulating the current fashions just to vex him. But if there was, Beatrice, devious and organized, would certainly be at the center of it.

He meant that as a compliment.

Connor continued. "If it is a conspiracy against you—and that's a big *if*—they would have had to know about the silk well in advance. How could any of them have known?" Connor asked, sounding a little confounded. He pushed his fingers through his hair.

Unfortunately, Dalton had an answer to that question.

"I gave it to her," he admitted grimly.

"You *gave* it to *her*."

"Yes."

"You gave our exclusive product to her."

"Yes."

"To our chief competitor."

"I did. As a gift."

"May I inquire as to WHY and also what the hell were you thinking?" Connor was suddenly spitting mad. "Do you need to be driven off to a sanitarium like Edward? You gave our primary competitor our exclusive new product in advance of launch? What happened to your plans for revenge?"

Dalton had been thinking that it would look gorgeous against her skin. He was thinking the shade was a perfect match for her spirit: vibrant, passionate, powerful and sweet all the same. He was thinking as a man who wanted to please his lover, not a competitor who ought to keep secrets from his rivals.

Dalton had been thinking more and more about Beatrice and less and less about revenge, his firmly held ambition for over a decade. It was a fire that went out without his anger to stoke it and . . . he wasn't angry. He was falling in love with her all over again. And when he let the love in, the anger faded. When the anger faded, he could see more clearly: his ambition to reign over retail in Manhattan was really just to impress her.

And yet this *thing* between them seemed to position them forever at odds.

Dalton did not want to be at odds with her.

If he was being honest in the quiet privacy of his innermost thoughts, he'd only ever wanted to love her and live with her.

This admission was something of a problem, as he'd spent the past sixteen years organizing his life around ruining the woman he really wanted to love . . . to make her love him?

What was wrong with the world that he had learned the only way to earn a woman's love was to ruthlessly earn a fortune at her expense?

"Might I remind you that it's not just your fortune on the line here, Dalton?" Connor said hotly. "I have much to gain—or lose—too."

"I know. I haven't forgotten."

He just didn't care in the same way he once did. Dalton yearned for Beatrice with a ferocious passion that even years of enmity couldn't put a dent in. He sought to win her in the only way the world had ever showed him—more money, more power—yet it wasn't working.

Now Dalton had to decide what mattered more: winning a battle or winning the girl.

Goodwin's Department Store

BEATRICE STOOD HAPPY and proud in a flurry of feminine energy and activity. There was Adeline making final tweaks to the models attired in her designs, seamstresses fluttered about dangerously with pins in their mouths and needles and threads, making last-second alterations. The air was tinged with girlish, nervous, excited chatter and laughter.

There were pretty dresses. A frenzy of activity. A friendly audience clamoring to see, for the first time, a dress *on* a woman's body before they bought it. New styles had been promised. And pockets. Nothing made a woman mad with delight like a dress with pockets.

It wasn't Wild Rose Pink but it was certainly something captivating. And the women were enchanted as models walked among them, carefully turning and deliberately showing themselves off at all angles because a dress and a woman's body existed in multiple dimensions and it took up space.

"I hate to admit it . . ." Adeline began to confide in Beatrice.

"But the only way this would be better is if you could have used the Wild Rose silk?" Beatrice finished her sentence. "I am thinking the same thing."

"You said it," Adeline replied. "Remind me why we are not?"

"Because he has some idea of revenge and ruining my store. I sometimes even fear he may be wooing me to get to it. I can't let him take down my dreams, and this store and everything it represents and everyone it serves. Not even over his exclusive Wild Rose Pink."

"Noble." Adeline nodded sagely.

"And I cannot let him win my store—or me," Beatrice continued. She wanted to say more, but her *something* with Dalton was still secret and certainly not to be discussed in a crowd so thick it felt like all the women in Manhattan were there. Everything was so complicated, in spite of her efforts to keep a neat division between rivals by day and lovers by night.

Her pride was at war with her desire and it felt . . . ridiculous.

"But does it really have to be either/or?" Adeline mused.

"But what is the alternative?" Beatrice asked.

"And/and." Adeline flashed a grin. "Must one of you have to lose in order for the other to win?"

"He's the one with the ideas about revenge and—"

"Women have a dreadful habit of thinking too much about what men want, and not enough about what we want," Adeline replied smartly.

"We respond rather than light up the path we want to travel. Like a beacon. What do you want, Beatrice? What does happy even look like to you?"

But Adeline was off before she could answer; a hemline was askew and it was an urgent crisis that required her immediate attention. Customers were waiting with bated breath and open purses.

Beatrice was alone with her thoughts. Alone as one could be in a mad flurry of activity and the hum of feminine chatter, and the cacophony of women shopping, which is to say, the joyous ruckus of a sound of women publicly owning their desires.

She had made this possible.

She had created this moment.

She had orchestrated this wonder of women seeing and experiencing the world tailored for them for the first time, supported by each other, and full of opportunities. *Be a beacon*, they had asked of her, demanded of her. She, who had nothing to lose could afford to risk all to give them everything.

She couldn't give that up.

This, this was what she wanted.

That's what she was thinking when Dalton stepped into view.

DALTON WAS NOT interested in all the women demonstrating the new fashions or the women purchasing them. He was not interested in all the ready-made garments for sale.

He only had eyes for one woman.

Beatrice caught his gaze and made her way through the crowd toward him. As if by mutual agreement, they had not seen each other these past few nights. Ever since he had asked her to wear his exclusive color and declare herself as his to all the world. Instead of making love, she had done this . . . this demonstration of her independence.

"I see what you did there—" Dalton said.

"I'm glad that you think I did something. I'd be insulted if you didn't."

He noticed that she was humming with the energy of one who persevered in the face of an obstacle with no expectation of triumph and who was surprised and delighted to find she'd won.

"What are we doing, Beatrice?" Dalton asked quietly, and she turned to give her full attention. His heart started to beat hard when her eyes met his.

"Rivals by day, lovers by night. Right?"

"That's what we *were* doing. Past tense."

"It got complicated, didn't it?"

"Can we go somewhere more quiet and private to talk?"

She nodded and motioned for him to follow and he did. She lead him away to the stairs, up to the fifth floor, in housewares, which was empty. Everyone was on the other floors.

A savvy salesgirl took one look at them and made herself busy on the far side of the floor, dusting an array of Tiffany lamps.

Beatrice leaned against a chest of drawers. It was on display in a staged bedroom, recently revamped. It did not escape his notice that the twin bed display had been replaced with a full-size one.

What did that mean? God, what was happening to him that he was now trying to read a woman's intentions in the arrangement of furniture on display?

"Talk to me, Dalton."

There was still something palpable between them, a smoldering-passion kind of something. He saw her hands reaching for him, then dropping to hide in the folds of her floral-printed not pink skirts. She wanted him, but wouldn't indulge.

"Tell me what you have against pink silk," he said. "Tell me why you are so intent on crushing it. After all, you have to admit it's so pretty."

"I have nothing against pink silk. I'm quite fond of it, especially Dalton's Wild Rose. But not if it's trying to ruin me. Not if I'm supposed to wear it as a sign of my submission to my competitor and/or lover."

"It's not possible for you and pink silk to peacefully exist in the same world at the same time?"

"You tell me." She lifted one brow. "And I know we're not talking about pink silk."

"We're not talking about pink silk."

"You're the one with a lifelong ambition to conquer. To deliberately devalue me so you can get me for a lower price. To *have* me. And I won't let you."

Dalton wanted to protest, to tell her she had it all wrong. But until very, very recently he had wanted to conquer, to run the store into the ground so he could buy it for a song, so he could be so powerful and her so vulnerable that he could have a chance with her. So he could have her parading around town in his exclusive pink silk, not so that everyone would know that she had given herself to him, but so he would know.

But when he thought about it, when he felt about it, that wasn't what he wanted at all. He wanted to love her and be loved by her. He didn't care what she wore—or didn't wear.

"Do you think actively working to ruin the source of my freedom and joy is going to get you the girl?"

Dalton lived in the world. He read the news and novels, saw the plays, grew upon the same stories, that a man needed a fortune at any cost if he was ever going to get the girl. Get. To have and to hold. But a woman wasn't a thing to have or hold, to possess or hold captive.

And oh, fuck, at last he felt like a duke. Her duke.

Having her but not really having her at all.

It wasn't what he wanted.

Dalton stepped aside. Giving them both a little breathing room.

"Did you know, Beatrice, that you weren't the only one wandering around a big empty house for sixteen years?"

Her eyes lifted up to his, searching, wanting to know more.

"Did you know that you weren't the only one yearning to be touched?" Dalton asked quietly so only she could hear because ruthless, powerful, millionaire tycoons such as himself didn't admit to such things. He knew such men kept such soft words bottled up inside, never to say them aloud, especially to a woman, in her territory.

But if felt so right and good to say it, to throw the weight off his shoulders.

He had not been alone. He had not wanted for company. But he been lonely.

"You were not the only one who had been lonely, Beatrice. You were not the only one hungering for touch and a connection. I've had all the success a man could dream of, and it's still not enough. What I'm missing is the connection I feel when I'm with you."

She was still. She was listening.

And the tension in his chest was easing.

He was actually saying these things. It was terrifying, exhilarating, and wonderful. It was like driving that automobile at top speed with the top down on a wide-open road. Like riding a bicycle down a country road and being aware for the first time of how limited you'd been your whole life and had never even known it. Until it was just you and the wheel and the wind in your hair.

"But men—" Beatrice protested.

"Tell me about men, Beatrice."

"It's just bodies. It's just a driving need. It doesn't mean anything."

"Lies. All lies," Dalton said, spilling the secret that men had been perpetuating for centuries. "Maybe we also want it to mean something."

"Well, you have a funny way of showing it," she retorted.

"True," Dalton admitted. "Men are idiots."

Beatrice was silent for a moment, clearly thinking, and he made himself stay still with that silence.

"So as for our rivals by day, lovers by night . . . what does this mean for us? I still cannot wear the silk," she said and he heard the question in her voice. Revelations about his feelings and humanity were all well and good but what did it mean for him and her in the here and now?

"What if I want more, Bea? What if I want more than a tumble in a store bed? What if I want more than a rivalry and more than revenge?"

There was a full-size bed right there. Made up in the finest linens and cashmere blankets and down feather pillows. Beatrice was the boss—she could order everyone away to afford them privacy.

"But, Wes, what if that's all I want?"

That slayed him. Right there in the middle of housewares, while leaning up against a finely crafted chest of drawers. What if this—a tumble in a department store bedroom, with a woman who only wanted a diversion—was the highest peak he could ever reach?

How positively tragic.

But Dalton was not ready to admit defeat, even if his concept of what it meant to win or lose was rapidly evolving.

"I have a proposal for you," he said and he had to laugh at the panic in her eyes. "Nothing serious," he quickly clarified. "One night. You, me, New York City. Let's leave our competition aside and just enjoy each other's company and see where things go."

"I believe the word you're looking for is *court-ship*."

"I believe you're right. What do you say?"

Chapter Twenty-seven

The Goodwin Residence
One West Thirty-Fourth Street
The next day

That evening Beatrice had plans. Plans which were best described simply as Wes Dalton. Her twenty-year-old self was thrilled at the prospect of a romantic evening out on the town with him—without a chaperone, too. Ah, the perks of being a scandalously divorced duchess!

But present-day Beatrice felt somewhat conflicted. She was on fire with anticipation to be with him, bare her body and soul to him. But it was clear he wanted more than that from her, more than she wanted to give.

But she had promised him a chance to woo her.

Tonight was the night.

A crash of contrary feelings were roiling within her as she stood at the drawing room window, peering out, waiting for the moment of his arrival so she could slip out without him coming to the drawing room.

Because Beatrice wasn't alone. Her mother sat near the fire, embroidering.

"You are all dressed up, Beatrice. What are your plans for the evening? I thought you declined the invitation from one of the Vanderbilt brothers."

"I did."

Beatrice paused, debating whether to share her real plans for the evening. It would be easy enough to say that she was joining some lady friends at a lecture or dinner party. But the truth was near to bursting out of her chest so she had to say something.

"I'm going out with Wes Dalton this evening."

Her mother did not even look up from her embroidery. "Interesting hour for a business meeting."

Beatrice kept her gaze focused on the window.

"I don't think it's quite entirely business."

"Ah. I see."

And so an awkward silence ensued. Admitting to one's mother that one was having an affair was not quite the done thing. It was not exactly a topic of polite conversation. And there was the fact that, at the moment, Beatrice was feeling unnervingly like a young girl of sixteen and not a woman of six and thirty, free to live her own life without explanation or apology.

"I'm not an eighteen-year-old debutante any-more, Mother. I'm divorced and already scandalous and if I want to spend an evening with a man, I can. I will take precautions not to be seen but—"

"Of course you can, especially if you take care not to be seen. Don't think that you are the first unmarried woman of a certain age to take advantage of your freedom."

Well, if that didn't stun her into momentary silence. Permission from her mother to have an affair, as long as she did it properly and circumspectly. That was unexpected.

"I just wish you wouldn't do so with . . . him," Estella said.

Her mother's dislike of Dalton was long overdue for a reckoning. Beatrice turned from the window to face her mother.

"Why don't you like him? That business with him and me was so long ago. He may have been a fortune hunter back then but he certainly isn't now. He has one of the three great fortunes of the age!"

"Are you sure he still isn't after the store?"

It was a moment before Beatrice answered. "No."

He had made his intentions clear to her: he wanted more than just a quick and casual romp. He wanted courtship and romance and possibly marriage. Thanks to the Married Woman's Property Act, she would still own the store if they did wed. But once their intimate lives were intertwined . . . it would be impossible to keep him and the store truly separate. He would still have claim over her body and time.

"Mother, why are you so sure that he is still after it and not me?"

"Besides the fact that he made an outrageous offer to buy it for more than it's worth? Besides the fact that he made it plain that it has been his life's ambition to own it?"

"Besides all that."

"He reminds me of your father."

Beatrice availed herself to the settee, wrinkled skirts be damned.

"You're going to have to explain that."

Her mother sighed and set down her embroidery.

"I was once like you, Beatrice. Remember, it was *my* father who had started the store. It was called Bergdorf's back then, and I followed him around, soaking up all the crumbs of information that came my way. I observed his innovations, his reasons. I saw how he trained the clerks and crafted his advertising copy. I delighted in setting up displays with him. I was just like you. Or rather, you were just like me."

"You wanted to run the store yourself."

"I did. Your father promised me that we would run the operation together. First he wooed me, then he charmed my father with his grand ideas and a fancy degree. And before I knew it, my father was selling the business to my husband and it became his. A wedding present."

Estella laughed and it was bitter.

"Then I had you and Edward and thus reasons to stay home."

"He even changed the name," Beatrice said softly.

"And then it wasn't mine anymore."

Beatrice realized then that the enormity of the loss hadn't lessened one bit. She could feel the ache of it.

Her mother resumed her embroidering. Stabbing the needle through the fabric and pulling the thread taut. All these feelings, unspoken, but let out in the push and pull of the needle and thread through bits of embroidery displayed throughout the house. Little monuments to all the women's feelings that had been left unspoken.

"But you seemed to like all the society stuff, Mother. You were forever going to parties and hosting teas and matchmaking."

"A woman's ambition cannot be created or destroyed. It can only change forms. It will manifest where it is allowed. Be that home, children, church, or social climbing. Or a career or business should she be allowed."

But I was not allowed.

The words didn't need to be said. They filled up the room anyway. They made it hard to breathe. All that tension that never, ever had a release.

Her mother's hands stilled as she looked up and met her daughter's gaze unflinchingly.

"Have your fun, Beatrice, but don't lose your head to him. You have a chance to live the un-lived lives that came before yours."

Oh, but what a weight for a woman to carry upon her shoulders.

It was the same crushing weight Beatrice felt when the well-meaning Ladies of Liberty held her up as a beacon to all the other women out there. Beatrice's success or failure was somehow an indication of what was possible for the future, and to make amends for the past.

What a burden and what a gift, all at once.

Beatrice stood and returned to the window, watching and wondering if any hours in the day were lived for herself alone. Was it so very wrong if she seized one or two, just for herself?

A carriage pulled by four white horses rolled into view. Dalton leapt down.

Beatrice turned to her mother.

"Thank you, Mama."

And then she was off, through the foyer and the front door and standing at the top of the stoop.

"No automobile?" she called down to Dalton.

"Apparently Prince Charming always arrives

in a carriage pulled by white horses. Well, here I am."

Oh, it was plain to see what he wanted. Her. All of her.

But what did she want?

The Top of the World

THE OFFICES OF *New York World* were in the tallest building in New York City and thus quite possibly the world. The terrace on the top floor was not open to the public—especially not at this late hour. But one of the perks of being a millionaire tycoon with friends in high places was the ability to call in a favor and obtain exclusive after-hours access to the best view in Manhattan. It was vitally important to pull out all the stops when trying to woo a woman as magnificent as Beatrice.

Dalton had a second chance. No one ever said Wes Dalton failed to seize an opportunity.

Beatrice sighed when she took in the view of the city, the river, the sky. "I am in awe and enchanted and utterly terrified all at once."

Me, too, Dalton thought. He wasn't thinking about the view.

"I thought I would show you my favorite view of the city," he said. "When you're down on the streets, it's a constant crush and hustle. But up here it's quiet and you can see how far we've all come."

"The city is so different than I remembered," Beatrice said, staring out into the night sky, a mix of stars and man-made lights, a vast expanse of sky and towers of steel and brick jutting up, insisting on making their presence known.

"You were gone so long."

"A lifetime, practically."

"A city block can change from year to year. I hardly remember what the city looked like last year, let alone when you left."

Then again, he hardly ever stopped to notice. He was always so busy making the journey from his mansion uptown to his palace downtown and back again, with the forays to parties and the theater. He hardly ever slowed down to observe everyone else's progress, so consumed he was with his own.

He led her around the corner, where a table had been set for dinner. There were candles in glass lanterns, fresh flowers, chilled champagne. A waiter stood nearby, ready to pour champagne and serve them food.

"Oooh, Dalton, you've outdone yourself. This is unexpected."

"My first rule of retail is to *surprise and delight. Always astonish the customer.*"

She laughed and turned to him. "You have rules?"

"Rules. Truths. Words to live by. Whatever you want to call it. The fact is, I didn't stumble my way to earning the title of merchant prince of Manhattan."

"Tell me everything," Beatrice said as she took a seat at the table.

"Tell my competitor all my trade secrets?" But then she smiled and he was lost.

"Well, if you're still trying to buy my store, then perhaps you had better keep your secrets to yourself."

There was a beat of silence as he considered. Hardly longer than a heartbeat of silence. He knew what she was asking.

This was his moment to decide and to let her know.

"The second rule is that a customer—most often a woman—should always have a choice," he said smoothly as if it were just conversation and he hadn't just surrendered. "Why offer one style of gloves when I can offer her a dozen? Because the other important rule is that a woman should always get what she wants."

"I think I like your rules."

"A woman—a customer—should always have the right to change her mind. No questions asked."

Dalton was speaking about returns. And by virtue of her position as president of her own retail operation, Beatrice was uniquely suited to understand the hard dollar amount that cost him every time a woman had a change of heart. He paid the price so she could walk away happy.

She was looking thoughtful now, staring off at the view of the city until she fixed the full force of her gaze on him.

"Do you ever think about the choices we made all those years ago?"

"All the time, since you returned," he said. "And almost all the time before that. Chances are I'd be nobody or nothing if I hadn't taken the money your parents offered. I like being somebody. Though I'm starting to wonder if it isn't everything."

"Would you take the money again?"

"Have you ever noticed something about the heroes in fairy tales and popular stories?" he asked and her eyes flashed with attention. "They are always princes. Royalty. Nobility. The wealthy. The duke always gets the girl."

She, who always had a quick retort, had nothing to say now because he was right.

"I thought," he continued, "that if I wanted to get the girl, I needed to be rich and powerful. And drive a carriage pulled by four white horses."

"You didn't need all that."

"Didn't I?" There was a moment of silence between them. Because all evidence suggested that he did. Just so he could be loved. "Would you say yes to the duke again?"

"I don't know," she sighed. "But I don't know that I would have chosen you, either. I had nothing but love for you, Wes. But I wish my choice hadn't been between two men, between all or nothing. I just wish I could have chosen myself."

"And now you finally have."

She said yes with no uncertainty and he understood. Beatrice was finally allowed to be *herself.* To fall in love with *herself,* to commit to no one but *herself.* He had nothing that could compete with that. He had a store and a name that carried some weight in this town—but she had her own. He had a fortune—but she wanted for nothing. He had a magnificent carriage pulled by four white horses but she was a witch who could summon a hack in the rain.

Dalton checked all the boxes for Prince Charming.

And all she wanted was to ride off into the sunset on her own.

But after the sunset?

"We made our choices and we have lived with them," he said. "But we are here, now free to do whatever we wish."

"I want . . ." She sighed and summoned the words. "I want something between all or nothing with you. But I don't want to give up my freedom. What do you think, Dalton?"

Would he be content with Beatrice at night only? To agree was to risk the greatest happiness or the greatest heartache. He hadn't gotten this far by playing it safe. So he raised his glass and said, "Rule—give a woman whatever she wants."

Chapter Twenty-eight

Later that night

$\mathcal{T}$he thing about being a divorced duchess is that there is very little one could do that would cause a scandal greater than divorcing a duke, which meant Beatrice was at tremendous liberty to do whatever she wished.

And if one wished to go home with a certain tycoon at a certain late hour, one could.

In fact, one most certainly did.

Dalton's carriage sped through the night—the streets blazingly empty at this hour—and stopped before a massive, wildly ornate mansion clearly designed to impress, and definitely over-compensating for something. She recognized it for what it was: a declaration in stone and money that he was a man of consequence.

She followed him from the carriage to the front door, hand in hand. It was late, it was dark. His mansion took up an entire city block so really, no one was close enough to see.

Beatrice hesitated at the threshold.

Her body was humming for the pleasure she knew she'd find with him on the other side. But it was going to mean something, maybe even more than she was ready to claim.

And so, she paused.

Then he slipped her hand in his, entwined their fingers, and looked at her, a question in his eyes. *Are you ready for what comes next?* She was on fire for it and nervous all the same. But it was Wes, her first love. He of the soulful blue eyes and burning ambition and plain yearning. He of the kisses that made her knees weak and the secret rules that were really the keys to his kingdom.

She stepped over the threshold.

The foyer was a vast marble affair, deliberately designed to impress and intimidate except that she was accustomed to such. Beatrice knew what it meant to live in a house like this. One could never truly be at leisure, one always felt a pressure to be worthy of it, to match it. And so she felt a little sorry for Dalton.

"So this is your house."

"It's where I sleep."

"My voice is echoing in your foyer," she said with a laugh. Which echoed. "It's like the duke's castle but with electric lights and central heating and running water."

"I have all the modern conveniences. Would you like a tour?"

"I'm not here to see your house, Wes."

She reached out for the lapels on his jacket, pulled him close, and lifted her mouth to claim his.

"Not wasting any time," he murmured as he broke the kiss to press his mouth to the curve of her neck.

"I think we've waited long enough for this, don't you?"

"You have no idea." He pulled out her hairpins and they skittered across the marble floor. Her hair tumbled down around her shoulders. Then he started on her dress, right here in the foyer.

Are you ready for what comes next?

Yes, God, yes.

She coyly undid the buttons on his vest. But then she ripped open his shirt, and buttons went flying. She laughed and the sound echoed. But she wasn't laughing anymore when she slid her palms against the firm planes of his chest. She lowered her head to tease one of his nipples with her tongue; his sharp hiss of breath made her feel like a queen.

"Beatrice," he murmured. "Bedroom."

And they stumbled their way there. Kissing. Undressing, leaving a scattered trail of clothes and things from the foyer, up the grand curving staircase, along the second-floor landing. And then her back was up against a heavy wooden door, Dalton's hands at her waist, his mouth claiming hers, her dress in a state of disarray, her heart pumping wildly.

And the night was only just getting started.

YEARS. *YEARS* DALTON had waited for this moment. Beatrice in his bedroom. Beatrice reaching out for him, her gaze so nakedly dark with desire for him. Beatrice touching him. Beatrice lifting her mouth to his for a kiss. He felt desired. He felt desire. He felt proud, triumphant even, to have this woman in his mansion, like he was finally worthy of her.

When it came down to it, he felt chosen.

It had all been for her.

He never really wanted revenge.

It had always been about the girl.

He had done nothing but work for sixteen years, all on the rare chance this moment could be real and not just a fantasy.

Years.

Now Beatrice was in his bedroom and they were going to make love.

He thought he might explode. The tightness in his chest. The suppressed roar in his throat. The pounding of his heart and the throbbing of his cock. He'd never felt so much, all at once.

He shrugged out of his jacket and his shirt, or what was left of it.

The removal of her dress was more complicated.

Nevertheless, he persisted.

For a moment he just looked at her, skin aglow in the moonlight. Puddles of silk and satin on the floor.

She said these things about her freedom, yet she was here and her lips were close and there was no mistaking the desire in her eyes. She wanted him. Just as much as she wanted her independence—but not more.

Her lips, inches from his.

Could he be content with *something* even if it wasn't *everything*?

Dalton honestly didn't know, but it was a risk he was going to take.

Especially when her hair tumbled around her shoulders and she wrapped her arms around him and kissed him on the mouth. Hot, sweet, dangerous all at once.

Sixteen years. One did not get this close and then slink off to sleep in the guest bedroom. Not when she brazenly toyed with the waistband of his trousers. Not when she looked at him like she'd been hungering for him for years. Not when she teased him with kisses.

So Dalton kissed her back.

He slid his hand around her waist, urging her against him to close that last little distance between them. He breathed her in and it did nothing to ease the tightness in his chest, the pounding of his heart, or the throbbing of his cock. Touching her only made him feel *more*.

"I fantasized about this," he whispered. "You. Me. Here."

She touched him, tracing her delicate duchess hands across his bare chest, lower. She was touching him brazenly, possessively.

I'm yours, he thought. *For better or for worse.*

And so began the clumsy, backward waltz toward the bed. Falling back in a tangle of limbs and kisses and pent-up feelings of desire. He wanted her and she just wanted to burn.

Rule: give the woman what she wants.

So he sucked her lip and dragged his hands along the curve of her thighs, her waist, up to her breasts. God. He'd never get enough of her breasts, full and so easily teased and aroused. When she was breathing hard and writhing for more, he moved lower, pressing a trail of kisses across her belly.

"Not exactly eighteen anymore," she murmured, stupidly apologetic.

He gave a little laugh. "Me, neither. And here you are, more beautiful than ever."

"You know just what to say to make a girl fall for you."

"The truth? It works wonders."

"Stop being so perfect."

He hovered over her, his strong arms supporting him. She could feel his arousal against her entrance, hot and hard. He gave her a rakish grin. "You don't really mean that, do you?"

"No. Yes. Dalton . . . just kiss me. Just take me."

BEATRICE LAY BACK on his bed, her hair tumbled around her. Nowhere she had to be, nowhere she'd rather be. Dalton above her. His body was glorious—all muscles and naked and hers to touch and pleasure. And his touch was exactly what she had been starving for.

He had been hell-bent on destroying her and tonight he was hell-bent on pleasing her.

Sigh. Even though she had been headstrong and outspoken and the wrench in his machine.

Not all men looked upon women like that with such lust, and maybe even love.

She knew. Oh, she knew.

She could just be herself. She could let go and enjoy herself. Thoroughly. Completely. Unapologetically.

He caressed her, everywhere, with a touch that was something like reverential but less delicate. Like he knew she wouldn't break. Like he was intent on enjoying her and learning her and knowing her. And she gave him the same attention—curve of his biceps, the planes of his chest that tapered to his waist and . . . the evidence of his arousal for her. She took the length of him in hand and the soft hiss from his lips made her feel like a siren.

He continued to kiss his way down her belly and lower still.

It was the easiest thing in the world to moan

softly in anticipation and part her legs when she felt the stubble of his cheeks on her inner thighs, when she was achingly aware of how close his mouth was to bringing her to climax.

"Ooooh," she sighed as she felt his mouth, hot and tender, expertly teasing and stroking her, making the pleasure and the pressure build and build. Her hands gripped the bedsheets.

He made up for years of cold loneliness with just his mouth. And his hands. And then things he said earlier and the promises she knew he would keep if she'd let him and *oh*.

"Oh, God." She breathed hard as he slid one then two fingers inside of her, stroking smoothly. She writhed around him, pulling him closer, holding him tighter. He was making her feel the *more* feeling. Like she couldn't get enough of his touch, or the intense way it made her feel.

More. She wanted *more* and she wasn't sorry.

She wanted *more* and he was giving and she was taking.

More. More. More.

The orgasm snuck up slowly and then hit her all at once.

She cried out her pleasure and he didn't stop.

There was still *more*.

Beatrice felt more alive than ever. She felt born again. She felt like she was flying. She felt free.

And before she could even catch her breath, he was moving to kiss her on the mouth, to capture the last of her cries, and his cock was throbbing at her sex, wanting more and she was wanting more, too.

Because when you are free to do whatever you want, when you are flying, when no scandal can touch you, when you are kissed like this, where there is love and lust and complications all tangled up, there is only one thing to do, one thing to say.

"Yes. More."

She was, apparently, insatiable and he was hot, hard, and ready for her.

"So tell me how you imagined this," she whispered, stroking the rigid length of him. She still hadn't quite caught her breath. Her heart was still beating wildly in her chest.

"It already doesn't compare," he said as he moved to straddle her, press his cock up against her sex. She sank into the mattress as his weight pressed down on her—was there any more exquisite feeling? She writhed a little, wanting him inside her, but still he teased.

He slid his fingers through her hair and kissed her deeply. For a moment. Before there was *more*.

His heart was thundering so hard Wes had to wonder if maybe a man could feel too much, all at once, and it would be his undoing. This wasn't his first time, it wasn't even the first time he cared about the woman he made love to, but it was the first time his heart and soul were inseparable from every touch, every whisper, every moan.

It was overwhelming as all hell.

His beloved Beatrice was here, in his bed, and he had just made her climax and her cries were still echoing in his head and doing things to his heart, and now she was naked beneath him saying, "Yes, more." And he was definitely going to explode.

So he kissed her, as if *that* would help him catch his breath and his wits. He gave up, gave in and when she wrapped her legs around his lower back he was done for. When she licked the sweat from his neck he wanted to die. But was there any better way to go than a tangle of hot, sweaty limbs and making love to the woman he loved best in the world?

He eased in. Inch by inch. It was a slow burn. A torture. But he'd waited *years* for this moment and by God he was going to savor every second of it.

Because this—Beatrice in his arms and all around him—it was everything he ever wanted. He knew that now. Ever since he first laid eyes on her and now it was better than he had ever imagined, and the devil only knew how he had imagined.

Her closed eyes, lashes upon her cheeks, her hair a tussled mess across his pillow. Her lips parted, soft moans of pleasure escaping. He kissed her.

He thrust in, harder now and harder again, and she sighed, "Yes."

And his heart was thundering with passion and madness all at once and all together. He thrust in again, deliberate full strokes. She grabbed a handful of his hair and kissed him. He linked his hand with hers and pinned her wrist to the bed and again she sighed, "Yes."

Her back arched up to meet him, dear God, and they found the rhythm that was a slow and steady beat to undo them both completely.

Everything he ever wanted. Losing his head and his heart with Beatrice.

Nothing else mattered, not the Marble Palace or this one, or all the years they had been stupid and so far apart. All the money in his bank account made no difference and he would have traded all of it for one more night like this.

There was only his body and hers, connected at last. The thundering of his heart, the throb of his cock, her heady moans as she cried out again. And then he was shouting his release, his body trembling.

He collapsed beside her.

"That was . . ." she started, breathless.

"Worth waiting for," he finished.

Chapter Twenty-nine

Goodwin's Department Store
A week later

*T*heir days had been filled with matters of business, but their nights had been nothing but pleasure. By some miracle they were both rivals and lovers. By some miracle, she was free to do whatever she wanted and what she wanted was Wes Dalton. On her terms. He met them, respected them, and it was almost enough for her to fall in love with him all over again.

Almost.

She was already aching for him at closing hour. She stood in her corner office, overlooking the end-of-day bustle on Broadway, feeling like a pirate queen on the prow of her ship.

And then she heard him.

Beatrice held her pose for a moment, letting him see her like this: silhouette of a woman before the overlarge window overlooking the city. Letting him see how this was her office, no matter that he once upon a time aspired to claiming it as his own.

Perhaps he still did? She didn't think so, but her mother's caution wasn't tremendously far from her thoughts.

She turned. Fixed her gaze on Dalton filling up the doorway. He wore a suit very, very well. She had ambitions to take it off him.

"Oh, hello, Dalton."

"I do believe we have an appointment," he said in a low, commanding voice.

"Urgent business," she replied.

His gazed dropped down to the buttons on her jacket. "Terribly urgent. It cannot wait."

"Then we better get down to it."

He closed the door behind him and strode across the room to stand just before her desk. Her large, strong, heavy oak desk. She had ideas about him and her and this desk.

Judging by his darkened gaze, he was of the same mind.

It started with a kiss across the desk. Until that was ridiculously uncomfortable and they laughed and she tugged his tie, leading him around to her side. His hands were on her waist, his mouth crashing onto hers. She wrapped her arms around him, threaded her fingers through his dark hair and kissed him deeply.

In a second he had her perched on the desk, her legs and skirts parted and hair tumbling down her back. The promise of this had powered her through the day and now the moment was here and she no longer wanted to think of departments or displays or lists or figures. Just *this*. She knew he felt the same.

His strong hands making short work of her dress.

His hot mouth blazing a trail of pleasure from her lips to lower and lower to her breasts, where did the wickedest things that had feeling the wickedest feelings. Like she was completely his, at his command.

And command he did; Dalton took control. Urging her legs apart. He kissed her there, teased with his tongue and fingers until she was writhing hard and crying out as the climax crashed over her.

She waited, breathlessly.

But not passively.

She had to touch him, too, feel the strong planes of his back, his arms around her as he stood and kissed her. This, this was what she'd been missing, what she had been hungering for. The sweet friction of his body against hers, the hardness of his cock wanting entrance, the drunkenness from his mouth on hers.

"Yes," she breathed, arching her back.

She felt him hard, throbbing with wanting. Or maybe that was her wanting. His touch, the scent of him, everything had her practically panting with desire for more of him, all of him.

But only if it meant something.

It had to mean something that he could kiss her with a passionate intensity that she thought of *more* and *forever*, and *Take off my clothes and take me right here, right now, on this desk where I conduct business.*

It had to mean something that he was the only man who would understand her—the real her, the woman she was becoming. Dalton understood her days, he knew just how she wanted to spend her nights. She couldn't imagine any other man sharing both those things with her.

She doubted any other man would meet her like this—her office, her terms—so agreeably and without judgment.

And all Dalton wanted was *meaning.*

She was thinking about it. If she was thinking at all. His thumbs were flitting over the dusky centers of her breasts, bared to him and the night, and it brought a soft hiss of pleasure to her lips. The man knew how to tease her.

And then, she stilled.

"What is it?"

"I . . . nothing."

He pulled back and gazed right into her eyes.

And then she heard it again. They both heard it again. Now that they both weren't breathing hard and driven to distraction.

They heard the sound of low voices and footsteps in the hall.

Dalton pressed a finger to her lips, motioning for her to stay silent. He pulled himself together and crept to the door before flinging it open with a loud bang that made her flinch with the sudden bang of it.

"Who's there?" His booming voice echoed down the empty hall. But there was no shaking the feeling that someone had been there. And they had both heard it. She wasn't crazy.

She had hoped she was crazy. She hoped she had imagined the sound tonight and all the other times that she'd been the last to leave or the first to arrive. The sound of footsteps, the click of a door locking, the feeling that someone was near.

She hastily buttoned her shirt—with whatever buttons remained; Dalton was proving perilous to her wardrobe but also lucrative to her buttons and trimmings department on the second floor. She met him at the door.

"Anyone there?" she asked.

"They're gone. Hopefully not thieves. Are you all right?"

She nodded. "We should go. I'm not quite in the mood now. Here."

He nodded, understanding.

Only when she went to close the door behind her—and lock it—did they see. It hadn't been thieves, but vandals.

Someone had painted the words Whore Go Home on the door.

Nothing had been stolen other than her peace of mind and sense of equilibrium. It was disturbing enough to see such violent language, especially directed at herself. But it was worse to consider that someone had been there while they had been intimate. They would have been close enough to hear. Or perhaps even see.

Beatrice turned away, revolted by the invasion of her privacy. But the fury bubbled up swiftly. How dare someone violate her sacred space, her privacy, her domain?

Again. This hadn't been the first time someone had snuck into the store to make mischief. But this was the first time she had been so terrifyingly close to it.

"Beatrice . . ."

But she was already bustling toward the closet where the cleaning things were kept and getting scraps of old cloth and soap and water to wash it off before the paint dried and settled in permanently. It wouldn't do for the staff to arrive first thing and see this.

Seeing the words *whore go home* painted on the door was no way to start the day.

Even though the hour was late, even though her lips were still warm and tingling from Dalton's kiss, she started to furiously scrub and scrub and scrub. The repetitive motion of cleaning soothed her; the immediately apparent effect of her efforts gave her back some sense of power and control.

And Dalton. Well, Dalton wasn't a man to stand idly by. Wordlessly, he picked up a cloth and started cleaning the higher parts where she couldn't reach. Side by side they worked, neither one of them remarking that this was hardly the evening plans they'd had in mind but nevertheless here they were.

And then it was all clean, like it had never happened, except it had.

"Are you all right?" Dalton asked.

"I'm fine."

"Actually fine or the way ladies say they're fine when they are actually experiencing a multitude of powerful emotions?"

"Yes, that one. Fine."

"I see." He was looking at her, she could feel it. She could feel his gaze searching every inch of her face, looking for the truth. And lowered her gaze. She didn't miss the sharp intake of his breath as he realized the truth.

"It wasn't the first time was it?"

"How did you know?"

"Someone smashed the mirrors. I was there."

"Right. I had forgotten."

He raised an eyebrow in disbelief. "I read about the vandalism to your reading room."

"Not the sort of news I hope to make."

"There were more. So many that you could forget one. Or even two."

Beatrice shrugged. "A few incidences here and there. Rude statements painted on walls of my office, broken typewriters, broken mirrors, that sort of thing. Idiotic pranks of an irate employee, most likely. We have Detective Hyde on the case."

Detective Hyde was operating in disguise in the store. It gave Beatrice peace of mind to know that someone was handling this so that she could handle everything else.

"Beatrice, it could be more than that."

"Nonsense. We are just women. We are just shopping."

"We both know there is no *just* about it. Think of what you represent, Beatrice."

"That again." She rolled her eyes.

Beatrice the Beacon. Hold her up and shine a light and make an example of her.

Like she wasn't a living breathing woman who just wanted an occupation that engaged her mind during the day and a man who engaged her body at night.

"Think of who stands to benefit if you were . . . scared off. Because, Beatrice, you have made the business vibrant and profitable again."

She couldn't say it and he was too much of a gentleman to make her. Edward. Her own brother. He had sufficient motive. But he was locked away at a sanitarium in Long Island. *Wasn't he?*

If it wasn't Edward, it could be any one of the ego-wounded former employees of the old incarnation of Goodwin's. Mr. Stevens, for example. It could be any number of men who were not hired in favor of women.

It could be any of the other department store owners—Macy, Fields, Wanamaker—who were jealous of her success and her prominence on The White List, which had overnight altered where Manhattan's women shopped.

"You are also, day by day, empowering a multitude of women. Beatrice, you are changing the game. And not everyone wants to change the game."

Not like him. Dalton rose to the occasion of her challenge like he was born for it, like it was a shock to the heart he needed to stay alive, like it was his idea of a good time to try harder. She was the bucket of water on everyone's fire, but to him she was the fuel that made the flames go higher.

She could almost love him for it.

Maybe she was even on the verge of really feeling something like love for this man who had once upon a time wanted to destroy her and was now helping her scrub rude words off the walls, even after their lovemaking had been interrupted.

The thought of love made her forget, for a second, that she was supposed to be scared.

"Too many people want to scare me off," she said. "Pity it won't work."

"They'll keep trying until it does," he said. Then he reached for her hand. "Let me protect you."

She laughed, and the sound echoed in the hall.

"Stay with me," he persisted. "You'll be safe at my home instead of vulnerable at your town house, where it's just you and your mother."

"For one thing, my mother is a dragon. For another, we have servants and locks, too."

"I'll escort you to and from the store each day, then."

"What? No! Good God, Dalton. I'm a grown woman, a divorcée. I don't need a chaperone."

She started to walk away, toward the exit.

"You need someone to protect you."

"*If* that were true, I would hire someone. I would hire a band of lady pirates to surround me with pistols, swords, and devastating wit."

"That's ridiculous."

"Is it? But I know some already."

"Beatrice, let's be serious. Let's be reasonable."

Oh, that was not to be borne. Beatrice stopped suddenly and whirled around to face him.

"Are you going to tell me to be calm next? Because you are saying the most offensive, ridiculous things a man could say to a woman. Be serious. Be reasonable. Be calm. As if I'm ridiculous, foolish, and hysterical. Is that what you think of me, Dalton?"

"No. You're the smartest, fiercest woman I know. But you are also being foolish and stubborn about this. Someone has been attacking you and your store and everything you represent. That only spells danger and I need you to be safe. Because I'm falling in love with you, Beatrice. All over again."

"Don't do this. Don't make love feel like a cage."

Chapter Thirty

Dalton's Department Store
The next day

*D*alton's, the department store, had an exquisite offering of fine jewelry on display and available for purchase. Dalton, the man, was considering it.

"Why are you looking at the diamond rings?" Connor asked warily.

"Well, I'm either going to start a new trend of men wearing diamond rings or I'm about to propose. One of the two. I'll let you guess."

Connor gave a low whistle. "That's one way of winning her store."

Dalton stilled. He had moved so far beyond his old ideas of revenge and ownership and destruction; he hadn't realized no one else knew the transformation that had taken place in his head and heart. He had one thought and one thought only: keeping Beatrice safe.

Hence this diamond ring that would declare

to one and all that she was a woman with all his power at her back. This ring held the promise of nights in his bed, where he could make love to her and know that she was safe, breathing softly and sleeping peacefully beside him.

With this ring, they would no longer be enemies, or lovers only by night. With this ring they could belong to each other and he would succeed at this feeling he'd been chasing all these years.

"This is not about revenge at all," he said. "I no longer want Goodwin's, the store."

"Really. No more revenge? No more competition? Our mad quest for the past sixteen years is over?" Connor was skeptical, which was understandable, maybe even angry. Dalton hadn't been around as much recently (because Beatrice) and hadn't been sharing the intimate personal details of his romance (because Beatrice). But Beatrice would understand, wouldn't she?

"Really and truly," Dalton replied. "I want no part of her store. I only want to be with her."

Goodwin's Department Store
An hour later

BEATRICE WAS CONCLUDING her interview with Detective Hyde about the string of unusual, ahem, activity that had been plaguing the store. There was a myriad of petty intrusions: broken lock on the staff door, the toys in the children's department strewn about the room, men's ties wrapped around the mouths of female mannequins. There was also the matter of the smashed mirrors, the trashed reading room, and those awful words painted across her office door last night, which Beatrice was informing the detective about. She'd been working late. She let the detective assume she was alone.

Detective Hyde was taking notes, her lips pressed in a firm line of disapproval. She *would* find who was behind this vandalism and she would bring the full force of the law down on him. She was so self-assured that Beatrice felt immediate relief. See—she didn't need to trade her freedom to Dalton for safety!

Speak of the devil—she looked up to see Dalton. In her office. In daylight.

Her heart did flip-flop things just the sight of him.

"I hope I'm not interrupting," he said.

"Come in, Dalton. Detective Hyde and I were just concluding."

She watched him observe Detective Hyde. She was the last woman Beatrice would want to meet in a dark alley; she was on the taller side, with a lean but muscled build, a wonderfully forgettable face that let her get away with anything. She was dressed in the attire of a cleaning woman, as it allowed her to operate in disguise and unnoticed in the store at any and all hours.

"Good morning, Detective Hyde. I'm glad to see you are investigating the matter."

"Matters," the detective corrected. And then she turned on him. "Where were you last night?"

Darn if Dalton didn't blush to have this stout matron, dressed in the uniform of a Goodwin's cleaning woman, demand to know what he'd been doing last night, where, with whom.

Beatrice laughed nervously and said, "It wasn't him, Detective."

The detective looked at them both and said, "I see."

Beatrice blushed.

"I suppose he knows about last night's vandalism?"

"He does."

"Who the devil would do such a thing?" Dalton wanted to know.

Detective Hyde shrugged. "I'm guessing the same person who did all the other things."

Beatrice saw him doing the math: the reading room destruction, the vandalization of her office door when he was here with her, the mirrors. And more still. She hadn't told him about the other little things. Not between their idle chatter and passionate kisses.

"Yes, Beatrice mentioned there were more. But I suspect she neglected to inform me of the full extent of the trouble."

"Just a few things," she said with a shrug. Because she could see the conclusion that he was coming to and she didn't like it one bit.

"You're in danger," he said. "I don't like it."

"Not particularly," Beatrice replied.

But Inspector Hyde said, "Maybe."

Beatrice watched the sudden transformation in Dalton as it sunk in. His eyes darkened, jaw tightened. And she saw him stand up taller, push his chest out, and do all the things men did to make themselves seem larger than life and intimidating.

It made her think of the duke, after she dared to stand up to him.

It made her feel like shrinking, in a misguided act of self-preservation.

"You're in danger," Dalton said again. "You need to leave here, immediately. We'll hire some additional security for the store and you, though it would be for the best if you stayed home. Safe."

"Don't do that." She sighed and closed her eyes. "Please don't do that high-handed hero thing where you stomp around and declare you must protect me at all costs and you use it as an excuse to lock me in your bedroom. I will not be shut away at home. Again."

"I wasn't going to do that."

She opened her eyes and gave him A Look. He'd literally just said he would do that.

"All right, I was about to do that. You have to

admit it wouldn't be the worst way to spend a few days." He gave her a rakish smile that promised more of last night, and Detective Hyde saw and made A Look. And now this was turning into a scene. Now Detective Hyde would know that she was romancing the enemy.

She might doubt Beatrice's commitment to the store, to the cause.

"Dalton . . "

"How about I get you a pistol instead?"

"I want no part of guns or weaponry."

"But I need you to be safe. I need to ensure that nothing bad will happen to you." And the need and wanting in his voice was plain and her heart ached because it was happening. The thing she was so afraid of: entanglement. Only this time it wouldn't be just a legal and monetary deal involving boatloads of lawyers. It was his heart and hers, their bodies, and the pleasures they shared last night. It was his fear. It would tie her up all the same and it scared her even more.

So it was with some trepidation that she asked, "What brings you here during regular business hours? Surely not this."

"Good afternoon to you, too."

"Good afternoon. But really—is there a business matter we need to discuss?"

"No. Yes. I do have a proposal of sorts. If we might have a moment alone?"

"Absolutely," Detective Hyde replied. "I have

an urgent matter of the utmost importance that requires my immediate attention that is also nothing to be concerned about at all whatsoever."

Beatrice closed her eyes for just a second of respite and when she opened them, Dalton was down on one knee before her, holding out a blue velvet box with a giant, pear-shaped diamond ring. This was a ring that made no whispered suggestions but bold declarations. This was a ring that would be heavy to wear.

"Beatrice, will you marry me?"

"No. Of course not. Why would you even ask?"

"With this ring, no one will trouble you. With this ring, the world will know that you have me to protect you. To cherish you. I can't lose you again, Beatrice. We have something that transcends years and continents and circumstances. Because you and I are uniquely suited to understand each other. We share passion and purpose. And we are *good* together, Beatrice. You know it as well as I. Dare I say, we even belong together?"

"I cannot, Dalton. I told you that. I told you that the other night, before . . ."

"You also said I could try to change your mind."

"There have been moments where I have thought *maybe*. But now you're here in my office, distracting me, demanding decisions and commitments, and saying I should go home and wait just to be safe. In other words, that I should shut myself away and flit around the castle. Well, I've done that already, and it's the last thing I want to do. So now I'm thinking . . . no."

"What if there is a child?" Dalton challenged. "I know you're not afraid of a scandal, but it's not fair to inflict it upon an unborn child."

"A noble, thoughtful, and decent sentiment that I do agree with. *If* there would be a child. But there will not be. And I know there will not be because I have taken precautions."

"You have taken precautions."

"Yes. They're not infallible but it's something." Beatrice sighed. "If only there was a pill one could just swallow and be assured there was no risk of conceiving."

"Indeed," Dalton said, rising to his feet with the grace and ease of a jungle cat. Even rejected, he was powerful and graceful and she wanted him.

But not enough.

"Assuming my precautions worked, there won't be a child and as such, there is no need to marry. And don't try to scare me into a match by mentioning a scandal should anyone find out about us. To say nothing of this scaremongering to make me wed you out of desperate need for safety."

"Give me a little credit, Beatrice. I'm not going to shame you into a match. I'm not going to terrorize you into my arms. That's not how I want to win."

"Glad to hear it."

He held the ring awkwardly. This hunk of strong, valuable, and eternal stone, bright and shiny and awkward between them. Beatrice looked at that ring, imagined it on her finger and all the women who looked at her as a beacon seeing that she belonged to another, to a man, to her rival. Wearing his ring, promising to *obey*.

She couldn't. She simply could not.

What would they think of her, their fiercely independent beacon, dimming her light to be with a man? Especially one who made no bones about wanting to dominate her professionally, who had said he wanted to see her lady land reduced to rubble? Who moments ago admitted wanting to stash her away in his castle?

She just couldn't.

Besides she still had doubts and sneaking suspicions.

"And besides, I cannot be certain this isn't some ploy to get Goodwin's."

"Do you really think I would *propose a lifetime of holy matrimony* just to get my hands on your store?" Dalton nearly shouted.

"It's been your burning ambition for the past sixteen years. I'm supposed to believe it just changed overnight?"

"Not overnight. Over the course of nights and days when I realized that the reason I've done everything I have done is for you. I thought it was revenge, I only wanted your love. That's my after."

"I'm you're after."

"I hope so."

And it was an enormous pressure, that, to be someone else's purpose and happiness, their nights and days. She felt overwhelmed and exhausted by it already. It was another tremendous burden for her slender shoulders.

"I just want to be with you, Beatrice. That is all I ever wanted."

She was not unmoved. She was a hot-blooded woman with a head and a body he pleasured expertly last night, and a heart that did have feelings for him. Because when they were good, they were *good*. Because he understood her and what made her tick in a way no one else ever had or likely ever would.

But she couldn't go back to married life. She couldn't give some man a say over what she did and with whom and where and why. She couldn't give up that space in her brain to worry about him and what he might think and feel. And if they had children—

Some would call her selfish. Beatrice didn't care. Why couldn't she be selfish?

"I don't want to give up my independence or my freedom, Dalton."

"I wouldn't keep you in a cage, Beatrice.

Gilded or otherwise. I'm not like him. For better or for worse."

"Oh, but it has already begun. Insisting I stay at your home, insisting on escorting me to and from work, insisting I do whatever you say so I can stay safe. To say nothing of the tug that I am already feeling."

"The tug?"

"If we were wed, I would feel the tug to return home when I wanted to work. I would feel the tug to consider you and your feelings and *us* in every decision—even though I presume we would still be competitors?" She lifted one brow and he didn't have an answer for that. "Suppose you wished for children? I don't know that I can give that to you. But I know I would feel the tug to be home with them and not here. Dalton, I want to be here."

She stood *here*. Behind her desk. In her office. Manhattan roaring outside her window. The floors below her hummed with female voices and feminine activity. Money and ideas and goods and services changed hands. Dreams were conceived and realized. Desires stoked and satisfied. And best of all, all these women had a space that wasn't home to just . . . be.

It was everything she ever wanted and she had it.

But it seemed Dalton would be the price she paid for it.

Dalton gave a bitter laugh.

"All the money I have earned, all the prestige I have accumulated, all the power I have gained, all the *years* of dawn-till-dusk work and dusk-till-dawn social climbing. All so I could be your damned hero. And it seems I have dedicated my life to all the wrong things. It seems that I'm working off an old script trying to catch up with a new woman."

"I'm sorry," she whispered. And she was sorry. "It doesn't have to be all-or-nothing, Dalton. We don't have to play by someone else's rules. We don't have to let anyone else dictate the terms of our happy-ever-after."

"You're a magnificent woman, Beatrice. I love you, Beatrice. Because I love you, I am terrified of losing you. Because I love you, I want more than stolen moments in elevators or quick tumbles in department-store beds. I want to hear your laughter echo in my foyer. I want to go to sleep and wake up next to you in my bed. I want a home. A life. A family. I want to feel that if my thousands of employees vanished tomorrow, I would still not be alone. Don't you want that, too?"

"I don't know," she admitted and he left—taking the ring with him—and not for the first time did she sit down at her desk and cry.

Chapter Thirty-one

Goodwin's Department Store
A few days later

*B*eatrice strolled through the sales floor of Goodwin's, reveling in the chorus of women's voices as they shopped and the strains of music played by an orchestra composed of entirely female musicians. Added to the mix was the clackety-clack of typewriters. There were dozens on display and customers were encouraged to try their hand at the machines and type whatever struck their fancy.

Beatrice loved looking at the notes. The paper sheets in the machines were full of lines and graphs about women's lives, messages to friends, notes to lovers, missed connections. They were sought-after reading material in the reading room. On the fourth floor, there were evening classes teaching typing.

She paused and breathed it all in. This, this was what mattered. This was what she had sought to create. A space where women could live their fullest lives, dream big dreams, and make them come true. It had certainly been such a space for Beatrice. Because of Goodwin's, she had everything she had ever craved: purpose and independence.

She had her freedom, too, but that had cost her. She wasn't thinking about what it took to escape the duke, but how it had hurt to refuse Dalton. She didn't regret it, but she certainly felt a sharp pang of something like loneliness, even in the middle of Goodwin's on a busy day.

There must have been thousands of people around her in the store but still she felt lonely.

Beatrice refused to dwell on it; instead she continued her tour through the store.

On the mezzanine of the grand central staircase, the Ladies of Liberty had established a table where they were soliciting signatures on a petition demanding women's right to vote. Women paused in the midst of their shopping to hear impassioned speeches about the rights they ought to have, as law-abiding and tax-paying citizens.

Something to think about between trying on gloves and underthings and purchasing packets of buttons and the new style of hat.

"How many names have you gotten so far today?" Beatrice asked.

"Hundreds at least," Harriet answered.

"And it's only one o'clock. We haven't even had the afternoon rush yet."

She ought to take a break from making her rounds of the store, but with Detective Hyde home sick—she'd worked herself into a fever—she didn't want to risk missing anything. Just in case. Hyde's warnings and Dalton's storming around, shouting about her safety had rattled her.

She couldn't let anything bad happen to this store.

Beatrice had once felt so powerless and disconnected. But now she had this marvelous space, where she could be the brightest version of herself. She had friends in the Ladies of Liberty who encouraged and supported her.

Now that she no longer had her nights with Dalton, this space was all she had.

This loud, boisterous, beautiful shop.

Amidst all the sounds of the store it was difficult to hear the first screams. It was hard to discern them among the swell of the string section in the orchestra, the cries for "Votes for women!" from the suffragists or the sound of hundreds of women asking a friend, "Should I get this dress, this corset, these gloves?"

The cries quickly increased in volume until there was no mistaking them.

"Fire!"

"Fire?" Beatrice looked questioningly at Harriet, who appeared concerned but unruffled.

It was only when Margaret bustled over, struggling to maintain a calm outward appearance, that Beatrice felt a cold knot in the pit of her stomach.

"I don't want to alarm you," she began but Beatrice was already alarmed. "There's a fire in the basement. I've rung for the fire department and they are on their way, but we should evacuate everyone just to be safe."

"Fire?"

"Fire."

Instead of the fragrance of fresh flowers, Beatrice breathed in the faint fragrance of smoke. Among the chatter, she started to hear the snap and crackle of a roaring fire. If she could hear it here, on the mezzanine, then it was not just a fire in the basement. She could hear the dull roar of it, smell its presence, and there was no denying it was roaring up hard and fast.

All around the store, one could see women pausing, wondering. *Do I smell smoke? Is there a fire?*

Yes and yes and they all started moving toward the doors en masse. Hundreds of them. Thousands of them. Clinging to friends and children and recently bought packages. Hundreds of them, thousands of them, spread across six floors, all vying for the same exit on the ground floor.

"Margaret, open the doors. Break the windows. Do whatever is necessary to get everyone outside."

Beatrice turned to go upstairs, and it was slow going against the direction of the crowd.

"What are you doing?"

"To calmly request our customers leave. Immediately."

Beatrice decided she would start at the top floor and make the rounds, and with the manner of a society matron hosting afternoon tea, graciously ask her customers to leave. Even though her heart felt lodged in her throat and she felt like she would be sick, right here near the display of bicycles she had fought so hard for.

But she was a debutante and a duchess and so she knew how to move through a crowd, radiating peace and loveliness no matter what she felt inside.

Please proceed calmly to the exit.

Please do take the stairs.

Please move with haste, but no need to worry!

But flames and smoke and screams of alarm outpaced her. She could hear the roar of the fire, coming up from the depths, she could hear the stampede of women and their shouts of alarm. She glanced down and saw the flames working their way through the millinery section, onward to ladies attire on the third floor.

She heard screams.

And she knew, oh God she knew, that this was the end of Goodwin's.

Everyone had to go—now. The fire was taking over.

Beatrice picked up her skirts and started to rush through each department, urging everyone to leave immediately. She tore through the ladies reading room, she interrupted the luncheon service, she alerted the staff in accounting. She was in the home furnishings department when she started to cough from the smoke and feel the heat on her skin.

Every fiber in her being screamed for her to leave. Her lungs wanted fresh air, her heart wanted to slow down, her brain told her to save herself.

She heard children crying.

The nursery! She had to get help evacuating the nursery!

The attendants were already lining up the children and carrying the babies. Beatrice ran to enlist shopgirls from other departments to assist their orderly evacuation and to console crying children and hysterical mothers rushing against the crowds and past the flames up to their darlings.

They made their way down the grand staircase. Step by step, with armfuls of wriggling toddlers, children clinging desperately to necks and skirts.

Beatrice couldn't stop now, but she lifted her eyes for just a second to take one last look.

Flames licked up the central pillars. Flames recklessly devoured all the merchandise—gowns and gloves and tea sets and place settings. Double beds, twin beds. None of it mattered, they burned all the same.

She watched the fire devour the place where she and Dalton had first locked eyes. The spot behind the pillar where they had first kissed. The fitting room where he'd brought her secret fantasy to life. All the places where passion got the better of them and love had blossomed.

All the moments of her life, gone.

The monument of her ambition, gone.

Her gift to fellow womankind, gone.

As long as these women got out—with their brains and hearts and tireless hours of service to families—as long as they survived, no real damage done.

She rushed past millions of dollars of merchandise going up in flame. No matter.

This building, now crumbling around her, was her home. Her history. Her memories. Goodbye to all that.

She would find out who did this. Who stole her dream from her, who wrecked this safe space, who stole this temple of joy and pleasure from women. She swore revenge.

If she lived.

She'd almost reached the doorway, almost reached safety when the child whose hand she'd been holding panicked and broke free and got separated. In the smoke and flames, Beatrice struggled to see her. Though her lungs screamed for her to go outside, Beatrice turned back to find that young girl and save her.

Dalton's Department Store

"GOOD MORNING, MR. DALTON," the shopgirl chirped at him as he walked past. He continued his stroll through the store with only the briefest nod of his head in acknowledgment.

He didn't have it in him to wink or say more.

All he could see was pink silk. Loads of the stuff. He never wanted to see it again, yet his warehouse and account books were groaning under the weight of all the excess of it. It was the color of failure and rejection. It reminded him of the flush stealing across Beatrice's skin as he made love to her, which reminded him that he would never behold such a sight again, which made him considering driving that automobile off the roof.

He turned to the nearest shopgirl.

"We need to get rid of this," he said. "All of it."

"Yes, Mr. Dalton. We'll mark it on sale."

"A public display of failure. Excellent."

The poor woman didn't know what to say to that other than, "Yes, Mr. Dalton."

For the first time in his life, Dalton didn't want to be on the sales floor in the midst of it all. Dalton could not find refuge in his office, either—the windows overlooked Broadway and Goodwin's and the windows to *her* office.

He could not even go home, the emptiness there always such a stark contrast to the voices rising to the rafters here. Home now held memories of her that he couldn't stand to remember.

He would have to sell it. Immediately.

Dalton had some idea of going downtown to Mrs. Claflin's Orchard Street Settlement House. It was a good excuse to get out of the store. Surely, there were no memories of Beatrice there. He felt like a cad for continually putting off Mrs. Claflin's invitation, and he had a notion that getting out of his own head would do him some good.

Some people had real problems. He just had a broken heart.

And maybe lost the will to live.

But otherwise, he was fine.

But that was before panicked murmurs rippled through the crowds in his store. That was before the doors burst open and a deluge of smoke-smudged women came crashing in, with alternating cries of "Fire!" and "Water!"

Dalton rushed toward them, ready to help. But out of nowhere, Connor grabbed his arm, his expression grave.

"There's a fire. At Goodwin's."

"I have to go to her."

"Go," Connor urged, eyes dark. "I'll take care of things here."

Dalton rushed through the revolving doors and skidded to a halt on Broadway when he saw the inferno raging. Flames were licking out of the windows. Swarms of women gathered on the

sidewalk, spilling into Broadway, blocking traffic. The fire department was there, doing their
best. But Dalton knew a hopeless case when he
saw one.

There was only one question: Where was
Beatrice?

He scanned the crowds and didn't see her
among the women who clutched each other, who
stood in small groups speaking in hushed tones,
women who wept into handkerchiefs.

He pushed through the crush, calling her name.
"Beatrice!"

He asked everyone, anyone, "Have you seen her?"

He saw them step back at the wild, panicked
look in his eyes. Dalton faintly registered that he
must seem like a madman.

But where was Beatrice?

What he felt was panic and terror because he
knew her, and so he knew that she would be the
last one out of the shop.

If she left at all.

Firefighters were doing the best they could to
contain the raging inferno. Their buckets and
hoses were woefully inefficient. Police officers
did their best to hold back the crowds.

Important work, that.

But he was the only one who knew to look
for her. And the only one mad enough to run in
after her.

"Sir!"

"Stop!"

Dalton pushed past the crying women, past the sweaty firefighters, past the officers in uniform. He ran toward the flames, toward the building as it started to crumble from within.

It was idiotic.

A stupid display of heroics.

But the world needed Beatrice. The world needed her, so vibrant and determined to live her best life and help other women do the same.

It was one thing to live alone in his mansion without her, lonely as all hell. He could do that. He had done that. He didn't want to but if that was his fate, then so be it.

But he had always been able to go through his days and nights knowing that she was out there, somewhere, dreaming under the same night sky, breathing the same air, feeling the same sunshine on her cheeks.

If he really loved her, he would be happy just knowing she was alive and living her best life, even if it meant she was living without him.

And if he loved her, really loved her, he wouldn't just stand by in her hour of need.

Dalton pushed past the officers and firefighters and their shouts to stop. He ran into the burning building, knowing full well that he might not come out alive.

If he died saving Beatrice, it would be the best thing he'd ever done.

Once inside, the smoke started to choke him immediately. The heat was unbearable. He pushed through, shouting her name. "Beatrice!" over and over until finally he heard her say, "Here I am!"

They were stuck behind some display counters, surrounded by flames and molten glass.

She looked so small, huddled on the ground near one of the marble pillars, trying to coax a small, terrified girl to leave. Dalton scooped up the child and turned to run to safety. Behind him Beatrice cried out and fell—she had twisted her ankle.

"Go!" she shouted. Fumes and flames were surrounding her. She wouldn't be able to crawl out fast enough and he could not carry them both at once. "Go!" she shouted again.

Dalton rushed toward the street and safely delivered the child into the arms of a police officer.

Then he turned and went back in for Beatrice.

Chapter Thirty-two

The Goodwin Residence
One West Thirty-Fourth Street
The next day

*I*f Beatrice was in no condition to travel downtown to Harriet's drawing room, then by God, Harriet's drawing room would come to her. In other words, the Ladies of Liberty came to call upon her at home, where she was stuck languishing in the drawing room.

Not only was she in a slightly injured state—a swollen ankle, some burns, a cough—but there was no place else to go.

Goodwin's store was good and gone, burned to ashes and rubble.

It was gone *on purpose*.

Thanks to Detective Hyde's diligent sleuthing—in disguise as a cleaning woman, whom no one ever really took notice of—and the police department's own subsequent investigations, the arsonist was swiftly apprehended.

"It is said that hell hath no fury like a woman scorned. But I reckon that hell hath no fury like a man with an ego wounded by a woman or a man who fears losing to a woman," Harriet said drily.

It had been none other than Sam Connor, Dalton's right-hand man, who had started the fire and who had been behind all the acts of vandalism. Beatrice had suspected Mr. Stevens or her own brother to be behind it. But Dalton's right-hand man?

She wished she were more surprised.

What really burned—and she did not use the word lightly—was that all her ambition and accomplishments had been undone by some man with a chip on his shoulder, who only saw what he stood to lose and who didn't think that the world was big enough for both Dalton's and Goodwin's.

Beatrice was shaken to her core. In pursuing her dreams, she had stoked the anger of men, unleashed their fury, and provided a brilliant, beautiful, feminine target for them to make their point. She had dragged her friends into the spotlight with her, making them targets, as well. She felt wretched.

"The police have him in custody. The evidence of his guilt is damning and I expect that he won't see the light of day outside a prison wall for a long, long time," said Arabella, who was one of the first female lawyers in the city. Her words provided some relief.

But what the Ladies of Liberty knew but dare not say: such men were like roaches. One might lock up one, but a million remained crawling through the city, disturbing one's equilibrium and ruining their days.

"Good riddance."

"Detective Hyde is livid that after all her undercover investigative work she was home sick with a fever on the day they struck," Beatrice said. "She is beside herself with guilt thinking she could have prevented it. I, as well."

"A woman's work is never done. She may never rest," Adeline said with a sigh.

"Connor was determined. If only he'd applied himself to a more useful pursuit, other than revenge," Harriet sniffed. "Like perhaps minding his own store's business."

"It is said that he thought Dalton wasn't doing enough to compete with Goodwin's."

"Was Dalton behind it?"

"I don't think so," Beatrice said. "I can't believe he would be."

"Well, he did rush into the fire to save you, so I'm inclined to believe in his innocence," Harriet said.

But still something sat heavy on Beatrice's chest. It was guilt, like somehow this was all her fault.

"I'm sorry," she blurted.

"Why on earth are you sorry?"

"Long ago, I made Dalton want revenge. And it was all he and Connor and been working toward for years, until I made Wes want to give it all up—and Connor feared he would lose everything he'd worked for. And now hundreds of shopgirls are without employment and wages. We have all lost our investment. We have lost the feminine space we have created. All because of my ambition. I should have just let them win."

"You cannot dim your light, Beatrice," Harriet said earnestly. She looked around the room at all the women gathered. "None of us can, especially not for any man. The world needs our light. It's how we see what needs to be done to make the world a better place."

"It just makes them so angry . . ." one woman said softly.

"If we lived in fear of men's anger, we would never do anything at all," Harriet said. It was the truth. If Beatrice were afraid of men and their anger, she would still be the Duchess of Montrose, choking on her own words and in a quiet and constant state of despair as she languished about the castle.

She supposed that was the point entirely. The threat of their violence was supposed to scare her into staying home and stay quiet and stay out of the way. To dim her light until it was extinguished entirely.

"So the question is, Beatrice, what will you do now?" Harriet asked. "I presume that you—and all of us—are constitutionally incapable of just letting a man get the last word. We are not women who sit idly by."

A roomful of expectant faces looked at her, waiting. Expectantly. They waited for her to present the answers, along with a plan, a map, a seating chart, and a paper pattern for the dress to wear for the occasion.

If she could manage it, she would have smiled because she was reminded of herself just a few months earlier as she'd challenged Dalton: *And then what will you do?*

What will you do with the rest of your life when the thing you had originally set out to do is now moot? She was young yet. She had money. Friends. Connections. She still had passion and ambition to burn, though perhaps she might not phrase it thusly any longer.

"I for one hope you'll rebuild," Ava said.

And then there was a chorus of female voices rising up all around. Calls for a bigger, taller, more stunningly beautiful store, the likes of which the world had never seen. They would fundraise for it. They would plan it and build it together.

"Marian could design something for you," Ava suggested. "She just graduated from architectural school."

"I'd be happy to help oversee construction," said Emily, who oversaw the Brooklyn Bridge construction years earlier.

"We're all ready to shop at this new store," someone said and a chorus of women agreed. Beatrice would build them a store worth waiting for. They dreamed out loud about what it would be like to make a monument to female consumption with no constraints. They plotted and discussed options and timelines and considered both the practicalities of such a project without limiting the scope of their dreams.

It was, of course, interrupted by a man.

The butler announced a caller.

Mr. Wes Dalton himself, looking every inch the powerful romantic hero in a dark, exquisitely tailed suit. A bruise on his cheek and a bandaged hand hinted at his recent heroics. He carried a newspaper.

All of a sudden, every one of the Ladies of Liberty remembered urgent appointments that necessitated their swift and immediate departures.

Dalton stood by, allowing them all to pass.

"Some have said that I'm a catch, but I guess that's before I sent a drawing room of women fleeing," he remarked drily.

Before she knew what was happening, the doors to the drawing room clicked shut softly and they were alone.

"Please, do sit," she said and he did, setting his newspaper down on the table between them. He leaned forward, his blue eyes full of concern and fixed on her.

"How are you, Beatrice?"

"To be honest, I've been better," she said drily, and he laughed and it thrilled her.

"Glad to see your sense of humor wasn't damaged."

"Have you come to say I told you so?"

"No. Although . . ."

"You could. You warned me about the dangers. You said I ought to stay home."

"But if you had stayed home, you wouldn't have been in a position to save the lives of your employees and customers," he said, and it made her breath catch and her heart stop because that sounded like an admission that he knew she belonged in her store, that it was where she was at her best and most useful.

Not at home, languishing.

And if he knew and he thought that and he was still here, even after she had refused his proposal, what did that mean for her and him and them together? What did she even want?

"So maybe I should say I told *you* so," she replied, trying and faltering at lighthearted conversation. Because he looked so handsome, so strong, so steady that she wanted nothing more than to curl up in his arms. She understood, finally, what kind of comfort and protection he'd been offering.

"If you wish."

"No, it doesn't matter now."

"I have come to apologize for . . . everything. There have been moments where I wished to burn Goodwin's to the ground but I never would have done it. Connor, on the other hand, feared losing everything we'd worked for. He'd feared losing to you. I hadn't known any of this until this morning."

"It seems some men can't handle a little competition," she said and it put in stark relief Dalton, who *could* handle competition with a woman. Who even seemed to enjoy it. Her heart did a little flip-flop. Because this man challenged her to do better, and she him.

Why, then, had she refused his proposal?

"I feel responsible. If I had been more attentive to Connor . . ." Beatrice could see the guilt racking his body. "I could have stopped him. I could have turned him in. I didn't touch the matches but I feel as guilty as if I'd started the fire myself."

"But you didn't. It's not your fault, Wes. And it's done and Connor will go to jail and the world will see what happens to second-best men when they go up against an army of women."

"I am deeply sorry for your loss," he said.

"Thank you," she said softly. And his apology meant more to her than anyone else's because he knew, in a way that no one else knew, what it meant to own and run and love a store. Especially this one. She swiped away one rebellious tear, and said, "I suppose you've made it up to me by rushing to my rescue like some storybook hero."

"You clung to me like a damsel in distress."

"So you claim. I don't recall that part at all."

"You'll just have to trust me."

Again, his gaze met hers. Beatrice could sense there was so much feeling churning beneath the surface of that inscrutable expression and finely pressed suit. Just as her heart was beating wildly beneath her ugly floral day dress that was her penance to wear because she, too, had ideas about competition and winning even if it meant not wearing that gorgeous pink silk of his.

And what for?

For a store? For the sake of winning?

What had she won anyway? She had no store and no Dalton.

She had refused the love of the one man who would love, cherish, and support her dreams. Oh, God. She bit her lip, choked back a sob. He was still here . . . he was still here . . . would he ask her again, now that she *knew* better?

Now that she knew she loved him?

Now that she knew she could trust him with her heart and ambitions?

"While I have come to see how you are faring, I have also come to tell you something," he said. "I wanted you to be the first to know that I'm retiring."

"What? But why?" she cried out. "You love your store. You *are* your store. And you have won!"

"Maybe, by default or by a technicality. And it sure as hell doesn't feel like winning. I no longer have the passion for it. I don't wish to best you, I don't wish to fight you, and I don't even care about the new season's merchandise," he said and she gasped.

"And what about the store? Are you really going to give it up? How could you?"

Hers had been stolen from her and he was just giving up, walking away!

"I have no interest in it anymore. I obviously cannot and will not give it over to Connor. I find there are philanthropic endeavors that require my attentions and my fortune. I will no longer partake in the day-to-day operations."

"But the store is you and you are the store. Your name is on the—" She stopped short. She was about to say *your name is on the building.* But it wasn't.

"No, it isn't. It never was."

"I am shocked. It's a good thing that I am lying down, otherwise I would faint."

"Smelling salts. First floor, past the staircase. Fifty cents."

"See! You belong in a department store. Dalton, you don't need to do this."

"You're the one who belongs in a department store," he said. That's all he had to say for her to know. He saw her and accepted what he saw. She felt seen, truly seen and in this moment, for the life of her, she couldn't remember why she'd said no to his proposal. His love for her was plain, and he was saying in so many words that he knew where she belonged and was at her best and wasn't going to fight her for it anymore.

Another rebellious tear made a run for it down her cheek. A mutiny. She who orchestrated hundreds of human employees could not get a few tears to follow orders and stay put.

"What will you do now?" Dalton asked. She just assumed he meant business.

"I'll rebuild, of course. It will take years, but it will keep me busy. You have caught me on my one day of being idle. . . . Just one. Tomorrow . . ."

She chattered on and he listened and after an appropriate interval he took his leave. He said, "Goodbye, Beatrice. Best of luck in your future endeavors."

And then he was gone and she was stuck languishing in the drawing room. Alone. Stuck with the fate she had done everything in her power to avoid. No Goodwin's. And no Dalton.

Just a newspaper that he'd left behind.

Chapter Thirty-three

*I*n the absence of anything else to do, Beatrice reached for the newspaper, with some idea of catching up on the news, or at least avoiding thinking about her own problems. After all, it wasn't like she had anything else to do, other than rest and try to recover.

But she'd hardly gotten past page four when she saw the most striking advertisement that had her heart racing.

There was no way not to see it. A full blank page with just a few little words. She knew like she knew her own name that these words were meant for her and her alone.

"Mother!" Beatrice shouted. "Mother!"

Estella rushed in, obviously fearing The Worst, as mothers tended to do.

"What is it?"

"Look." Beatrice thrust the newspaper at her.

"Oh, my God, Beatrice, I thought something was actually wrong," her mother said, pressing her hand to her heart. "But you only wished to show me something in the newspaper."

"Not just something. Everything. Well, almost everything. Look."

She did.

The advertisement read:

**FOR SALE: ONE RETAIL EMPIRE
DALTON'S IS AVAILABLE FOR PURCHASE
BEST OFFER**

"Well I'll be damned," Estella said softly.

"I know."

"I thought the store, and success, were all he ever wanted."

"Me, too."

"With Goodwin's gone, he has no real competitor. Yet the merchant prince is giving up the throne."

"I thought the store was all I ever wanted. But now I am not so sure," she said. Her voice cracked as she said, "Love complicates things, I suppose."

Her mother sat down beside her and clasped her hands.

"Beatrice—I'm so sorry. As a mother, you try to do what is best for your children. I thought he was just a fortune hunter like all the others, but one who would break your heart and leave you penniless. I was only trying to protect you. I was only trying to do what was best."

"I didn't believe enough then, either. And neither did he. But now . . ."

His intentions could not be any clearer.

There would be no more competition.

"He obviously meant for you to see this," Estella said.

"I know. But what does he want to happen because of it?"

"It's time for you to stop thinking about what he wants. Or what you should do. Or what I or anyone else expects. You have nothing holding you down or holding you back now, Beatrice. You have a blank slate to create the life you want. This time, I'll help."

What did she want? The same thing she'd always wanted. Purpose-filled days and passion-filled nights. But now she saw a new way of making that dream become real and it seemed Dalton saw it, too.

They weren't competitors after all and they were meant to be together.

"I know exactly what we need to do," Beatrice said in the confident voice she'd learned to project from somewhere deep inside. "Mother, can you please go down to Dalton's and buy all the pink silk they have in stock?"

"Happily. Especially if it means you'll stop wearing these ghastly floral dresses. But I daresay they'd be lovely on the upholstery . . ."

"We can discuss redecorating later. I'm about to create my own happy-ever-after. But first, I need the right dress."

Chapter Thirty-four

The House of Adeline

*B*eatrice's heart hadn't stopped racing since she saw the advertisement. Dalton selling Dalton's was the last thing she ever expected and yet it made perfect sense all the same. And as for that best offer? She knew him, body and mind, heart and soul. She had an idea of an offer he couldn't refuse and one that would beat all the others he was sure to get.

As soon as her mother returned with sufficient quantities of pink silk, Beatrice took it all to The House of Adeline.

"I need you to make me a dress," Beatrice said to Adeline as soon as they were alone in the fitting area. "Out of this."

"This" was yards and yards of the Wild Rose silk, carefully wrapped and folded and waiting to be crafted into something exquisite. It was begging to be touched, to be loved, to be proudly displayed. Between this fabric and Adeline's gowns, Beatrice was going to be dressed to conquer the world.

Thank goodness—she was nervous about what she intended to do.

"Oooh," Adeline sighed. "I've been dying to create gowns out of this. Of course I would never, because of our crusade. What changed?"

"I presume you saw the advertisement in the newspaper?"

"Of course. I'm sure someone on some farm out West has yet to see it, but it's only a matter of time. But everyone in Manhattan has certainly been made aware that the great wonderland that is Dalton's is for sale. I assume you're going to make an offer."

"Of course."

Adeline's eyes lit up. "How much?"

"Oh, he doesn't want just money. Anyone can give him that. He wants something more, and I intend to give it to him."

"So you need the perfect dress, made in the fabric that is exclusively his and that declares in no uncertain terms that the battle between you two is over."

"Exactly."

The dress would be the easy part. She had just the right offer for him, too. She was certain enough that he would say yes. But it was the realities of *after* that had her in a state of stomach-aching anxiety.

Beatrice still had qualms about the after.

"But first, before I make this monumental and irrevocable step, I need you to tell me something."

"Hmm." Adeline was already stretching the measuring tape, recording the exact length of her arm and the span of her wrist. She'd been waiting weeks to make dresses with this silk, she would not waste a second now.

"You have found love with an impressive, important, and powerful man and you are going to marry him. But you are also not giving up your own dressmaking empire, or your friends. So I need to know, how do you do it? How do you have a relationship with a man without losing yourself?"

Adeline smiled and sighed and put down her measuring tape.

"It's not easy. You have to know your own heart and mind. You need to *own* your heart and mind. But never forget that hearts and heads can expand if you let them. There is room for so, so much love. You can love him and love your work at the same time, Beatrice. Remember, it needn't be either/or. It can be and/and."

"I think we can do that . . . now."

"Also," Adeline continued seriously, her hand on Beatrice's arm. "You need to be able to leave at any time and support yourself respectably. Because if you can leave at any time, you can freely choose to stay. For love."

And with those words, Beatrice thought that perhaps her work wasn't an obstacle to their life together after all. It gave her another purpose besides a marriage and money in her dress pockets; it meant that she could afford to choose to stay with Dalton or leave. Maybe it meant they could have a fighting chance at being together simply because of love and not of need.

Especially if her head and heart could expand enough for both. There was no good reason why her head and heart could not expand infinitely.

"But, Adeline, don't you feel the tug? The tug between work and home, and yourself and your lover?"

"Of course I feel the tug." Adeline laughed. "I don't know that someone will never feel it. I just damned well hope that my duke feels it just as strongly. Look, Beatrice, love is messy. It's hard and complicated and it's not easy. But if we don't embrace that hard part, then we don't get the good stuff."

"You make it sound so simple."

"We could probably make it far more complicated but honestly, who has the time? We have things to do."

Beatrice finally let go of the breath she had been holding and it came out in a burst of soft laughter. It would be a mess! It would be complicated! But with real love and their determination, they could fashion themselves a happy-ever-after.

She was going to do the thing she was scared of most in the world, for the thing she loved most in the world, with the man she desired most in the world. If there was ever a man she would take this chance on, it was him.

It could be a disaster. But she had already survived disasters, hadn't she?

It could also be glorious.

"How soon can you make the dress?"

"I can do it before you change your mind if that's what you're asking."

Chapter Thirty-five

Dalton's Department Store
His office

Dalton was packing up the few personal effects of his office on the top floor when Beatrice, a vision in pink silk, strolled in like she already owned the place. His heartbeat quickened like she hadn't refused him.

"I've been waiting for you," he said by way of greeting. Ever since he'd placed that advertisement in the newspaper, he'd known he could expect her to waltz in with an offer. She wasn't one to accept defeat or stay home for the rest of her life. She was too ambitious, too determined for that.

So, he'd expected her.

"Here I am, at long last. How do you like my dress?"

She did a slow turn to show off every flutter and fold of the Wild Rose Pink silk grown. He had an appreciation for women's fashion and noted the artistry. But what really had his heart stopping was an appreciation for what it meant for Beatrice to walk down Broadway wearing his exclusive color.

He dared to hope this wasn't just a business meeting.

"You in my silk looks better than I imagined. And trust me, I had imagined. Though most of my fantasies involved removing it."

She quirked a smile. "You're going to sell a lot of this silk now. You'll make a fortune. Another one."

"Too bad I'm quitting."

"And selling."

"I'm assuming you've come to make an offer."

She came to stand just before his desk and pressed her palms on the surface and leaned forward. His gaze dropped to her breasts straining against that silk.

"Of course. And not just any offer, either. I'm going to make you the best offer you're going to get from anyone in Manhattan, and thus, the world."

"Let's hear it."

"Three thousand dollars."

Dalton laughed. The store generated millions in revenue each year, and each season only garnered more sales and more profits. This store had made him the third greatest fortune of the Gilded Age. He sold three thousand dollars' worth of gloves. On Thursdays. At lunch.

"Macy offered me five million. Wanamaker offered me upward of that."

"Oh, I'm not offering just three thousand cash dollars. I'm also going to give you something money can't buy."

"Now I'm intrigued," he said, but his voice was rough, betraying all the heart-racing hope and tightening in his chest. Beatrice, here, in that color, hinting at offers and promises was enough to make him explode with hope.

"I'd like to propose a partnership." She perched on his desk now, a vision of pink silk and pink lips. He was very interested in partnerships. "Let's call it Dalton Goodwin. I'll own the store outright and do what I like with it. And I will also be your wife."

"Are you proposing marriage to me? Is this some ploy to get my store?"

"I also offered three thousand dollars," she said. "No, Dalton, this is not a ploy to get your store. I still have my name, my land, and a tidy sum from insurance. I could rebuild Goodwin's starting this afternoon if I wanted to. But if you're selling anyway, why not sell it to me? You know I would do great things with what you have built. You know your legacy—our legacy—would be in good hands."

This was true.

She was so much more inspired than Wanamaker.

"But I don't care what happens to my store anymore," he said. "I'm really only interested in you. And me."

"I won't promise you children," she said. "I won't promise that I will be home in time for dinner or that I won't speak of business at the breakfast table. But I will love you, Dalton, in the way that only I can. Fully and completely, unapologetically and without reservations. I know you, Dalton, like no one else does. The man you were and the man you are. And I want to be with you to see the man you become. So if you think you can share me, I think I can share a little bit of me, too."

Well, if this wasn't everything he'd ever wanted. Beatrice, the best most beautiful and rule-breaking version of herself coming to him, offering herself to him. Offering a lifetime of love and laughter and being together. On terms he could very much accept.

But he'd been wounded before. His heart was pounding. And he was nervous that this was too good to be true. She was honest with him about what their marriage might look like, so he'd test her with the same.

"I mean it when I say I'm quitting. I intend to devote my time and fortune to philanthropic efforts," he said.

"I know some philanthropically focused society women who will be delighted to welcome you into their fold."

"You'll have to support us financially. I'm going to give my fortune away."

"I think I can manage."

"I have plans to sell the mansion and live more simply."

"Castles are overrated."

"You're proposing a marriage."

"A merger, a marriage. Whatever you wish to call it. You and me. Together. In sickness and health, in business and pleasure, but definitely happily ever after."

Dalton stepped from behind the desk to stand before her. He breathed her in. This bold, beautiful woman wanted to be with him just for himself and not for his prestige or power or fortune. She wanted to be by his side while he took new risks. She wanted to be in his bed, for the rest of their lives.

For the first time he truly felt like the most powerful, unstoppable man in the world.

"In all the stories, it's the man who proposes," he pointed out.

"You and your rules," she sighed. "I think all that matters is we end up together and make our own happy-ever-after. Don't you?"

Dalton pulled her into his arms and said, "I do."

His mouth met hers and they kissed, like it was everything he'd ever wanted, like his heart was going to explode with the pleasure of it, like nothing else in the world mattered. Not the bustle of Broadway outside his office window, not the six floors of commerce and desire below them, not all the years they had missed out on.

All that mattered was this moment, here and now, and the promise of forever.

"Wait—" he said as something occurred to him. Dalton stepped back and reached into his desk drawer for a certain blue velvet box. Then he dropped to one knee and opened the box to reveal a diamond ring. He was all in favor of the unconventional if it meant being with Beatrice, but he couldn't completely shake tradition.

"Shall we, Beatrice?"

"Yes," she sighed. "Yes, we shall."

Dalton slipped the ring on her finger. And they kissed, mouths and hearts colliding, losing track of where he ended and she began. They kissed like it was the only thing that mattered.

Epilogue

New York City, 1899
Four years later

$\mathcal{D}$alton never ceased to be in awe of the sight of Beatrice standing before the windows of her office, formerly his. She had such a commanding presence as she surveyed the city outside—the crush on Broadway and the former construction site across the street where Goodwin's used to stand.

She cut a fine figure in her deep blue tailored day dress and jacket.

This was the version of Beatrice Dalton-Goodwin that the world got to see. The impressive business-woman, the fierce advocate for women's rights, a lady always ready to lend a helping hand to others.

And then there was the version of Beatrice that only he got to know. For instance, he happened to know that underneath she wore the most wicked and wonderful undergarments in that Wild Rose Pink silk. The pink silk, soft skin, quiet whispers and moans version that was for him and him alone.

As if sensing him, she turned and smiled and said, "Oh, hello, Dalton." It still took his breath away.

She took a long, indulgent look at him in his suit and he grinned. The missus did like the way he looked in a suit; almost as much as she liked how he looked without it.

"Shall we?"

"We shall."

They linked arms and he proudly escorted her from the office to the sales floor, down the impressive central staircase, past housewares and ladies attire and home furnishings and personal accessories. She'd made some changes to the store and the decor, all to keep up with changing times, all of which ensured that the store—now called Dalton-Goodwin's—was still the premier shopping destination in Manhattan and thus the world. There was still no name on the building; everyone just knew.

Dalton didn't miss it and the store was now her domain. He had found his *after* and he'd never been happier. His days were now kept busy with his philanthropic endeavors. It was hard work spending the third greatest fortune of the age, but he was up to the task. They were off to a launch celebration now for one project that was of particular interest to them both.

"Good afternoon, Mrs. Dalton. Mr. Dalton."

Shopgirls greeted them by name, with smiles as they passed through the main floor, with perfumes, cosmetics, drinks, and other little things. They joined the crush of customers browsing and pursuing as they made their way from the register to the door, carrying their purchases in distinct pink bags. There was no need to print the name of the store on them. Everyone just knew.

"It looks like you have quite the crush," he said as they could barely get across Broadway, to where Goodwin's used to stand. A crowd of mostly women had gathered. He recognized Beatrice's friends, but there were many women who simply must have seen the advertisement in the newspaper about today's event.

"We should have shut down the street."

"You might have to yet."

Something special was happening today.

A christening, of sorts.

A ribbon cutting.

Four years earlier, Goodwin's had been burned to the ground in an act of arson by an angry man who couldn't handle losing out to a woman. He had tried to send a message to Beatrice and all the other women like her: shut up and go home. A lesser man or woman might have been scared, but Beatrice and her friends were made of stern stuff.

The rubble had been cleared.

Plans had been drawn up by Marian Morgan, architect. Construction had commenced and gone on and on and on, and now the building was finally done.

The original Goodwin's could never be replaced. But in its place rose another building, magnificent in its own way. It was a residential building called The Goodwin full of apartment flats, exclusively for single women.

Ten floors of small apartments that were safe, clean, and affordable. The Goodwin would provide a room of one's own for shopgirls, typists, secretaries, and future lady bosses, or any woman who needed a safe place to lay her head while striking out alone in the world.

Upon arrival, Beatrice and Dalton were swarmed by her friends Harriet, Ava, Adeline, Daisy, and Eunice.

"Should we smash a bottle of champagne against it, like a ship?" Ava asked.

"And waste a bottle of champagne?" Harriet retorted. "Absolutely not."

"Good point."

After some speeches and congratulations, Beatrice cut the giant Wild Rose Pink ribbon. The crowd cheered. After, Beatrice pulled him aside with a mischievous gleam in her eye.

"Meet me at the store later?" she whispered. "Let's say housewares, at closing hour?"

"There's nowhere I'd rather be than with you," he murmured. And then Dalton swept her into a kiss that had the crowd cheering and girls pretending to swoon.

Love was much, much sweeter than revenge.

Author's Note

$\mathcal{O}$ne of the themes in my Gilded Age Girls Club series has been reclaiming "girl stuff" that is so often deemed frivolous and inconsequential. Like romance novels, traditionally lady-centric stuff like dresses with pockets, lipstick, and shopping, is often dismissed even though—or maybe because—these things have been so empowering to women. Not just in how they make a woman feel, but because they put money in the pocket of her dress.

So, shopping. The Gilded Age is the Golden Age of the department store. Innovations like the fixed price, the ability to browse with no obligation to buy, stunning visual displays, and female salesclerks made them friendly and welcoming places to be. Many of them also offered amenities like nurseries, beauty parlors, post offices, restaurants, and libraries. As the stores got bigger—and they were massive palaces of retail—they became a destination, a place to go for the day.

As these stores increasingly appealed to women, they also became safe spaces for women to go—on their own, or at least without a man or a chaperone. Thus the department store was the first public space where respectable women could go independently without ruining their reputations. The Ladies' Mile—a stretch of Broadway around Union Square—was the first area in New York City where respectable middle-class women could go out on their own. Once people got familiar with women being out in public to go shopping, they began to push the boundaries and go everywhere else.

Similar to department stores, women's clubs were also popping up in this time period. The Ladies of Liberty Club is modeled on The Sorosis Society. According to the *New York Times*, this club "inaugurated and epitomized the women's club movement and was itself one of the most influential organizations for women in late nineteenth-century America." Their purpose was to further the educational and social opportunities of women. The members included activists, writers, female physicians and ministers, a fashion magazine editor, businesswomen, and even Emily Warren Roebling, the woman who oversaw the construction of the Brooklyn Bridge. These clubs gave women opportunities to learn, to practice speaking in public (!), and to normalize the idea of women getting out of the house and taking an active role in public affairs. It was no small thing.

Retail is the perfect business for a woman like Beatrice, who is desperate to get out of the house and do something. She's inspired by two real-life women: Consuelo Vanderbilt and Margaret Getchell. Consuelo, as many people know, was forced to abandon her true love and marry the Duke of Marlborough by her mother, Alva, a force in high society. The marriage ended in divorce years later. It should be noted that Alva also divorced, remarried, and went on to be a prominent supporter of the suffrage movement.

Beatrice's work was inspired by Margaret Getchell, whose biography is called *America's First Lady Boss*, so you can imagine how fast I bought that one! In the early 1860s Margaret was hired by Richard Macy himself as an entry level clerk. Thanks to her talent for math, she was soon promoted to bookkeeper and trained other clerks, and before long was promoted to an executive position due to the many innovations she implemented that made Macy's a success, such as adding new departments, creating stunning visual displays in the windows, adding a soda fountain, and convincing Mr. Macy to use his personal red star logo as the company's logo. She also dressed cats up in baby clothes for a popular window display and basically unleashed American's obsession with cat pictures. Margaret was the superintendent of a million-dollar business with two hundred employees—but she gave up her salary when her husband was made partner and worked unpaid until her death in 1880, at just thirty-eight. The character of Margaret in this book is another tribute to her.

Margaret's personal motto was "Be everywhere, do everything and never fail to astonish the customer," which I gave to Wes Dalton. He is loosely inspired by real-life guy Alexander Turney Stewart who was called the Merchant Prince of Manhattan and whose retail business earned him one of the great fortunes of the age. He died one of the richest men in New York (behind a Vanderbilt and an Astor). After his death, John Wanamaker bought his store on the Ladies' Mile and reopened it under his own name. I will also note that Stewart was a poor Irish immigrant when he started out. A small windfall—an inheritance from his grandfather—gave him the capital to start his business.

Some other characters who have real-life counterparts: Harriet Burnett is inspired by Jane Cunningham Croly, founder of the women's club movement in the United States. Harriet's partner, Ava Lumley, is inspired by Elsie de Wolfe who was the first professional interior decorator. Adeline the dressmaker has parallels to Madame Demorest, who popularized the paper pattern, published a monthly magazine, and decided fashion for American women for decades. Daisy Swann, the cosmetics inventor, was based on Harriet Hubbard Ayer, Helena Rubinstein, and Elizabeth Arden. Martha Matilda Harper is real—she pioneered the franchise hair salon and invented the reclining shampoo chair. The briefly mentioned architect Marian Morgan is inspired by Julia Morgan, one of the first female architects and the designer of Hearst Castle.

Josephine Shaw Lowell was real, as was her "White List," which highlighted the companies that were treating their female employees right. In other words, instead of a boycott she started a "buycott" to attempt to harness women's purchasing power to make a positive difference in the world. Lastly, I got the idea for my Detective Hyde from the *New York Times* obituary of Isabella Goodwin, a police matron who went undercover as a maid in a boarding house to help nab the suspect of a bank heist. (Someone please write this as a standalone romance.)

Beatrice's insistence on a display about bicycles is no coincidence. According to Susan B. Anthony herself, bicycling "has done more to emancipate women than anything else in the world." Bicycling for women was really championed by suffragist Frances Willard who, when she died, was one of the most famous and beloved women in America. She wrote a little book called *How I Learned to Ride the Bicycle*, which is a wonderful meditation on what it means for a woman to have the freedom a bicycle affords—and also how necessary it is for women's fashions to change to allow her more freedom to ride. I will be forever grateful to Bill Strickland for teaching me about her.

In the process of researching this series, I have been delighted to discover so many dynamic, innovative, and successful REAL women—and that they keep popping up in each other's life stories. I was also enraged that I hadn't heard of them before. Based on history textbooks and what's taught in school, we're given to think that women were just languishing at home in the drawing room, doing nothing of great consequence. This is the noble duty of the historical romance novel: to rediscover and breathe life back into these women's lives so we can learn and revere our otherwise ignored history.

One last thing—you may notice that Wes and Beatrice don't have a baby in the epilogue. In all my years of research in the genre I have never found The Law that says every happy ending must have a baby or two or ten. So this HEA is for the readers whose idea of happiness does not include children and for those who struggle with having one (I feel you). So imagine what you will for Wes and Beatrice. Because happy-ever-afters are ours to create and define.

Acknowledgments

Many thanks to everyone who helped make this book possible: the wonderful team at Avon Books, my friends in Romancelandia, and my supportive family (especially Tony). Special thanks to Mama Rodale for a love of romance and shopping.